Last Meal

Based on the True Story of the Bloody Benders

Dr. Paul A. Ibbetson

No Compromise Media

ISBN: 1536893412
ISBN-13: 978-1536893410

DEDICATION

I dedicate this book to Fern Woods who kept my interest in the Bloody Benders strong since childhood. She was a great caretaker of Cherryvale history.

CONTENTS

1 PRESENT DAY: THE INVESTIGATION BEGINS

The smell of human decay hung in the air. No matter which way the wind blew the stench of death seemed to cling to every scent brought forth by the Kansas prairie. It was the first thing Detective Robert Johnson noticed as his horse began to climb what was rapidly being called "Bender's Mound." Death was ahead of him, and if the reports were accurate, it would be something worse than he had ever seen in his hard fought life.

Johnson was a detective for the Clint Parker Security Agency. The man was thirty-five years old and had a muscled frame. His blond hair was complemented by a rugged face, complete with two, thin knife scars, which ran down his left cheek. His eyes were piercingly blue and penetrating. His physical attributes highlighted his tenacious ability to finish the most daunting of tasks. Johnson was a "finisher." He was what the esteemed Clint Parker called, "The best man to put on the trail of cold-blooded killers." The ex-civil war soldier was fast with a gun and deadly with a blade. More importantly, he encompassed both the deadly grit of a frontiersman with the cognitive abilities of what was being termed, "the modern day criminal investigator." Most importantly, Johnson didn't work for love of money. This set him apart from a great many men who carried a badge. He was not a slave to drink or any other vice, which differentiated him from most of the rest.

Johnson, a highly effective deputy, had left a sheriff's position in Dodge City, Kansas to join Clint Parker five years previous, when the man had broken business relations with Alan Pinkerton. It was their combined, driven nature to succeed where others fail, which drew Parker and Johnson together. Clint Parker and Alan Pinkerton together had founded the highly successful Pinkerton Detective Agency following their service together in the Union Army during the war. Both men had served as military intelligence and together they had created a special branch of spies, which collected critical intelligence on Confederate troop movements. When not in conflict with one another, they were a masterful team. Together, they created information gathering techniques such as shadowing suspects, advanced surveillance, and working undercover using various alias names. The two had successfully thwarted an assassination attempt on President Abraham Lincoln in Baltimore, Maryland.

They had agreed that a formal organization should be created to protect the President but it had not yet come to fruition when Lincoln was assassinated in the Ford Theatre. The President's death had strained their relationship, but it was Pinkerton's fruitless quest to kill or capture the train and bank robber Jesse James that had split their partnership.

Jesse James was an elusive rogue along with his gang of outlaws, which required being dealt with. The Railroad was quick to hire the Pinkerton Detective agency, which was filled with former military men and had the slogan "we never sleep." However, their usual efficiency was fruitless against a gentleman thief who had extensive ties to the local communities. James was akin to a modern day Robin Hood, and finally the Railroad stopped funding Pinkerton's attempts to catch the gang. Pinkerton, who was too prideful to relent, started spending company money in continued attempts to capture the robber. That was the end for Parker who took his company shares and went his own. There was no surprise that the Clink Parker Security Agency was created, or that both men would be become harsh competitors. It was in their blood. Since the split, the battle between the two agencies had remained constant. Pinkerton had the money, the name, and the press. Parker had a handful of highly capable people, and they made a living but not much more. What the Clint Parker Security Agency needed was a golden moment, a media worthy event. Something to place them in the public consciousness. The Bender murders in Kansas could very well be that moment. Sure, the Pinkerton Agency and every other bounty hunter for five states around would be attempting to collect the two-thousand dollar reward offered by Kansas Governor, Thomas Osborn. Notice of the reward was in the copy of the newspaper Johnson now carried, but the money wasn't all of it. If Clint Parker's men could make the capture, their credibility would be near equal with their rival. In fact, the Pinkerton agency had made it that much easier for them. Despite having three times as many men and extensive funds, the agency had over extended itself putting large amounts of assets into assisting the Spanish government quell a revolution in

Cuba. There was a real opportunity here, but it wouldn't last forever.

The teams of horses alongside the trail were an obvious precursor to the number of onlookers, which would be present at the top of the mound. To reach the mound itself required riding a two mile incline of dirt track commonly known as the Osage Trail. The trail, which went near the Bender Inn, was part of a much longer route. It had been used to forcibly move local Indians south from the state to newly created Indian reservations in Oklahoma and Texas.

Now the trail was a fairly high traffic transit route for travelers moving across the state and beyond. Bender's Mound was unique for several reasons. Of course, in this area of southeast Kansas, any noticeable elevation from the common flat terrain was unique. But this trail, which lead to Bender's Inn, was flanked on both sides by a tree row with a mix of medium sized hedge, hackberries and oaks. For the traveler moving across the state, the trees brought a welcomed bit of shade on what was mostly a tree-less Kansas plain. For Johnson, the trees had a bothersome connection to the dead bodies he was about to observe as his horse made the apex.

At the top of the mound the road evened out, and after only a quarter mile, to the south, about one-hundred yards off the road was the Bender Inn, or at least what was left of it. Had it not been for the reports of mass murder, the farm would have looked very normal. Rest stops like these were common place. The small house was close enough for the crudely written and misspelled sign that stated, "grocry" to be seen, clearly signifying that supplies could be acquired therein. The flip-side of the sign had the proper spelling "groceries" written in a fine hand.

Unfortunately, hundreds, no make that thousands of people now surrounded the property, including the house, which had been uprooted and moved twenty five yards from its foundation. Pieces of the homestead had been destroyed during the move, and it was obvious to Johnson that onlookers were also starting to take pieces of the dwelling as souvenirs.

A makeshift hitching post had been set up by the local justice of the peace, George Majors. He served the nearby town of Cherryvale, which was about to be incorporated, and had a Bender history of its own. Majors had designated the hitching post for law enforcement horses only, and a young boy was being paid to make sure nothing was stolen. The boy told Johnson that Constable

Majors was in the orchard south of the home with the diggers. The "diggers" was a term that had new meaning on top of Bender's Mound. The *Thayer Headlight* newspaper, which was in Johnson's saddlebag, was over four days old. It stated that four bodies had been discovered in the orchard south of the main house and more digging was underway. The newspaper staff also questioned the missing status of their own editor as possibly tied to criminal events at the Bender Inn. It was in the orchard the first of the bodies had been located.

The newspaper had already identified several of the initially discovered dead. Bill McCrotty's body had been identified. The man had lived near Osage Mission and was known to a few locals, plus he had a very distinguishable tattoo on his left arm that read, "W.F. McCrotty" with a picture of the American Flag below the inscription. Ben Brown who had been in route from Cedarvale to Chautaqua County had also been identified by family. Two additional unidentified male bodies had also been unearthed from shallow graves in the orchard and were awaiting identification.

George Majors knew Johnson was coming and met him near the orchard.

"It's a damn mess out here. Every day we unearth more misery." He said as he spit a mouthful of tobacco, which shot out in a long, brown arc. Majors was fifty-five years old and had the red nose of an enthusiastic drinker. The summer heat was not agreeing with him and large beads of sweat poured from his beat-red face. He swabbed aggressively at his brow with a worn handkerchief.

The Constable had twenty-five men working shovels, and they were slowly expanding their perimeter in the orchard. As a crime scene, there was almost zero containment. Many of the locals were helping to keep most of the public from being directly under foot in the orchard but the Bender's farm had received national attention, and evidence was being trampled almost as soon as it was discovered. Majors brought with him several documents, which had been wired through the Clint Parker Security Agency. Johnson would read everything his agency had amassed on the Benders from the newspaper in the town of Thayer and other sources. That was his next destination. The Bender trail was getting colder by the moment, but he had to see the crime scene, take it in, with all his senses.

Majors advised him diggers had discovered the body of local doctor, William York. This discovery had inflamed the locals who held the doctor in high regard. Since the discovery, several lynch mobs had been formed and were already running wild in hopes of finding the killers. As bad as trigger happy farmers was the doctor's youngest brother, Colonel Edwin York, from Ft. Scott who was on the war path for blood and had no intention of bringing the Benders to trial. Majors advised Johnson that the doctor's second brother, Alexander York, a sitting Kansas Senator had petitioned Governor Osborne to put up a bounty for the Benders. Despite giving anyone who could collect the reward a stake in seeing the Benders brought to justice, Majors warned that the doctor's brother, Colonel Edwin York, would have no reluctance of running over anyone he felt got in the way of catching these criminals. Colonel York had also relinquished a sizable amount of his own personal fortune to hire men beyond the soldiers under his command. Johnson would soon be heading in their same direction and he planned to arrest the Benders before Colonel York and his men could put them to a rope or worse.

After he had been briefed by the constable, and collected all the teletype communications, Johnson did what made him better than most detectives of the age; he stood back and fully observed the scene. He walked by the open graves and scrutinized the corpses despite some hard looks from the crowd. He walked the Bender house, he checked the shed and barn, and did a cursory observation of a tunnel system below the house's foundation. Then, from different vantage points, he observed the farm from atop Bender's Mound. Everything he observed would be written down and he would refer to his notes again and again over the course of the investigation. One thing became readily apparent. The Bender farm had been created to be a highly effective kill zone. As he had noticed from his approach to Bender's Mound, one could not see any activity from a distance. Even the hordes of people and the grave diggers were obscured by the apple orchard. Was this simply fortuitous for the Benders, or had they planted the orchard themselves? Next, was this section of the Osage Trail. Because of the tree row, anyone coming through the trail from either direction north or south toward the Bender Inn would be blocked from seeing activity on the property until less than a quarter mile away. However, from the high ground of Bender mound, and Johnson had confirmed this on both sides of the property, one could see anyone approaching from over five miles away. His military instincts began to kick in, and the value of this high ground had to have played a part in what happened here. He hoped the documents he carried would confirm the theories that were building in his mind.

Back toward the orchard screams arose, which tore Johnson from his thoughts. The screams came from women and were followed by the shouting of men. The crowd, which had migrated to the trail side of the property started moving back towards the orchard. Something was going on.

Johnson followed behind the main surge of people and observed what was happening without being knocked about by the crowd. There were several rounds of wailing from the crowd, which seemed to carry on the wind like a dark cloud. Whatever it was that had been discovered, it appeared to be the worst yet. Soon Johnson quietly made his way to the point of interest.

The disturbance was brought about by a newly discovered grave that held two bodies. The Loncher family, who had come in from out of state, were present, as were almost anyone who had missing family members or friends from the last three years. The Loncher family identified the bodies immediately as George Loncher and his seven year-old daughter Mary Ann. George Loncher's body had been stripped, and he had been stabbed several times. Whatever had happened to him, it had been violent and more so than any of the discovered bodies so far. Until now, all the victims had been adult males. All had skulls which had been crushed, and in the case where the bodies were well enough intact to properly view, all had had their throats slashed. Until the discovery of George Loncher, none of the victims had been stabbed.

Now the depths of the Bender atrocities would reach new heights—the killing of a child. By God's grace the young girl had not been stripped, and she still wore a light blue dress and white stockings. A single black slipper was on her left foot, the other presumably still somewhere in the shallow grave. Her skin was porcelain white, and combined with her blonde hair, which still shined, seemed to take on the quality of a doll. Johnson wondered if this was simply his mind trying to reject the reality of what had been done to such an innocent. He quickly cleared his thoughts and observed the scene as an investigator. The back of the girl's head had not been smashed and her throat had not been cut. In fact, there were no visible marks upon her body from a cursory inspection. Whatever had happened to this child was brought about by a process different from the others. However, the end result had been the same, death and burial in a shallow grave. The

Harmony Grove church attendees, who had been singing
hymns all afternoon, had been on break but the new
discovery brought them back with a new round of "Safe in
the arms of Jesus." Johnson had heard loose talk in the
crowd earlier that day that Kate and her brother John
Bender had been regular attendees to the church and that
Kate may have even taught Sunday school. The grand
parents of the dead child soon made their way to the
grave, and a new round of wailing began. Johnson had
seen enough.

The detective mounted his horse and prepared to
go north to Thayer, when again another ruckus arose from
behind him. Now, a body was being pulled from the
property's well. He had walked by the well several times
without thinking about anything out of the ordinary. The
boy who had been watching his horse had seen an object
shining deep in the water and had gotten the attention of
two nearby citizens who had hooked the body of a full
grown male. From the greyish color of the man's skin and
the bloated nature of his body, he had been partially
submerged in the water for most likely near on a month.
The man's clothes were fancy and he was obviously
someone of means, but in his state identification could
take some time. A wave a vomiting swept through the

crowd as the thick, putrid smell of rotting flesh hit the wind. More than a small number of onlookers had drunk from the water of the well throughout the day, which brought more vomiting and renewed wailing.

My God, what really happened here? Johnson thought to himself as he left the newest revelation of carnage behind him for the trail.

2 THE TRAIN ROBBERY

The sun was starting to set and normally he would have stopped for the night, had a meal, and waited until morning to continue. Travelling at night was a dangerous and often fool hardy action on the Kansas plains. While the threat was no longer Indian attacks, any injury could mean death, and the open prairie left most travelers on their own to fend for themselves. Johnson shook his head. This was exactly what made so many people easy prey for the Benders. This family offered food and a few hours rest, shelter from the rain, security from unknown dangers. Stopping at the Bender Inn was akin to doing everything rational a person on the trail was taught to do.

It was 2:00 a.m. when Johnson's horse trotted into Thayer. The man's muscles were tired and he had a slight headache. It wasn't a surprise. For the last day and a half he had been on a train and horse, with only a few hours on foot, and that was spent at the gruesome Bender farm. He hoped to get a solid meal before taking what would most likely be another train ride to Humboldt, Kansas. The Bender's wagon and half-starved horses had been confirmed abandoned just outside of the city of Thayer. Meeting him at the town's train station was Jim Snoddy, a marshall from Ft. Scott, and Colonel C.J. Peckham. The two had collected the ticket agent's initial accounts of the Bender family boarding the Thayer train with tickets on the Leavenworth, Lawrence & Galveston Railroad bound for Humboldt. Johnson would interview ticket agent Jon Tinsdale who took the Bender's fare and watched them board. If his story appeared valid, he would move onto the next leg of the quest—to find the Benders in Humboldt. It wouldn't take long for all the potential witness accounts to dry up, and then Johnson would be on his own. On most occasions, he worked best that way.

As happened often in high profile cases, witnesses were unreliable. The Bender murders were now at the apex of its notoriety. Some would be attempting to profit from it and in the end, as was the case with Lincoln's murderer, if the Benders stayed on the run long, anyone seen near them would feel the pressure to forget what they saw. Thus was the case with Jon Tinsdale. The man had been interviewed many times, with the last being by the rabid Colonel Edwin York and his growing posse, now numbering over seventy-five men. Had it not been for the marshall and Peckham, the colonel's lynch mob might have beaten the fifty-year-old train agent to death. As it was, the bruises on his cheeks and head were still swollen from the knocks he had taken three days previous. Tinsdale was just starting his day when he saw the three men waiting for him inside the ticket office. His head sagged as he prepared himself for another grilling. This is how it often was. Any notoriety he might have felt early on was gone and now the man was most likely wishing he had never gotten involved at all. Johnson could read people instantly, and, more importantly, he knew how to deal with the people he read. Quietly, he sent the two other men to the café and said he would meet with them shortly. Walking up slowly to Tinsdale, he extended his hand to the man and spoke in a kind voice.

"Mr. Tinsdale, I just want to thank you for doing your civic duty. I'm sorry if everyone doesn't know and appreciate how important it is to get the facts on this killing in our state."

The man was taken back by the Johnson's words and his demeanor softened. Quietly and without aggression, Johnson had the ticket agent walk him through the description of the group who boarded the train to Humboldt. There was a strong, stocky man with black hair in his fifties. This had to be Pa Bender. He described a short, thick, woman of the same age with black hair and a sour disposition, no doubt Ma Bender. Then there was a young man, maybe twenty-five years old with a light frame, brown hair, and child-like eyes. This was the description of John Bender Jr. Lastly, was Kate Bender. She was described as in her early twenties, pretty, and having a lovely smile. Johnson had no doubt it was the Benders who entered the train. Tinsdale swore their tickets were bound for Humboldt. Where would they go from there, he would have to find out for himself.

It was here Johnson showed, once again, his advanced skills as an investigator. Having built a level of trust with the witness, he dug deeper. First, he asked Tinsdale what additional information Colonel York had asked during his interview, the interview that had left him with bruises and cuts on his face.

"Not a blasted thing!" Tinsdale exclaimed, tentatively touching his swollen cheek before continuing,

"That's the whole messy thing of it. I would have told him anything he wanted to know and he wouldn't have had to knock the tar out of me to get it! The man's uncorked! His chickens have flown the coup! He just wanted to know where them Benders was off to, and he was going to beat me a little no matter what!"

Johnson gave the man a dollar to get some salve for his face from the mercantile. Tinsdale's face beamed with appreciation. Now it was time to attempt to gather information that maybe no one had collected.

In the same non-threatening tone, Johnson inquired, "Mr. Tinsdale, clear your mind if you will, and think back to that day. Please tell me anything you saw, heard, heck even smelled with these folks. Tell me anything that may have seemed odd in any way."

Tinsdale did what he was asked and soon the two men were talking again. This time Johnson was taking notes. When they were done, they shook hands and the detective bought his own train ticket to Humboldt and collected a new set of messages from the teletype office. The detective met quickly with Snoddy and Peckham. They promised to keep an eye on Tinsdale and to do their best to look out for his welfare. The detective told them the ticket agent might very well end up being an important witness in the Bender's murder trial should it someday take place.

The train left Thayer at 8:00 a.m. and began its steady trek to Humboldt. Johnson walked all the public cars and even looked through the storage compartments to see if any clues to the Benders might have been left behind. When nothing of importance was found, he spoke to the workers from the conductor to the line hands, and no one remembered the Bender family. More than likely the family had stayed in a private car, away from the public. Certainly their train ticket afforded them this option. One of the bits of private information Tinsdale had passed on was that the family that took this train were very wealthy. The ticket master said that the older man who purchased their tickets had a money roll he guessed had to contain several thousands of dollars. Furthermore, being an employee that was accustomed to observing travelers carrying money said, the young man in the group had two front pockets full of what, in his experience, were most likely large cash rolls.

"Not safe traveling like that, but people do it all the time," Tinsdale had told Johnson privately.

The detective had given Tinsdale another dollar to keep their private talk quiet should he be asked the same questions again. It appeared the Bender family had the means to go anywhere they wanted. He would have to be careful to consider all possible means of transportation open to these killers. Heaven help any half-cocked bandit who attempted to take the Bender's money.

In the privacy of his own sleeper car, Johnson spread out the teletypes and other information he had collected on the Bender's background from the agency. He had been dispatched from Dodge City to the southeast portion of the state, and the Benders had been gone from the inn for at least two weeks. They could be on the other side of the planet by now. Time was a factor, to say the least. Many were attempting to collect the Governor's reward, a bounty initiated by Dr. York's second brother, Alexander M. York, who served as a Kansas Senator. The truth would be that few would actually examine the small details, which would inevitably lead to the Bender's capture. Johnson wanted to know as much about the family as possible. As he physically tracked them, four additional men from the agency were collecting background information from places as close to the crime scene as Cherryvale, Kansas to as far as New York City, where at least a portion of the family may have come from.

Thumbing through the messages sent from his agency, it showed that on September 19, 1869 John Bender Sr. had purchased a 160 acre plot on the northeast corner of section thirteen, range seventeen. Johnson looked at the plot on the county map. Next, John Bender Jr. purchased a 160 acre plot but chose not to get a normal rectangular plot next to his father. Instead, he chose an irregular plot one eighth of a mile wide and a mile long, all of it to the north of John Bender Sr.'s claim. Again, Johnson viewed it on the map, and an idea formed in his mind. Was the unusual land plot for John Bender Jr.'s claim solely for the purpose of keeping new settlements from getting too close to where Bender Inn would be built and operated? What he did know was the closest neighbors on the county map were the Toll brothers' property three-quarters of a mile to the north, the Tyke cabin a mile to the south, and the Brockman Trading post on the other side of the hill. Only two of the rooftops of the three structures from the neighboring properties could be seen from the heights of Bender mound. Johnson had to believe that the Benders had factored in their activities' visibility to their neighbors when they built their homestead.

Then there was the home itself. Though the documentation was sparse here, it did appear that John Bender Sr. and John Bender Jr. made the first journey to Kansas without the wife and daughter. Johnson thumbed through the stack of papers to attempt to pin down the specifics but did not find anything other than receipts for the wood purchases made by the men at the Cherryvale Lumberyard. In hand written notes the clerk at the lumberyard stated the men worked for months on the home, and they were on the land parcels well before the women arrived. It wasn't that strange for men to precede the women when families moved across the country but with the activities of the Benders', the detective didn't want to take anything for granted.

The father and son also made several purchases from the Brockman Trading Post. Johnson scrutinized the receipts and a series of purchases caught his eye. The receipts of interest were several purchases for quick seeds. These were apple tree seeds, which grew and matured faster than traditional seeds. Both apple trees and other fruit seedlings and seeds were purchase at a large rate and almost immediately from the time the Bender men arrived.

They had either created, or greatly bolstered, the orchard found near the Bender Inn. The seeds were very expensive and probably special ordered. Johnson took down some notes to send off in his next teletype to the agency for them to inquire if the men had also planted an orchard on John Bender Jr.'s property. It was probably nothing, but he included in his teletype message for someone to scout the John Bender Jr. claim on the outside chance criminal activity may have taken place there. Johnson did not like to leave any stone unturned.

As interesting as the Bender's purchases were, so was what they bought very little of, crop seed. They had three-hundred and sixty acres between the two men, and they had purchased only enough seed to plant about forty acres. From the Independence cattle auction receipts it showed they originally owned eight head of cattle: three Holstein milk cows, an Angus bull and four Angus cows. They later enlarged their herd by four heifers and most likely had lost two calves during the blizzard of '69. No matter how a person figured it, they had not used the majority of their land for either farming or for cattle. This lack of land use should have caught people's attention. Had anyone ever inquired about this? Johnson wrote in his notes to follow up on this.

The train hit a bump which sent several papers that were in the detective's lap tumbling to the ground. He gathered them and then decided to take a short break. His eye's burned, and his body was ready for a reprieve. After exiting the sleeper car he made his way to the train's bar and ordered himself a whiskey. The warm liquid burned its way down his throat. He was willing to allow himself one, maybe two more shots, but that was his limit. While a few drinks would loosen his tired muscles, he never allowed liquor to weaken his mind or reflexes.

Some were saying the Benders were already out of the country. Johnson thought this to be unlikely. No, he couldn't rule anything out, but the evidence wasn't creating a picture that fit with a bunch that would cut and run quickly from a country as vast as America, and why would they? For all intents and purposes, they had collected big in Kansas.

Tracing their expenditures and Johnson's own observations, Tinsdale's statement of the Benders being flush with cash made logical sense. Majors, the local constable from Cherryvale, had told the detective there were no horses left in the stable when the Benders departed. Even with the number of bodies that had been discovered so far, the horses, wagons, and personal effects of the dead including cash would have been sizable. It just seemed they were too good at what they did to flee the country completely, unless retirement was their plan. Did killers ever retire?

In retrospect, the Benders really didn't need to farm to survive; killing people was bringing in more than enough revenue. Had their entire appearance as an immigrant farm family making a few extra dollars with a makeshift inn been a full-fledged criminal front? It could not be ruled out.

Johnson had noted the Bender Inn was unusually sparse. Even though the house had been moved, it was basically intact when Johnson got on the scene and he looked it over carefully. There was a complete lack of hominess. It was as if the family had never truly shared any normal experiences of day-to-day life there. It was a very cold place to walk through. No pictures on the walls, no books, nothing that showed the place to be more than a sparse location of business, or, maybe more aptly, a kill zone. Only one rug was present in the house and that one was completely utilitarian to cover a trap door under the kitchen table. The full reasons behind the kitchen's trap door were still unknown but Johnson had his speculations, and they weren't pretty.

Johnson read through all the teletypes and the large stack of papers Constable Majors had provided. Using the abilities acquired from his training through the Clint Parker Security Agency he began to create a profile on John Bender Sr. He would create a profile for each member of the family though it would easier when he got more information on the men. After all, they were the leaders of the family, and were presumptively thought by everyone to be the actual killers. Now, there was no doubt that Ma Bender and her daughter Kate would also hang as accomplices if the group was caught, but that would be mostly for shunning their Christian duty to expose the Bender men for their deeds. Even though no one had yet to prove in a court of law what had really transpired at the Bender Inn, Johnson was no fool. The women had to know what was happening around them and whether it was out of fear, or something else, they had remained silent. They were also as guilty as sin.

The train made a short stop in Humboldt, and here the decision of where to go next became more difficult. The detective contacted the train conductor and through talk and money convinced him to hold the train that would have left the station after a mere fifteen minutes.

First, he sent a lengthy message by way of the telegraph office, to Clint Parker himself, the owner of the detective agency in New York. Johnson sent in his observations so far and requested information be collected through Majors in Cherryvale about any strange deaths in southeast Kansas before the Bender Inn was constructed. He also asked for the last location of the Bender family before arriving in Kansas. In addition, he asked about an orchard being present on the John Bender Jr. property. From what he understood, no crops or cattle were present on the property and he had a theory that was growing about why that was, but it was something he was not ready to share yet.

Two ticket clerks claimed to have seen the Bender family at the Humboldt station. Ticket clerk, Ron Sparks, stated the family split into two groups, with John Bender Jr. and Kate taking the MK&T train south to the terminus in Red River County near Denison, Texas. John Bender Sr. and Ma Bender where reported to have bought the extension trip and stayed on the Humboldt train to Kansas City. Conversely, Harry Odelly said the entire family boarded the train south to Texas. The documentation was inconclusive as four tickets had been purchased for trips in both directions. Johnson used his conversation and observational abilities to make a critical decision. At the onset he learned that Colonel York had already interviewed both men and himself had gone towards Kansas City where John Bender Sr. and his wife were reported to have headed. With his posse now at numbers growing every day, he had sent fifty men south toward Texas. These men would be on horseback and would no doubt take shortcuts from the train's full route to hit the station stops as quickly as possible. It's what most lawmen would do but most men weren't Robert Johnson. What Colonel York and his men didn't allow for was seeing any locations where the Benders might jump from the train. Johnson would take the train ride now, no matter which direction he chose to go later, in an attempt to follow the Benders along their actual journey.

In Humboldt Johnson observed the Bender's use of money to attempt to misdirect some of the followers from their trail. For the tickets collectors, having been grilled over their story several times, along with the conflicts in their tales, had created a personal animosity between the two and they couldn't even stay in the same room with each other. Both men said they had clearly seen what happened, and the other one was a liar.

Harry Odelly was a seventy-five-year-old Irishman and had worked for the railroad for twenty-nine years. Whether he was concerned about losing his job at his advanced age or had a pre-existing heart condition, the man sweated profusely while being interviewed and was tremendously agitated. Johnson could only presume his tension level while in the presence of Colonel York and his thugs. On the other hand, Ron Sparks, a young man of about twenty years was excited about the investigation and very engaging.

Johnson utilized his detecting skills and observed the young man carefully before talking to him. Sparks was an orphan who at eighteen was given a job by the railroad partly because he had been abandoned on the train as a newborn and several of trainmen had an affinity for the then baby, now a young man in pursuit of employment. In addition, Sparks had lots of energy and worked for the railroad's meager entrance wage. One thing was for sure, a person of his station could not afford the new outfit his employer stated he now wore to work. Even today, the young man while in average clothes wore a three-dollar hat, new boots, and from the smell of the face cologne that still lingered near his person, had received a high-end shave that morning which often ran as much as thirty-five cents. Johnson surmised as a first level train employee, he probably made not a penny past twenty-five dollars a month. Sparks had recently come into money and it wasn't an inheritance.

Johnson separated the boy from his employer and interrogated the young man for three hours. He was using precious time he didn't have, but finding the truth of whether or not the Benders had run in different directions was critical. The detective knew the questions he had to ask, and more importantly, how to ask them. Not once did he threaten violence, an obvious tactic that had been implemented by Colonel York, and one that was usually short sighted. From his knowledge in the field, he had learned people seldom gave reliable information when being tortured. Smart men used facts and evidence to catch people in lies and break them without ever leaving a physical mark.

After three hours, Sparks had been forced to the truth. His new money had indeed been collected from a bribe of seventy-five dollars from John Bender Sr. He was instructed to tell authorities the Benders had taken two trains when it fact the family had stayed together and were headed for Texas. The bribe was a literal fortune, but as he spoke, it appeared that the boy may have been influenced by the reported beauty of Kate Bender. It was clear by his testimony Sparks had instantly fallen in love with the girl, who promised to come back for him in a month if he held up his part of the deal.

Sparks's deception was serious business and could be construed as aiding and abetting. To the crimes now attributed to the Benders, the young ticket agent could easily hang. This did not sit well with the detective. He was adept at judging people's character and Sparks was simply a love struck kid who had come across the wrong people at the wrong time. The detective made a deal with the ticket agent, which he felt was both ethical and practical. He would not tell local law enforcement about the boy's false statements and after a month, the boy would contact both Jim Snoddy and Colonel C.J. Peckham and alter his account. He would say that after reflecting on the incident, he did not feel certain his recollection was accurate. Johnson walked him through how to explain how the excitement over the incident had temporarily overwhelmed him. The boy was made to repeat every word. If done correctly, Sparks would avoid a hangman's noose, regardless if the Benders were, or were not, caught. In addition, Sparks agreed to anonymously send the other ticket agent, Harry Odelly, half of the remaining Bender payoff money. This equaled twenty-five dollars and would go a long way to reduce the old man's tension over his ordeals of the past few weeks. It seemed like the right thing to do. Johnson told the local authorities his interview with Sparks failed to turn up anything new and his decision to take the next train to Terminus in Red River County near Denison, Texas was just a random choice.

The ticket for the MK&T, which was part of the Union Pacific Railroad was not cheap, but unlike half of Colonel York's men. Johnson was on the right trail. The train pulled out promptly at 2:30 p.m. and would work its way into Oklahoma by late that evening. Johnson would get at least three hours sleep in his private car before the evening meal.

The first full stop would be in Vinita, Oklahoma, and while the town was not much to look at, it had a teletype office where the detective hoped to get more information pertinent to the investigation. Traveling from one state to another was like entering a new world. The United States was getting smaller, and communications faster, but in Oklahoma most citizens and great number of law enforcement wouldn't know much of anything about the Kansas murders. The further south they went, it would be more of the same.

Johnson took the downtime on the train to clean his weapons. He had acquired his Sharps rifle in 1862 when his skill as a sharp shooter was recognized by the Union Army. His aim was deadly and the Sharps rifle, which held a .50 caliber 475 grain projectile, could drop a buffalo as effectively as it could a confederate soldier. The Civil War seemed to never leave Johnson's mind as it was here he learned the secret trade of observation, concealment and when need be, killing. These were skills that would later be further developed by the detective agency for the purpose of law enforcement. His rifle was a weapon from the war but his revolver was a weapon of the future. He carried the new Colt Peacemaker. It was a .45 caliber single shot pistol that would become the official sidearm of the U.S. Army next year. His ability to procure this masterful piece of technology was a byproduct of his employer Clint Parker's past affiliation with the Army, and the usefulness of the agency in government matters. Lastly, Johnson cleaned his bowie knife, which he had used twice in brawls in Dodge City. While the detective was deadly at long distances with the rifle, if need be, he could do the same at close range.

Johnson was dismayed to see there were no communications for him to receive at the Vinita office, other than additional money which he received gratefully. He carried an unhealthy amount of cash with him at all times. The agency had long since trained their detectives that more information could be obtained through carefully crafted bribes and opportunistic purchases than through violence.

In McAlester and Atoka Johnson temporarily left the train and made casual inquiries in town. No one matching the Bender's descriptions had acquired supplies of any kind from the locals. In fact, no one had seen them at all. Johnson had to keep looking. Somewhere there had to be a person who held that special bit of information that would help him narrow in his search.

By 9:00 a.m. on the third day he had almost traversed the state of Oklahoma. Johnson was asleep in his private car when the sound of gun fire made him jump from his fold-out bed. At first the shots sounded like hail hitting a metal roof top. It was nothing more than a *ting! ting! ting!* sound, which moved closer quickly until two bullets came crashing through the shuttered main window of the sleeper cab. The rounds landed three feet from Johnson, who already had his hands on the Sharps rifle. The bullets entered the cab through the shutters, and along with the commotion taking place outside made it evident

that some sort of siege was taking place. At least twenty-
five men on horseback were racing toward the moving
train. They all had rifles in hand, and all but two wore
bandanas covering their faces. Johnson, who made it his
business to know all the outlaws who currently had
bounties on their heads, quickly recognized the outlaws
John Kenny and Don "cold-hand" Frange. The gang
belonged to Kenny and they were also known as the Rio
Grande Posse. Despite being only the second in
command, Frange had actually killed three times as many
men. The group was notorious as train robbers and cattle
rustlers in New Mexico, and their presence this far east
was strange. Johnson took aim from his sleeper car and
shot a single rider, who was trailing the main group, off his
horse. The action was moving quickly to the center of the
train.

As was the case with long distance railroad travel,
the mail cars were usually placed in the center of the train.
The passenger cars were toward the rear, followed by
supply cars, which would carry lumber and cattle with the
mail cars in the center with everything from letters to
steam trunks of clothing all the way to the more precious
items such as company payroll, and bank transfers of gold
and coin. Coal cars would be near the main engine to fuel

the entire system. Trains such as these would have up to three large, steel safes, which could, at times, be stuffed to the brim with payroll currency of every sort.

In the heyday of Pinkerton's contract with the railroad the detective agency had utilized a myriad of crafty plans to thwart train robberies. They had mounted Gatling guns inside the mail cars, which could belch a deadly stream of bullets in seconds. They had filled cattle cars full of armed detectives on horseback, and through this ingenuity had wiped out entire gangs at a time. Had it not been for the exorbitant amount of money Alan Pinkerton had managed to receive in contract to catch or kill the members of the James and Younger gang and his inability to deliver after being paid, this train might also have been armed with a Pinkerton defense.

Instead, the train had a meager response ready for such an attack. Johnson had noted four armed men, possibly ex-army, but most likely just railroad labor hands that had been handed a pistol or a rifle, who would ride with the money within the mail cars. There were probably two more men either deputized as "train police" or hired muscle somewhere on the train. All-in-all it would be far from what was needed to stop the robbery.

Beyond the mail cars would be the coal cars, which would fuel the boilers of the train's engine. As Johnson exited his sleeper car and made his was down the hallway, he knew the train robbers would do one of two things. They would either follow the James and Younger model, and keep the train moving at least at three-quarters speed, hit the mail car and flee quickly, or they would do what the stupid robbers did; they would shut the train down, rob the mail car and then progress to the passenger cars and rob the travelers individually. This often ended with additional loss of life and higher occasions of rape and other crimes. Jesse James had understood that while the booty from the passengers might slightly increase the overall take, it also took a lot of time and there was never a certainty of just who might be traveling onboard. The Long Boot gang had lost seven of their men when attempting to rob the passengers of a Missouri train when, to their surprise, they encountered the Jenus brothers, two notorious "quick draw" shooters from the state.

There were probably fifty to sixty passengers slated for the trip to Denton, Texas. Since half would be residents of the state, no doubt headed home, it was certain there would be lots of armed passengers. As Johnson entered the second passenger's car gunfire erupted again. Many of the passengers were indeed firing on the robbers, and they were taking fire in return. Women screamed and children cried as bullets bounced around the inner hull of the passenger car, tearing through seat cushions and breaking glass. A man in a brown suit vest fired wildly out the window until a bullet to the chest sent him crashing hard to the floor. A young man of fifteen was struck in the shoulder by a stray bullet as he tried to cover his sister. Fortunately, the robbers rode by quickly, and soon the gun fire in the second car stopped and commenced in the next car forward. Worse yet, Johnson saw what appeared to be the dead body of the conductor on the ground as the train moved forward. To confirm someone else was behind the controls, the train started to slow down. The Kenny gang was going to stop the MK&T, and it was going to be a blood bath unless he acted now.

Against his better judgment, Johnson exited the passenger car and made his way to the

rooftop. From there, he began to run toward the conductor's station, jumping from car to car. It didn't take long to get near of the mail car, which was the central point of action. Here the four hired railroad guards were fighting for their lives to keep robbers from entering the car. Men on horseback were firing into the car from both sides and several riders had climbed aboard and were firing through the windows. It would be only a few minutes before the guards would be dead and the mail car would be boarded.

Johnson stopped five cars away and went to a knee. From this location he was seventy-five yards away from the robbers and would be firing from a still moving train. As he raised his rifle and took aim at the men clinging to the outside of the mail car, he slowed his breathing and relaxed his mind. He squeezed gently on the trigger and the rifle jumped against his shoulder. The bullet struck one of the robber's in the back sending him falling to the ground. Two more robbers fell before John Kenny, who was in the process of shutting the train down, realized something bad was happening.

It was his experience as a war-time sniper that had trained Johnson to stay back from the action and out of view. Even when Kenny remounted his horse and rode back to the mail car, he, like his men, had no idea where the bullets were coming from. Behind them was open Texas prairie for miles. The passengers in the travel cars didn't have the proper angle to hit the men attacking the mail car, and yet well-aimed bullets continued to strike the men attempting enter the car.

Finally, Kenny saw Johnson, but not before seven of his men had been killed. The leader of the gang and several others began to fire at the top of the train car but Johnson was already on the move. He had struck a blow to the gang, but he no longer had the element of surprise. Worse yet, the train was almost at a stop. Johnson had to think quickly as Don Frange and five other men moved swiftly in on him, firing as they advanced. Frange loved to kill, and he had a knack for staying alive while doing it. It was reported he had been shot fifteen times during his life, and it was the devil that kept him alive.

Johnson could have made a last stand with the passengers in one of the cars. There were guns there, and the men who were capable would no doubt fight to the end to defend their families. When the train did, in fact, come to a complete stop everyone knew it was a fight or die situation. However, Johnson refused to focus more gunfire on a passenger car comprised of families simply because he had decided to take a last stand there. If he was lucky, maybe he could draw the fire elsewhere. As bullets bounced around him he entered a cattle car. The trailer was full of agitated Santa Gertrudis, and Johnson was as

41

apt to get stomped to death as shot. Still the large, red, wild eyed cows slowed Kenny's men who had dismounted on both ends of the cattle car and were attempting to trap him in the middle. The cattle were packed in tightly, which reduced their ability to kick one another. It also made moving through the herd slow going. The Santa Gertrudis, with their large body weight, were lucrative, but they were a wild breed and they all sensed Johnson, who was now hunched down in the center of the car. The cows grunted in anger as Kenny's men slowly and quietly worked their way toward the location where the detective was hiding. Their revolvers were in their holsters as to shoot without a definite target here was too dangerous.

The gunfire that had been going on from the passengers cars was now over. Johnson could only guess how many travelers had been killed, but no doubt Kenny's men now had control of the survivors. He had to think fast. He had maybe a couple of minutes until he would be completely cornered. It was then an idea came to him. Not the best idea, mind you, but certainly one that was better than waiting to die. Crawling past a large bull who eyed him with such ferocity it was certain had he had the room, would have stomped him to death, Johnson made his way to the center door of the cattle car. Quietly, he grabbed hold of the handle. He knew that when he opened the cattle door the Santa Gertrudis would charge for freedom. Even being right at the exit offered him only a small chance of avoiding being trampled to death. However, his chances of survival were much better than that of the men within the cattle car, who now closed in on him. Getting himself into position, he waited for what he knew would come next. Within seconds a giant explosion rocked the train as a dynamite charge was ignited from within the mail car. Kenny's men had blown the lid from one of the metal safes. This was the distraction Johnson needed. The cows bellowed in fear and fury, and at that exact same moment Johnson slide open the door. He flung himself underneath the train as hooves flew over his body. The men pursuing him within the cattle car were trampled. The guards on both sides of the train who were serving as lookouts had their attention to the open plains and none of them saw Johnson make his way toward the mail car. That is, no one except Frange, who had sent his men in, but had not personally entered the cattle car. Frange was forty-five-years-old with a long black beard, which was slowly turning white. When his mouth was not full of whiskey, it was full of chewing tobacco, and he was known for spitting tobacco on the corpses of those he gunned down. A long brown tobacco-filled arc of spittle shot from

Frange's mouth as he signaled three additional riders to dismount and follow him. Frange and his men began to work their way down the train line attempting to find Johnson's location under the train cars. There were desperate few places for the detective to hide.

Johnson took a defensive stance along the caboose. Despite its limited cover, it was his only option. For miles in all directions there was nothing but open range, and if he ran, the robbers would easily ride him down on horseback and put a bullet in his back. The only thing working in his favor was that most of Kenny's men were busy collecting the spoils of the robbery and all but the deranged killer, Frange, and three additional men, too afraid to directly oppose him, were closing in. At that moment, it was a simple matter of distance, time, and bullets. Johnson never wasted a shot and his ammunition level was fine, but that wasn't his concern. Frange and his men were charging at him from both sides of the train. They fired as they ran. At fifty yards out their shots were short and far off the mark. Johnson exhaled slowly as he pulled the trigger on the Sharp rifle. A bullet hit one of the men in the chest, killing him instantly. At twenty-five yards the bullets from the three remaining men's pistols sent dirt dancing around his boots where he knelt along the caboose's massive wheels. Johnson's next shot hit the man nearest Frange in the left leg, sending him crashing to the ground in pain. A bullet ricocheted off the hull of the caboose, which sent chards of metal into the detective's cheek. The men were closing too fast. As Johnson squared the rifle's sight on Frange, a bullet struck him in the shoulder, knocking him backwards to the grounds. The Sharps rifle went spiraling in the opposite direct. The detective realized every second counted for his survival and shrugged off the roaring pain in his left shoulder and drew his pistol as the first advancing robber came upon him rapidly. In his haste, the man almost over ran the detective and he stirred up a dirt cloud as his boots slid to a stop two feet from Johnson who was still on his back. The man was breathing hard and mucus ran from his nose as he jerked his pistol toward Johnson and shot. Fire flew from the gun's barrel, but despite being only feet away, he missed. Cursing, through rotted teeth the man stepped even closer and steadied his aim and fired again. This time there was only a "*click*" sound as the hammer hit the firing pin. The robber's pistol was empty. From his back, Johnson placed the end of his pistol on the man's boot and fired. The bullet traveled through the man's right foot exiting out his heal in a gush of blood and bone. Before the outlaw could hit the ground Johnson had squared and fired on Frange who was less than twelve feet away. The bullet went high and took the man's black cowboy hat off his head. Frange fell to the ground as Johnson rolled to a different position. When the dust settled, the two men sat on the hot hard Texas prairie no further than six feet away with pistols point at one another. A single drop of crimson slid its way down Frange's forehead. The detective's round had almost sealed the deal but Don "cold hand" Frange was more than just alive; he was angry.

"You don't die that easy," Frange said, wiping the blood from his head.

"Might say the same for you," Johnson returned, weighing his options.

There was a commotion coming from the center of the train, and soon additional gunshots sounded.

"I think your boys have some new problems," Johnson said motioning with his head toward the train's mail car.

Frange grunted in anger as he saw his gang fleeing to the west. They were being chased by at least twenty men on horseback. The men wore long, gray coats and their tall, white Stetson hats clearly marked them as Texas Rangers.

"Rangers don't stop once they're on the hunt. You, Kenny, and your gang are done." Johnson worked his way to his feet as did the man before him.

Frange spat a long stream of tobacco in Johnson's direction and spoke, "It was bound to happen sometime. At least I'll know you'll die with me." His eyes were cold and his smile had a hungry darkness about it.

However, his smiled faded when Johnson returned it and began to walk toward him with his pistol still raised.

"You're an idiot, Frange. An idiot with an empty gun." Johnson laughed.

"To hell it's…" Frange was interrupted by the detective. "You fired three times at the cattle car, twice on your approach, and then that chicken shit shot while I was on the ground boot shooting your friend. That's six shots, and oh, don't even try to convince yourself that you reloaded along the way cause you didn't. Blood thirsty killers like you never take the time to count bullets and never think down the road."

Frange cocked his pistol as did Johnson. "Bullshit. This ain't nothing but a trick," Frange responded as sweat formed on his forehead.

"Oh really?" Johnson lowered his gun as the commotion at the center of train was coming their way. "Then, by all means, take the first shot because I'm taking the second one and putting a bullet between your eyes. You might as well know you're not only a murderer and a thief, but also an idiot, before your die."

Frange was breathing hard. He was scared, and it was apparent. His gun hand shook but in the end, his killer instinct was going to win out against his fear of death. Johnson could see that killer glint return in his eyes, and had it not been an approaching Ranger who yelled at them both to put down their guns, Frange would have pulled the trigger. At the sound of the Ranger's approach, the man's attention was split and his head turned toward the approaching lawman. Within a flash, Johnson raised his pistol, fired, and put a round into the man's skull. Frange fell in a heap and Johnson dropped his pistol as three more Rangers quickly surrounded him.

Over the next two hours, the Rangers went through Johnsons papers and verified his employment with the Clint Parker Security Agency. Though he thought a couple of times about checking Frange's pistol, which lay in the dirt, the detective refrained from examining the gun to see if it had, in fact, been empty. Some mysteries were okay to leave unanswered. The outlaw was dead and he was alive, that was enough. The capture of the Benders was his goal and he would focus all his efforts on tracking them down.

Two local doctors were brought to the site and began treating the train passengers. Fortunately, only five had been killed which paled in comparison to the John Kenny gang, which had lost thirteen. Other than Kenny and five of his men, who were fleeing with the cash and gold stolen from the train, and the group of Rangers currently on their heels, was the remaining outlaw Johnson had shot in the foot. The man's name was John Greentree, and currently he was in the back of the second doctor's wagon. As was customary during robberies of any kind, criminals got medical attention only after every victim had been attended to. The man's belt had been synched around his ankle to keep him from bleeding out, and he had been tossed in the wagon to wait his turn. When his turn did come, the doctor's prognosis was quick and to the point. The foot would be amputated and the stump cauterized. His chances were fifty-fifty he would die during the procedure as painkillers were too scarce to waste on a worthless outlaw, who would certainly hang after a short trial.

Johnson spoke with the Rangers about any information they might have about the Bender family while the captain of the Rangers argued with the senior doctor that a sedative had to be used on Greentree. This wasn't out of compassion. The Rangers needed a survivor of the gunfight to bring to trial as they believed the surrounding communities needed a trial and a hanging to be convinced the Rangers were effective at bringing justice and order to the territory. Greentree, who was already turning white from blood loss, was too afraid to try and plead his own case and simply watched everything transpiring in shivering silence. It wasn't until the man heard Johnson's questions about the Benders that he spoke.

"I seen them Benders you looking for, mister," he said in a weak, trembling, voice.

Johnson walked to the wagon and examined the man's face. Even as the pain twisted the man's facial features, the detective knew from his own observational skills the train robber was telling the truth. "Tell me everything you know," Johnson said quietly.

Greentree looked to a large bottle of laudanum, which sat in the doctor's black leather bag. The white haired doctor, who still carried an angry scowl, broke from his argument with the Ranger and grabbed the bag with both hands. He spoke in a sharp voice, "Like I was telling these lawmen, we don't have the resources to waste precious painkillers on no good varmints like this!"

Johnson handed the man several dollar bills saying, "Just a few sips doctor, for a greater good I assure you."

The doctor eyed the money with the knowledge it would be enough to purchase several bottles of the high powered painkiller. The scowl, which had been on his face, softened and he stuffed the bills in his pocket and placed the leather bag back in the wagon and walked away. Johnson motioned for the Rangers to give him space and when he was alone with Greentree, he removed the bottle from the bag and allowed the man to drink enough to take the edge off the pain but not enough to cloud his brain. When the man was settled Johnson asked his questions.

"Tell me what you know about the Benders. Take your time." Johnson held the bottle out to the man and shook it gently as if to remind him there was still more of it available. The detective was glad when the man accurately described the family. The Benders had indeed made their way into Texas and to Johnson's surprise, they had joined an outlaw colony near the border of Texas and Mexico.

The Benders were said to still be there. The detective knew the Benders had to be crafty to have committed their deadly deeds for as long as they did without being noticed, but taking refuge with a band of cattle rustlers and train robbers seemed out of place. That is, unless his initial assumptions about the family were way off base.

The doctor removed a bone saw from the front of the wagon and had collected the three Rangers who would help restrain the man while his foot was removed. Johnson had seen this process too many times on the battlefield during the war, and didn't need to watch it again. The detective had allowed the man three drinks from the bottle of laudanum and was about to end his interrogation of the man when the robber offered one last piece of information.

"You know you're all wrong about that bunch," he said through slurred lips.

"How so?" Johnson asked.

"They ain't no family, at least not like you'd think it. And that old man, Bender, ain't leading nothing," The man's eyes were beginning to droop.

Johnson gave him a shake and he continued, "The girl runs the bunch; she'll be running the whole colony in six months."

"You're talking about the daughter, Kate Bender?" Johnson inquired dubious of the man's statements.

"She ain't no real daughter, and that ain't no real family, as I already said, but yeah, the one they call Kate. She's craftier than John Kenny could ever be, and more deadly than that butcher Frange."

The Doctor and the Rangers were now directly behind Johnson, and it was time for the robber to say goodbye to his foot. Despite an unhappy look from the doctor, Johnson allowed Greentree a final pull from the bottle. As he turned to leave the men to their grislily work, Greentree made one last statement. "Detective, don't keep after that Bender bunch. Just let them be. It ain't worth no bounty. That Kate Bender is no outlaw. I know outlaws and I've seen the worst. She's a witch and worse than that, she walks with the devil."

3 NOVEMBER 1870: A CRIMINAL
OPERATION BEGINS

Insert Kate and Ma Bender waited patiently to be picked up at the Ottawa train station. They had been traveling on trains for several days, and the world had changed greatly over the miles from Polk, Ohio, or even Ashland County, to where they were now. Compared to the tall trees of Ohio, Kansas seemed like a flat wasteland of open pasture.

However, as Kate Bender's beautiful, green eyes surveyed the people walking back and forth throughout the station, she saw opportunity. This trip was the culmination of long, careful planning and it would reap the family a great bounty. Well, the family entity they had created. They were well practiced not to address each other in any form but their fictitious, Bender family titles. Kate had made them practice until they all but believed it to be a reality. Still, somewhere in the back of her mind the truth was still there; they were all really strangers to one another.

There was John Flickinger, a large man born in Germany with a penchant for physical violence. He was born in 1815 and at fifty-six years of age, was as strong as an ox from years of working fishing nets and lugging crates of the daily catch along the docks of New York. Despite being able to speak decent English, Flickinger, under Kate's direction seldom spoke to anyone. It was simpler and more believable for people to avoid conversations with the often angry Pa Bender, than to allow the man's temper to disrupt their criminal enterprise. There was no mistaking what they had come to do. They had come to kill and to steal, and they would get rich doing it.

Though over a year had passed in the preparation for the move to southeast Kansas, they had already honed their skills for this venture in Polk, Ohio. In fact, had it not been for Kate's intuition and ability to read people, they might have continued their small criminal enterprise there, which would have led to inevitable capture. As had been the case for years the beautiful German girl knew exactly when action had to be taken to avoid detection. There were extraordinary reasons for this. Eliza Griffith, who now traveled by the name Kate Bender, had help from a most unbelievable origin.

Through the train station window they both saw Pa and John Jr. dismount from their flatbed wagon, which would take them to their new home. The wagon was strong and sturdy but not flashy or overly expensive. It was a purchase that would fit in well with the locals. John Jr.'s cloths were stained with sweat and he looked as though he was in need of a haircut. If there was one thing the boy could do it was play a part. Kate always thought of John Jr., whose real name was John Gebhart, as a boy despite the fact he was slightly older than her at twenty-two years old. John Jr.'s mind was like that of a child's. He was not daft by any means. His factual features were handsome and his body was straight and strong. On short term inspection his mental faculties appeared no different than anyone else. However, if someone spent extended amounts of time with the boy it became apparent he saw the world differently.

Within the criminal enterprise known as the Bender family, no one was innocent. However, Kate considered John Jr. to be the closest to qualify despite having committed eight murders himself in Ohio. John Jr.

had been slated for commitment to the Willard Asylum for the Insane in New York. Kate knew, or better said, had been shown, he was important to her future work. With a handful of money, and a few falsely signed forms, he was released into her custody. John Jr. loved Kate but it was not in a sexual manner. His love was like that of a brother, a companion, a friend. For John Jr., the Bender's killing and robbery was like a game that never ended. He understood that what they were doing was murder, and it was wrong, but even so, Kate gave a blessing to it and that brought him joy. As long as Kate was happy, he was happy. In his mind, that made him blameless and clean.

John Jr.'s mind would often wonder and occasionally he would laugh in a way that was too childlike for a grown man. But with that said, when in the presence of Kate, he could focus and learn and do. Kate taught him how to flawlessly portray himself as her husband or brother. It was decided that John Jr. would play the part of a brother while in Kansas, as he enjoyed this character most, and Kate liked the opportunities afforded her when appearing single.

Ma Bender's real name was Almira Meik, and she was, in fact, Kate's biological mother. Despite this they were nearly strangers. Meik was a man hunter and a deadly gold digger and she had a lust for the finer things only men

of wealth could provide. Kate assumed her mother had
been attractive in her youth but all of her living
recollections of Ma were of an aging, dumpy woman with
a bitter disposition towards life. What she could do, what
she taught Kate to do, was act lovingly toward men and to
manipulate them for personal gain. Ma could, when she
desired, transform herself into an angelic creature, which
could stroke the egos and control the insecurities of
powerful men. Alas, she did not have the ability to
withstand the day-to-day rigors of marriage, and within a
year or two her husbands would see through her
deceptions, to the bitter woman she actually was. Afraid of
losing her fine living, Ma would dispatch her husbands and
live as a wealthy widow for as long as the money held out.
Kate's mother was a poisoner. She was a master in the
usage of liquid and culinary poisons. Arsenic, cyanide,
mercury, belladonna, wolfsbane, foxglove and a number of
other herbs could be crafted into a tool of death by the
woman. Ma knew how to administer poison in ways that
were undetectable and brought about few questions of foul
play. Most often Ma killed her men slowly over time.
These sorts of deaths were usually seen as natural
sicknesses running their course. In all, she'd poisoned nine
husbands over seventeen years. Two had actually gotten
sick of natural causes, and Kate's mother had poisoned the

doctor prescribed medicines to speed up their demise. She was good, and Kate learned not only the art of poisoning from her but the more important art of role playing and feminine deception. In the latter, she became an amazing specialist.

On the train bench Ma massaged her neck and absentmindedly caressed two of the four large steam trunks the women had brought with them. Ma was fifty-six years old and suffered from a bad back. Long trips of any kind eventually caused her discomfort, but she, as well as the rest of the group who now traveled as the Bender family, knew Kate was right to signal their departure from Ohio. Kate was always right, and her decisions had never failed to keep them ahead of the law and flush with cash. The items within their luggage ranged from the common to the ghastly. There were several expensive dresses from New York, which would have caught the eye of any local. They had changed out of these two states ago and into plain dresses, which would fit the simple look for women on the plains. Their large stock of jewelry, some bought in fancy stores, and others taken from the cold, dead fingers of their victims in Ohio, where stored in ornate wooden boxes, and probably would not be seen while they were in Kansas. Two-thirds of an entire steam truck was full of Ma's vials and satchels of poisons. Kate had tried to get her mother to leave these items out of state but it was no use. Even though their plans for Kansas would not require these deadly concoctions, the old women just would not give them up.

The entire group had discussed and agreed to the parts each would play. In Kansas, Ma would not be seeking out rich bachelors or widowers with an end game of separating them from their money. She was now too old for seduction and her killing methods took too long. Instead, she would have a silent role and assist Kate who would shoulder all of the major decisions for the group. The men would be the muscle, and when violence was needed, as it had in Ohio, they would dole it out under her direction. Even Pa with his violent nature had agreed to this prior to the Ohio experiment. Kate had delivered to them a huge monetary reward with the promise that in Kansas, they would make enough money to retire for life.

In another steam trunk were stacks of pictures of Labette and Montgomery County, Kansas. These pictures include the vantage points of the new homestead and all visual points of their property line in relation to their neighbors. It was after looking at hundreds of photos of the open properties that Kate had made the decision on the tracks they would purchase. The Indian land, which had been opened to the public, was vast, but they had special needs. Their test run in Ohio had taught them that much. The Bender Inn would be located on high ground and out of visual range of the train lines. They had learned trains carried hundreds of eyes and they would need privacy for their work. As good fortune would have it, Kate had seen the trees that flanked both sides of the dirt trail that led to their homestead. The seldom seen tree lines in this state obscured activity on the trail nearest their new property and gave additional cover to activities that might be transpiring at the inn.

Still, there was more work that had to be done before Kate and Ma could arrive. Along with building the inn, barn, and a house, Pa and John Jr. were directed to plant an extensive apple orchard on both purchased properties. As was seen in the photos, both land tracks had a few small apple trees, but under Kate's direction, the men had planted at least fifty fast growing apple trees, on both properties. They also planted additional trees of various types down to the road way to fill any open, visual gaps of the road to their property as seen from a distance. The cost of the work was immense, and the men had to buy their supplies at over ten different vendors to avoid suspicion. Fortunately, the one thing they had plenty of was money. In one steamer trunk alone was thirty thousand dollars in cash. The other trunks all held currency in one form or another. To most, they would have been seen as rich beyond belief but Kate knew that the lifestyle she and Ma required would require more, much more.

Fluent German was spoken as the group united. They laughed and hugged one another in the train station. Despite the fact that Ma and Pa hated one another, and that the entire band of thieves and killers were governed by a twenty-one-year-old girl, they appeared in public like another loving immigrant family, that had relocated to make their mark in the mostly untouched center of America. They looked normal and, thus, unremarkable.

On the lengthy wagon ride to their claims, they spoke at length about their operational plans. Pa gave a point by point breakdown of everything they had put into place. The big man was allowed to drink from a liquor bottle while he gave his account. Pa's first vice was whiskey, and it could be a problem as he was always an angry drunk. He had become enamored with a brand called Old Forestor, which was a stout Kentucky bourbon whiskey. Ironically, the brand was far from old, having been released only about a year ago by a man named George Garvin Brown. Pa sang his praises for the former pharmaceutical salesman turned bourbon-merchant. During her initial embrace with Pa at the station she had smelled his breath and was pleased to see he had not been drinking earlier in the day. Limiting Pa's drinking would be her job and she would handle it as she had in Ohio. Within the secret knowledge of the created Bender family, Pa's second vice was Kate herself. Once a month, maybe more if it was required, Kate and Pa would go to the seclusion of the barn and his desires both normal and exotic would be satisfied. This was Kate's power over the large man with the black hair and crooked nose. Whereas he would have beaten the brains out of a man for similar requests, Pa would willingly obey almost all orders from Kate. Her hold over him was great and it had to be.

Sex was of little consequence to Kate Bender beyond what it could get her, and that was a lot. She understood the physical act was traditionally associated with love and she could overwhelm any man with her abilities in the bedroom. Beyond a sisterly bond of friendship to John Jr., she had no true emotional ties to the group. Certainly nothing she would call love. However, if love was real at all she felt it only toward her true benefactor, and he was still in Ohio.

Kate smiled as she observed Pa's gaze upon her. The months without her touch had worn on him, and it was obvious he wanted her. That was good, and she enjoyed the notion she would make him wait even longer to be satisfied. There were things that would have to be done almost immediately upon their arrival, and she wanted the big man moving quickly to her orders. To this effect, she made Ma sit with Pa up front, while she and John Jr. sat under blankets in the back of the wagon. The wool blankets were thick and shielded their bodies against the cold November winds.

On the open Kansas plain, John Jr. bellowed his childish laugh, and no one admonished him. Despite the serious work that was ahead of them, Kate enjoyed a moment of light-hearted play. After they had enjoyed several hours of simple fun, Kate began whispering in John Jr.'s ear. In a sweet voice she cajoled her pretend brother as she gently collected critical information on what had really taken place in her absence. Everything from how many times Pa had beaten him, to just how many murders they could take credit for here already. Oh yes, despite her orders to the contrary, Kate knew Pa could not go a year without extinguishing a life. He wouldn't be able to hold his inner anger that long. The darkness within him was too powerful not to escape at least once. She only hoped he had not placed the whole family under suspicion before they could get their criminal operation off and running.

"Oh, mercies of the abyss!" she said quietly through clenched teeth when John Jr. recounted three murders Pa had committed within a few miles of their new home, all in the course of the last eleven months. This was blasted bad fortune. They might have to abandon this place they had so carefully selected. No matter what, she would have to deal with this and have everything right before her benefactor arrived. It had to be perfect by then.

4 NOVEMBER 1870: UNEXPECTED

BODIES

Ma and Kate compared their photographs with the actual landscape as they approached the inn. Indeed it all appeared the same in real life as depicted in the pictures. In fact, it was better. The increased tree line over the trail that led to the inn made it all but impossible to see travelers as they climbed the hill that would take them past the Bender establishment. The inn was sparse but completely functional. As they unpacked the wagon, Kate walked the area around the main house. They were truly on the high ground, and she had watched closely to make sure the home could not be seen from their approach. She smiled when she saw they had one-way viewing of their neighbors from their lofted position. The top of the Toll brother's cabin and their entire herd of cattle could be seen by the Benders from the trail's front entrance to their home. The Tolls were about three-quarters of a mile away to the northeast. They were the closest neighbor, and thus, the biggest threat to their privacy. While the elevation of the property lines kept the Tolls from being able to view Bender activity from their homestead, these neighbors would be on the road that took them by the front of the property on a regular basis. There would have to be special precautions taken to keep these neighbors from seeing more than they should.

To the south was the Tykes family. Mr. and Mrs. Tykes were a middle aged couple who lived alone, and their cabin was not in visual range. Any chance observations by these people from their pasture ground were completely blocked by the fast growing apple orchard, which was flourishing on the south side of the property. On the west side of the mound was the Brockman Trading Post. It was run by the brothers, Ern and Rudolph. Pa and John Jr. had purchased several times from the post which had ingratiated them to the owners. Kate would slowly meet all the neighbors and discover their desires and weaknesses and use it all to the Bender's advantage.

As strategically planned with the property purchase, the well visited Brockman Trading Post had no view of the Bender inn. Better yet, other than trespassers on foot, the inn could only be accessed by the Osage Trail dirt road. From the entrance of the property, a person could see almost two miles down the trail in both directions, while anyone on the trail approaching the Bender Inn saw only the thick tree line.

The inn itself was a good one hundred yards south of the property's entrance. This distance had been meticulously measured by Pa and John Jr. before the home was built, upon explicit instructions from Kate. Anyone approaching the inn would see nothing until they were directly in front of the inn and even then, regular travelers would never think twice about what was happening inside the small rest stop.

While the November air was cold, and the trip back to the Bender's new home had been a long one, they were in good spirits. Pa had even waved to Billy Tolls who had been walking two pregnant cows along the roadway. The boy eagerly returned the wave looking for several moments at Kate, who gave him her best smile. The neighbor showed no look of concern, only the regular excitement country folk exude when new faces pop up. Kate would scrutinize each neighbor even more now, with the new knowledge blood had been spilled prior to her arrival. So far so good. She was pleased with the nearest neighbor's demeanor towards them, and he would remember the pleasant appearance the group made together in the wagon. They would look like a typical family. Maybe not overly loving, but this was a family living on the plains of Kansas. People here weren't pampered or as proper as city folk. She would find out exactly what passed as normal, and the Benders would be that. Appearances were everything. Soon she would begin molding how each and every member of the clan portrayed

themselves in public. That is, if Pa had not already
destroyed their chances in Kansas.

First, she would reassert her authority as leader of
the gang. They were all smiles and laughter as the steam
trunks were unloaded and brought into the house. Inside,
the two women surveyed the home. It was plain. The
house was a one-room dwelling with cloth partitions.
There were two makeshift bedrooms, one for the men and
one for the women. There was a small living room, which
contained two rocking chairs, a small wooden shelf, and a
coat rack. The kitchen area had a wood stove and pantry
with extra shelves where supply stocks for travelers would
be stored. A wooden kitchen table was present and was
flanked by two homemade chairs. Two additional stools
sat in the corner which would allow all the members of the
family to eat together, but directly after their use, they
would be removed. For the work that was ahead of them,
they needed to create a specific mental picture for
travelers. It was simple, food would be served to a single
traveler and that person would eat in the company of Kate
Bender, who would provide pleasant conversation and
take their order for any supplies the inn had in stock for
their continued trip. Men could eat, resupply, and in some
cases nap on a small wooden cot, and then get back on the

trail. For many, this would be exactly how things would transpire. For others, things would take a darker turn.

Inside the house the men explained how they had built the home, and acquired the materials to create the barn and stables yet to be seen. Kate had been all smiles, and even Ma was uncharacteristically happy. That would certainly change over time. Without warning Kate slapped Pa hard across the face.

"What the hell?" the big man shouted in shock. His large body began to shake and fire began to burn in his eyes. To his shock, Kate struck him again and this time with her fist. She had the speed of a rattlesnake, and though Pa would have killed a man for the same, the second blow made him freeze. The daughter of the fictitious family shouted in the man's face, maintaining their practiced family roles.

"Damn you, Pa! What did I say when I sent you two on this important mission?" Kate's face was red with anger and somehow, she appeared much more frightening than the big man. There was a moment of silence, and Pa took in a breath as if to attempt to answer the question, but before he could speak he was struck again. This time Kate hit the man high on his left ear. Pa growled in anger and pain. It was clear he wanted to tear the young girl apart but it was also clear he wasn't going to do it.

"I told you to stay out of trouble! I said do what needs to be done here quietly! Smile if someone talks to you, say hello, and then speak a little German and most will just go away happy and content." The girl's hands tightened into fists, and it appeared she would strike the man again, but she didn't. Instead, she stood on her tip toes and stroked the man's stubbled-chin. Three red marks were forming on his face, and she pretended to be unaware of the damage she had done. In a soft tone, she spoke, never breaking character with the roles they had given each other. "Pa, we have to careful all the time. Yes, there are less people here than there are in the city." She ran her hand across the man's cheek and he closed his eyes in what was most likely erotic bliss. Noticing this she smiled but tapped her finger on his nose until his eyes were open again, and continued, "But, gossip runs twice as high in the countryside. Remember Polk City? Remember the chatter about missing travelers, and those were just train folk. John Jr. says you went and killed three people. Do we even know if they were travelers from outside the area?"

Kate looked directly John Jr. who shook his that they were not all outsiders.

"Damn it, Pa! Makes it even harder, and you know it!" Her eyes watched Pa glance toward John Jr., and she spoke quickly. "Don't even get mad at John Jr.! You know what you done, and it's all on you!" Pa's eye's shot back to the floor.

Kate signaled to Ma, and John Jr. who sat down upon wooden stools. She pulled out a chair and motioned for Pa to take a seat as well. Her facial features were now soft but determined. She had that look that always preceded the delegating of orders. Taking in a long breath she patted John Jr. on the shoulder and then sat in the last chair before speaking. "Okay, we are going to go through all the details of your little indiscretions, Pa, and then, we're going to do what needs to be done to make sure it doesn't come back on us."

For the next week Kate worked to cover the tracks of the three murders Pa had committed before the women's arrival. As she had surmised, he had been drunk at the time of all three killings. Even Pa admitted that much. The first man had been trespassing near the southeast property line. Pa and John Jr. had been fishing in Drum Creek when the man had gotten on Pa's bad side. To Pa's defense, the man, whose papers had identified him as Donald Jones, had been the more intoxicated of the two. After a short fight, Pa had drowned Jones in the creek. Kate listened quietly and asked questions when they were needed. When she wanted complete honesty, she always verified details with John Jr. There were times when his accounts were truly childlike but he would never tell her a lie. Pa would lie, and she knew it. Fortunately, at the moment he was on his best behavior as he understood what would happen if they were captured. He also knew any likelihood of a future trip with her to the barn hinged on this matter being wrapped up quickly. Donald Jones had a letter in his pocket which identified him as having lived in Parsons, Kansas, thus making him a relative local. After the needless killing, the two men had buried the body off the Bender property.

"We took him a quarter mile from the creek up on the Bradley claim and buried him deep. I can't say he'll not come up, but it won't be on our land," John Jr. said in his usual honest way. He quickly added, "Plus, that neighbor Mr. Bradley is one hated man. We seen him in all kinds of arguments at the feed store, the lumber yard, you name it. Everybody hates him, bad Kate! I bet all kinds of people would be happy to pin a killing on him."

John Jr.'s observational skills were as sharp as any child's and while he might not understand all the nuances and subtleties of what his eyes gazed upon, his accounts were usually accurate. The men had watched the newspapers for four months and there had been no reports related to Jones. Kate was satisfied the Drum

Creek fisherman's body would stay quietly tucked away on Bradley's property. However, there would be no more fishing for the men on Drum Creek. Pa brought forth all of the items taken from the man's body. They included three personal letters, a rusted pocket watch, and five dollars and seven cents. Despite having brought thousands of dollars with them from the year's work previous to setting up the Bender Inn, the men knew they were not allowed to spend any of the money taken from a victim of a new kill. It was the ultimate rule of the gang. Within their surreal world of murder and theft, they had one unbreakable form of solidarity: they would not steal from each other. If the man had only one dollar in his pock, it had to be split four ways. Kate verified the haul, as meager as it was, with Ma, and the money was stored separately from all other cash, to be evenly split at a later time. The Bender Inn treasure chest had now officially been created.

The second and third murders happened at nearly the same time. John Jr. gave a full account while Pa remained silent with a look of shame etched across his grizzled face. It was nearly a year previous and during one of the hardest winters locals had seen in a generation. The snow had started falling in mid—October and it hadn't stop until mid-February. The snowdrifts and the white-outs, where visibility was only inches from a person's face had been hard on everyone. For Pa and John Jr. it was especially difficult as they were on a rigid timeline to have the inn and barns built and have the entire homestead prepared for Kate's arrival and they were behind.

They had built the simple home first and had shelter from the elements but the horse stalls and barn had not been completed in time. It was their lack of experience at being either ranchers or farmers that caused them a great deal of strife. Even Kate's meticulous instruction on the creation of the buildings, and the photos they were to take of everything, including their progress, said nothing about how they were to purchase the livestock. With the distance between the women and men, and the time it took to send coded letters back and forth, Pa took it upon himself to make the decision on the purchasing of the animals. Things did not turn out well. In what was a late year cattle auction in Independence, they bought six head of cows, three of them almost to term. It seemed like a solid purchase as they had gotten the animals at a more than fair price. Pa made the purchase as the men set the foundation for the barn. They assumed that within the next thirty days they would have the barn completed in plenty of time for winter. What neither of them knew was that a few weeks later, their work sight would be covered in snow in what was later called the Blizzard of '69 and it would rage for months. Without proper cover the cows died one by one. John Jr. almost wept when he spoke about the baby calves freezing to death beside their mothers. Pa became most belligerent during this time and drank heavily.

John Jr. had convinced Pa to bring the horses inside the house which probably saved them. When the first short break in the blizzard came Pa demanded they go to Cherryvale to the lumberyard and collect additional wood to start back in on the barn.

"It was mighty peculiar to make the trip. I mean, we still couldn't see well out there, but the horses were getting skittish all cramped up in the house, and Pa wouldn't hear different," John Jr. said still timid to look at the big man.

Kate nodded for the young man to continue. She knew exactly why the pretend leader of their fictitious family would have struck out into the elements during such bad weather. His inner hate was boiling over, and the man was going to make someone pay. It was inevitable without her presence this would happen, and had it not been someone else he had killed, it probably would have been John Jr. Did the young man with the simple mind know this? Had he left the little house that day with knowledge that someone was going to take his place on the altar of Pa's rage? Kate cleared her mind of these questions as they were not relevant to the problems before them.

It turned out the Bowdry sisters, Annie and Analisa, both teenagers, were fated to meet Pa and John Jr. that stormy day. As with the Bender men, the Bowdry sisters had no business being out as another round of the snow storm was already beginning to build up. The girls had struck out, unbeknownst to their parents, to help clean the Baptist church in preparation for the upcoming Sunday service. The locals had attached rope lines along the side of the main roads to Cherryvale to accommodate the foot travel during the winter season. The Bowdry girls were returning from the Church and were west bound when the falling snowflakes turned from heavy to a stormy sea of white. When visibility became zero, the girls clutched the cold rope and moved forward with their heads down. Whether it was faith or simply their knowledge that they were only a few miles from home, the girls didn't move in a panic. Yes, their parents would be upset about their unannounced departure, but in the end, their blessed service for the congregation would overshadow a childish act of defiance.

Pa had drank the entire six miles to Cherryvale and had almost gotten into a fight with the owner of the lumberyard. After making his purchase the men headed home. The horses had trouble pulling the wagon as their vision was obscured by the snow and the mighty winds. The roadway appeared abandoned. Halfway home even Pa began to shout over the wind his reservations about leaving the house.

"There weren't no way to tell where the side of the road was. It was just a stupid act of misfortune for all parties concerned!" John Jr. looked towards Pa as he spoke with a quivering voice.

As it happened, the team of horses strayed to the edge of the road far too close to the rope line meant for foot travelers. For the girls, it was most likely the whaling of the storm that covered the sound of the approaching wagon.

"It was like that little girl was a ghost and she just materialized right under that horse," Pa said, speaking for the first time. An emotion that might be seen as sadness swept across his face.

Patiently, Kate pressed her finger to her lips and John Jr. continued the account. The horse had trampled Analisa and John Jr. saw the life leave her eyes before he could dismount the wagon. Annie began to scream as a ring of blood began to expand from her sister's lifeless body turning the white snow to red. John Jr. attempted to calm the girl but she would not be consoled. Annie let go of the rope and began to run blindly to the west screaming for her father. Slurring curse words, Pa jumped from the wagon and gave pursuit. John Jr. ran after them but by the time he caught up, Pa was on top of the girl with his hands around her throat. John Jr. swore that even through the wind of the storm he heard little Annie's neck snap. Kate looked again to Pa, and this time there was no sorrow in his eyes. Instead, there was a shadow of the angry bloodlust, which had originally taken him out into the storm. Whether he had seen the girl as a lose end, someone who might expose them to a charge of murder, was unknown. What was known to Kate was somewhere, deep within his dark recesses, he had enjoyed killing the second girl. Kate recognized she should have been repulsed. She almost longed for the feelings of regret at the children's deaths that flowed from John Jr. but she realized she felt nothing. Well, nothing that would resemble a normal human emotion. She was angry at Pa for his carelessness and even angrier when she was told that the bodies were left on the side of the road where they were found months later during the first thaws. The fact the grieving town wrote the deaths off as an act of God, a product of the blizzard, was of only small consolation. This was blatant irresponsibility on the part of Pa, and she would have to rein him in or they would certainly hang in Kansas.

The girls had no property to confiscate except for a black covered Bible. It was general in appearance and had no inscriptions on the inside. Obviously it must have been a new acquisition to one of the girls. Kate took the Bible and slammed it into Pa's chest with enough force to take his breath away.

She spoke in her authoritative voice, "This is your penance old man! Every day at two o'clock whether rain, sleet, or shine you will sit on that front porch and read from this Bible for one hour. People will come by and they will say, 'there's old man Bender reading God's word. He may be a grumpy old cuss but he's surely a true believer and that makes up for everything else.'"

Pa wanted to protest but kept his mouth shut as she continued, "When these folks come by, some will be neighbors, some we're going to feed and send on, and some we're going to kill, you're going to smile at them all and shake that Bible in their direction like you're ready to go to the promised land."

Kate's eyes moved across the entire family and she growled as she spoke. "The time is now! This is what we've worked for and everybody will be watching us. We can't make stupid mistakes! From here on out no one dies unless I say. It's time for this place to get on a paying basis."

5 MR. PIPPS

Despite the gang's readiness to start their criminal operation at the inn, Kate refused to make the first selection among the travelers that stopped for food and supplies. Instead, she told them they needed to practice the legitimate operation of the place. There was some truth in it. A routine was created for each member of the bunch. Pa and John Jr. would check the cows and feed the four sheep and three goats they owned. Ma would take the food scraps to the six pigs, which were penned just outside the barn. Kate would feed the chickens and wash clothes near the well, which was thirty-feet from the house. When spring came, the men would plant forty acres of wheat, which would feed the family and allow some trade at the mercantile in town. All of these activities had a practical use but more importantly, if visitors from town came by, it allowed all the family to be seen at different parts of the farm. It was the cover they needed to draw attention away from their real work.

Off the north side of the house John Jr. began preparation for a sizeable garden. Here he would plant potatoes, carrots, lettuce, green beans, and other vegetables. Even now he worked there measuring out the plots and removing small trees from the planting bed. In the warm months he would be there every day starting in the late morning and often until dusk. The true purpose of his work was not food. From the vantage point of the garden John Jr. could see people approaching the inn on the Osage Trail from the east or the west for almost two miles out. When someone approached, he would alert Kate who would make a decision on who would live and who would die. Outside the Benders were never out of yelling distance of one another. If Kate made a decision on the fate of a rider from a distance, and sometimes she did, John Jr. or Pa would yell "Get supper ready!" This was the signal that set the entire gang into motion to commit their deadly deeds. From inside the house, Ma would step up on a short stool and start hanging the bed spread curtain, which served as the partition for the kitchen and dining room from the rest of the house. She would later clean the blood and other traces of the kill from the covers for their reuse. Pa would make sure the kill weapons were in place while John Jr. watched the riders approach, and as importantly, the presence of others who might show up at the last moment. The entire operation in Kansas would be a recreation of the Ohio experiment. Food would always be ready on the stove and Kate would wait with the traveler, they were always male and always single riders. She would smile and visit with the traveler while Pa or John Jr. approached the man from behind. The bed spread would hide their approach. The man's head would be silhouetted against the sheet and the blow the traveler would receive to the back of the skull usually caused instant death. Whether it did or not, Kate would use a straight razor and slit the victim's throat to ensure the deed had been finalized. For now, the plan was for the bodies to be loaded into the wagon and transported to John Jr.'s separate claim and buried in the apple orchard on that property.

As always, Pa was getting anxious and even John Jr. couldn't understand why they were not doing what had been their trade for some time. Ma, whose eyes always scanned everything with the cold calculations of a coiled viper remained silent when discussions of the gang's inactivity were brought up. A month after the women had arrived, Kate said they were still not ready. To keep the gang busy, she road with Pa to South Coffeyville and Parsons. Here they sought out men of low morals to fence the horses, saddles, and other large items they would take from their victims. These large items, things that could be seen by others traveling by the inn had to be removed quickly. Pa and John Jr. would take these pieces of property from the inn by nightfall to fences who would buy them at reduced prices. As was the case in the past with the fences, Pa made the initial inquiries with Kate quietly at his side. Later, she would decide who they would, and would not, do business with. In short order the selections were made. A very seedy man in south Coffeyville by the name of Churchill Mongroly was selected as a fence for the horses, wagons, and other related goods. Mongroly, who illegally owned slaves at this late date past the war, had several legitimate businesses which gave cover for his illegal ventures, which included human trafficking, prostitution, and stolen goods. Part of his illegal proceeds lined the pockets of the local marshal which protected him from arrest. Mongroly took his stolen items straight into Oklahoma to sale. In Independence, a vendor on the outskirts of town served as a fence for jewelry and other items of gold and silver. In Parsons, the McCure Brothers quietly bought and sold guns, knives and anything else they saw of value. These items were then transported into Missouri. With the locations to sell their stolen property now acquired, even more pressure came to bear on Kate to start selecting victims and for the gang to make their first group kill at the inn. Night after night people stopped, ate, bought supplies, and left. As men of apparent means sat eating evening dinner at the kitchen table, it became harder for Kate to keep her position that they should not begin the process they had become so proficient at in Ohio. They were killers after all. Still, Kate shook her head that it was not yet time.

The reason for her delay had to remain a secret from the group. If they knew the truth they would either consider her mad or they might just believe her. Either way, she would lose her power over them and her leadership of the gang. That was not going to happen.

"Where are you, Mr. Pipps?" Kate said under her breath as she sat on the front porch of the inn looking at the full moon, which had risen in late December. They were just about to go into a new year and her benefactor was still behind them in the journey to Kansas. Mr. Pipps, what a mysterious person he was. Kate chuckled as she attempted to square the man in her mind. Could she actually call him a person anymore?

6 MORE THAN HUMAN

Kate had met Raul Cladios Pipperstein III almost eleven years ago. She had been ten-years old at the time. She and Ma lived in German-town in New York City. Ma maintained a mid-range apartment in the once flamboyant Regalle Motel. She was in the last years of her gold digging marriage pursuits and the two maintained the façade of wealth, living off the estates of her departed husbands. It was a desperate lifestyle. Most of the time Kate was on the streets as Ma required their apartment all hours of the day for male callers. The last thing men of affluence wanted to see was a child in the house. The young girl had seen all manner of violence and debauchery in the alleyways and side streets of the city, but she had also experience kindness and what she identified as love. The latter two came from the man she came to identify as Mr. Pipps. Mr.

Pipps was a vagabond, one of the many homeless in the city. He often slept on the stone steps that led to Kate's apartment. Steam from the apartment building's boiler room, deep in the basement, would seep out of the deep cracks in the building's front steps, and many of the street people found warmth during the cold nights at this location.

Kate was innocent then, and the kind words of "good morning, miss" and "have a lovely evening, miss" from the man in rags was enough to start small conversations, which led to a friendship. Within the harshness of the city, Mr. Pipps became Kate's best and only friend. Though never asked, Kate began to bring bread scraps to the man and their conversations became more frequent and longer in duration. Even at this young age Kate was extremely observant and her mind worked faster than her years. Without it being told, she observed her new friend had at one time been very affluent. His cloths, though rags today, were garments of the rich. A long black leather coat hung from what had once been wide, powerful shoulders. His shirt had once been white silk, and his boots were from fine leather, though soiled and torn by then. The man had a tall, black brimmed hat, something akin to what a pirate captain might wear on the high seas. Despite being hunched over and old, the man had to be at least six-feet-five inches tall and once had been a powerful specimen. He often pulled out an old soiled handkerchief from his pocket when his coughing fits got worse than usual. Kate observed the old rag was monogramed with his initials RCP. Mr. Pipps was a man who had come from money. The question that always danced in Kate's young mind was how the man had come to this condition.

After a time, her visits with Mr. Pipps became the highlight of her day. When the man was not present at the steps of the apartment as she passed, a frown would remain on her face for the duration of the day. Ma was very opposed to the girl's interactions with the homeless man, and soon she stopped sharing her conversation with her. Mr. Pipps had been born in Europe and his tales of foreign lands were mesmerizing. He had come to America to expand his fortune and had soon acquired land and two ships to market products from locations across the world. His fortune had doubled and then doubled again. As he told it, the last treasure he sought was a fine woman to share both his love and growing empire with. He found it in a young English girl by the name of Katherine Settlemen. Katherine was the love of his life and soon became the entire focus of his existence. Then things went horribly wrong. Kate never fully understood the reason for the cryptic nature of the explanation of what had transpired between Katherine and Mr. Pipps. At first he thought the woman had died of sickness. It seemed apparent she was no longer among the living and her friend was grief stricken over the loss. However, the years passed and conversations would periodically veer onto the subject, and it seemed less and less as if Katherine had indeed succumbed to sickness. Over the next five years Kate learned that Mr. Pipps had an unhealthy love for drink and often he would swig from a silver flask, which was age worn and dented. When the alcohol had him, his recollections of Katherine would be become morose, and at times bizarre. Stories of love and romance would turn into strange tales of deceit and betrayal. Kate never knew for sure if it was the liquor or his growing ill health that made for his strange babblings, but the full truth of what had happened to Katherine, and the man's fall to ruin, remained a mystery.

One day Mr. Pipps was no longer on the steps of the apartment complex. While this, in and of itself, was not a complete oddity, when it was followed by another day, and then another, and then a week, Kate feared the worst. After a month had passed, Kate stopped hoping to see her friend waiting for her with his tired but friendly smile. To a ten-year-old, Mr. Pipps had appeared like an old man. As a young teenager of fifteen Kate understood that Mr. Pipps was not so old, as he was abused by life.

For the next year life went on for Kate. Ma retired from gold digging as time had caught up to her. The illusion of prosperity they had managed for most of her life was replaced by the reality of poverty. Ma took up washing clothes out of the apartment and Kate began stealing on the streets. As a child, she had learned to be quick of hand and subtle of movement. She could lift wallets and watches as good as any pickpocket, but as her body grew, she began to attract the men. Ma was only too happy to begin prepping her for the gold digging trade, but Kate had no interest in marrying men and going through the long process of killing off a mate. This left only one other option, prostitution.

Kate excelled in manipulating men for money using her body. Ma's fleeting connections with the aristocratic German population allowed her a beginning of her new trade with few physical altercations. It was lucrative work when compared to begging or purse snatching but at best it kept the two only at the edge of destitution. Kate aspired for more. The death of her street friend combined with the routine selling of her body to strangers had extinguish any ideas of what love was, or if it ever really existed. Instead, she now thirsted for true wealth and the long-term security it could provide.

It was just after her eighteenth birthday that Mr. Pipps returned. That is, something akin to Mr. Pipps. The first time she saw him she was walking a side street near the park. There, at a distance, sat Mr. Pipps on a bench. She remembered the pigeons that scurried about his feet. Even though he was a long ways a way, she knew immediately it was him. It appeared he was looking directly at her, and she felt his presence. By the time she made her way across the street he was gone. Had it been just wishful thinking? Was it just the last remnants of grief in what was left in her heart, which was quickly turning to stone? She did not have to ponder these questions for long. Mr. Pipps began to show up everywhere and in the most peculiar places. She saw him standing along the railing of the Lion's exhibit at the City Zoo. She saw him standing by a team of horses and then moments later he was sitting atop a tree branch near a government building. Yes, it was Mr. Pipps but certainly not the same man she had known. His cloths were the same, but he held his body differently. He no longer had the physical frame of a man once strong, now broken. His body in the present had power and exuded uncharacteristic strength. Kate remembered this clearly and the new Mr. Pipps only wished to commune with her from a distance. Several times she attempted to run to her old friend, and he would jump across building tops and dash between carriages with unearthly ability.

After several instances of frustration over her inability to touch and hold her old friend, Kate made peace with it and started to become accustomed to Mr. Pipps's returned presence in her life. One day, after a long night working the streets, she neared the apartment complex she still shared with Ma. As the building came into view, there under the illumination of the street lamps was Mr. Pipps. It was like déjà vu to see her old friend sitting leisurely upon the cement steps. Despite the shadows created by the low lighting, she saw Mr. Pipps lean up and look directly at her and begin making signals to her with his gloved hands. The hand talk! How could she have forgotten this? The two had created an intricate number of hand signals, which in time had become their own private language. At the time it had been both practical and fun. Because Ma had hated Mr. Pipps from the onset, when she would be walking home with her mother in the evenings and would see Mr. Pipps at a distance, she would flash him signals, and he would evacuate the area and, thus, a conflict. Their private hand talk had been used when Kate wanted to bring Mr. Pipps food or warnings about the police, who periodically rousted the homeless from the residential areas. A tear, something she thought long gone from her emotional library, fell from her cheek when Mr. Pipps signaled his greeting and then placed both hands upon his heart. The girl immediately returned the sign and their reunited bond strengthened.

Over the next ten months Mr. Pipps reasserted his place within Kate's life. She now saw him every day, and though their hand signals should have limited their conversations, it did not. For some reason, and Kate was in perpetual internal conflict over why, the two began to sense and interpret each other's thoughts. The hand signals soon became only a validation of what their minds were already sharing. This extra-sensory process was both joyous and vexing for Kate at the same time. She loved Mr. Pipps and admitted she also needed his presence. He had arrived as her savior in a desperate time of need.

Kate's relationship with her mother had always been that of two strangers. Now, with Ma's gold digging days behind her, their survival fell solely upon her. She was not ready for the responsibility. Worse yet, Ma now carried a resentment against her because of her own loss of power as a bread winner. The girl could not monetarily provide as her mother had done, and Ma was getting anxious for a return to her higher standard of living. Kate was wondering if in time, her mother would poison her food as she had done to so many men. Something had to change soon for Kate, and it seemed Mr. Pipps understood her plight.

Soon her friend started to direct Kate in her immediate course of action. The girl was only too happy to comply, as Mr. Pipps seemed to have an uncanny ability to direct her toward prosperous gains. At first it was simple things such as which men to approach on the street for an evening seduction. Mr. Pipps who would seem to show up when needed, would point a finger at a man, and through their mental connection she would know the content of his mind and she would comply. These johns, pre-selected by her benefactor would be gentlemen, who would also render payments for services much higher than the norm. Within a short time, Ma's temper had been satiated, as additional funds were flowing into the household. Kate replaced her worn dresses with new ones and she began to wear hats of higher quality. Mr. Pipps had bettered her life in a short amount of time. This was an unchallenged fact; however, Kate sensed this was just the beginning. Mr. Pipps had more in store for her and whatever it was, she wanted it.

As was the case that Kate's benefactor directed to her to take certain actions, he also directed her to avoid certain people. It was in this she learned the consequences of disobeying a directive from Mr. Pipps. Every day Kate would leave the apartment and make her way toward Gerald's Street. Here within the German town district were the upscale dance halls and pubs for the wealthier German residents. Along with the other working girls, Kate would frequent the establishments and seek out patrons for her services. Kate's ability to size up people was beyond her years and experience on the streets. Still, like many of the prostitutes around her, there were always the deceptive johns with either no money in their pockets or worse, bad intentions in his heart.

Kate's good fortune was that she had Mr. Pipps who up to this point had shown the extraordinary ability to pick out the cream of the crop. He seemed to never be wrong, and had she fully understood this then, she would have denied her own headstrong nature and followed his instruction when her benefactor directed her to avoid a certain man on the street that night. His name was Horace Jones, or that was how he introduced himself when he approached her. He was a tall man of about six-two and his body was fit. He wore fine clothes, which were recently pressed. A gold chain, which was no doubt connected to a watch in his pocket, shimmered as he walked. The man's teeth were white like ivory, and when he moved close to her to inquire about her plans for the evening, he smelled of fine cologne. His shave was recent, as if the hot cream had just been toweled from his face.

"Excuse me, my lady, might I have the pleasure of your company this evening?" His voice was sweet, and he bowed as he took her hand, never taking his piercing, blue eyes off of her. He met every criteria of a wealthy and safe john. Kate laughed at his introduction and gave him her best smile. Within moments they had made an oral contract, which was customary of the street. This was also of positive note as there would be no confusion later about the monetary exchange that would take place. If she was lucky, the man would tip above and beyond the flat fee which might very well allow her to end her day early and be richer for her efforts.

The man's eyes weren't just blue, they were as blue as the ocean in summer. His smile was pretty; that was the thought that shot into her mind. It could have been the man's good looks or something else that distracted her from the fact she had not yet seen her friend. It was not until the wealthy man had taken her arm and was walking her toward the street she saw him. Mr. Pipps was standing in the street, which was uncharacteristic for him, as horses and carriages shot by his body at dangerously close distances. His disapproval was obvious. He shook his head vigorously, which made his long brimmed hat flap back and forth. Kate's first reaction was to obey the warning and pull free of the man but then she saw the fine carriage he owned and the private driver, and her old instincts kick in. He would indeed be a lucrative john. She made the decision and got into the carriage, and they were off. Several more times she saw Mr. Pipps. Once he was standing on a walkway bridge and then again amongst the throngs of people on the streets. He shook his head each time, and his thoughts entered her brain as a warning call to flee. Unfortunately, Kate had already agreed to the service, and it was bad form to break an oral contract with a john. But, it wasn't that, some stubborn part of her felt she knew better than Mr. Pipps, and she would show him.

"You are a magnificent creature, my dear," the man said as he handed her a bouquet of flowers he had already purchased.

He's is a high spender, she thought as she accepted the gift and gave the man a gentle kiss on the cheek. He simply smiled in return and patted her hand. The journey took them to the Morring Hotel, an upscale establishment for short term stays and discrete romantic interludes. Many a rich man would have been all over her during the ride but not Mr. Horace Jones. He must truly be a refined man and wanted to wait for the privacy of the room. At the hotel the man signed in with a foreign name as was customary in places such as these and escorted her to a room on the third floor. Kate would never forget the thick red carpeting of the Morring Hotel or the long empty hallway they walked to get to their room. She could still smell the man's cologne. It was something exotic and certainly expensive. He let go of her arm and inserted the key into the lock. The door opened and he walked inside. She followed. Just another transaction, another hour, maybe two, of meaningless physical congress, and her life would be hers once again. As she was about to follow the man into the room she heard a sound behind her and turned. The door on the other side of the hall was open and just inside the door was Mr. Pipps. He was a mere ten feet away, the closest she had been to him since his reappearance. Oddly enough, even at this distance, the long brim of his hat shadowed his face and most of his features except his eyes. His eyes glowed as red hot coals, and his skin was as leathery as his long brown coat. He shook with anger. Kate pondered later if his rage had been a product of her defiance or his knowledge of what was about to befall her. One thing was for certain, what Mr. Pipps did know was only moments from transpiring. No more than seconds after her benefactor's appearance a voice sounded behind her.

"Shall you come in, my precious thing?" the voice was sweet like honey, and Kate turned, smiling, to face the man as his fist smashed into her face. The next few hours were disjointed moments of consciousness and horror. When Horace Jones left the Morring Hotel it was with the full expectation his prostitute of the evening was dead. In fact, that was close to the case. Kate had suffered multiple broken bones and had been abused to a level that was medieval. For a month she mended in the St. Michael Hospital. As the medication dulled her pain, her mind swam in an ocean of depression and regret. Thrice a day, attendants came in and moved her body from one side, to her back, and then to another side to avoid bed sores and to maintain proper circulation in her mending body. The process itself was excruciating each time, to the point of tears. However, there was an upside to this regiment. For six hours each day she faced the window of her room and through it she saw life in the form of children playing, and birds flying about as if there were no cares in the world. There was Mr. Pipps sitting on a park bench or standing near a statue or where ever she seemed to need him. He was always there, always watching over her. He never left his post.

Ma came to the hospital and paid the medical bill, which kept her from being thrown out of the facility, but she did not visit. The doctors, deeming her hospital stay was about to come to a conclusion, where weaning her off the medications she certainly would not be able to afford after her dismissal. For two days Kate was in the throes of agony. Her body ached and her insides, her private parts the man had abused the worst felt as though they had been removed with a dull knife.

It was during this time of great pain Kate began to question Mr. Pipps and then herself. Yes, he had been right about a great many things including Horace Jones, but what did that mean? She had seen him up close and this was not the Mr. Pipps she had known. She had tried to tell herself her departed friend had returned in better health but she knew that was not completely true. Truth be told, his physical capabilities were not of this Earth, and what of his other abilities? Could he see the future? Was he an angel watching out for her? She laughed as the notion was not in her belief system to ponder. With that said, the being that had been before her in the Morring Hotel would not fall into any classification of an angel based on any standard religion she had ever heard of. Was he a demon? Her thoughts moved on.

The most likely reality, and one that concerned her now, was that she had gone utterly insane. As the pain in her body made her grit her teeth, she faced the truth of it as a condemned criminal might face the reality of a firing squad. Only walking through the cold facts would keep her mind busy, and avoid her desire to scream at the top of her lungs. Mr. Pipps had been near death before his disappearance and since his return, she had neither touched nor spoken directly to him. To any normal person, she had no way to prove he was actually real. His ability to appear whenever she needed him seemed uncannily like a creation of the mind. Could Mr. Pipps simply be a figment of her imagination? She had been arrested more than once while on the streets and had seen the mentally infirmed restrained within muzzles and strait jackets. She had heard these people talk to invisible companions and babble about nonsensical things. Was she now one of these people? Was she about to become one? Could it be she was one diagnosis away from being classified as insane and transported to an asylum where doctors would drill holes in her head, or worse? Was this the change that was coming to her life? She was the most unsure of things she had ever been in her life but the young girl was not going to give in to these notions yet. She owed Mr. Pipps, whether he was real or imagined, that much.

One week later she was released. She was still sore but she walked out of the hospital under her own power.

The smell of the city was refreshing in contrast to the sterile scents mixed with lingering death, which seemed to be everywhere within the hospital. She walked deep into the city park and found a bench near a wooded area. It was a peaceful place where she could sit in the shade and watch the squirrels jump between the branches. She had to come to grips with moving on after the grievous violation that had taken place to her body.

"Why move on? Why not get revenge?" a voice sounded in her mind. It was like gravel in her head and it was laced with both bitterness and sadness. Sitting atop a hanging branch on a nearby tree was her benefactor. His body was partially cloaked within the shadows of the upper branches, and had it not been for their special bond she expected she would have never seen him. It was a man's voice. It was Mr. Pipps's voice, but Kate could not say with absolute certainty she had not created it. Still, she entertained the questions that had been forwarded. "What do you mean? Are you suggesting I hunt down this wolf who has all but ripped me to pieces?"

The long brim of his hat moved up and down as he nodded the affirmative. Kate could sense a smile ripple across the nondescript features of his face. However, his eyes, which still glowed red, reflected seriousness. Kate smiled back, as she could sense the hatred Mr. Pipps felt for her attacker and she knew deep within her was the same burning desire for him to suffer beyond belief. A vision of a straight razor blade dancing across the man's throat, and him being drowned within a lake of blood shot through her mind. It was the first time she had entertained a thought of this gruesome nature and she was not sure if it came from her own mind or in some unfathomable way had been placed there by her benefactor. Even though she expected to be repulsed by the vision, to her shock, she was not. Instead, she felt an energy flow through her, and with it a feeling of limitless power. In this vision, she was the wielder of the blade, and the throat being slit was not just that of Mr. Horace Jones, but all of humanity. It was at this moment she sensed a great and wonderful mission was before her. At least if Mr. Pipps was truly real.

As if sensing he was about to be addressed, her benefactor kicked his feet forward and leaned to attention upon the tree limb. This action seemed to excite a few birds nearby, which flew away at the same moment.

"Okay, let's find this man and kill him. However, I need you to do something of the upmost importance for me. I need you to prove to me you're real. I need to know beyond a shadow of a doubt."

Mr. Pipps dropped from the tree grabbing hold of a smaller branch with a single gloved hand to stop his fall.

For a few moments he swung from back and forth on the limb like a large monkey. Then, with an athletic grace the girl had never seen before, he dropped to the ground and ran to her at an unearthly speed. Stopping five feet away from her, he tipped his long brimmed hat, and she felt his power move through her. They were about to start an amazing journey together, and she wanted all of it.

An agreement had been struck. Mr. Pipps would reveal himself to be more than a figment of Kate's imagination, and together they would kill the rapist Horace Jones. This was a deal Kate was not only happy to accept but eager to see its execution. Mr. Pipps on the other hand seemed to work on his own timeline. At the onset it appeared to the girl her elusive and unnatural friend was either attempting to test her patience or something else equaling vexing.

Kate had assumed their mission would entail stalking the prey. They needed to find Horace Jones and discover his routine. From this intelligence gathering they could formulate a plan of attack. Unfortunately, for an entire month following her release from the hospital, Kate spent her time doing everything else but closing in on the rapist. Day after day Kate would walk to the pubs and chit-chat with men who would buy her drinks and leave her small tips in exchange for light, provocative love talk. She was still too damaged to rejoin the sex trade, but for the price of a smile, and a laugh, she did pocket enough to survive.

Each evening, she would also seek out Mr. Pipps, who was always somewhere near. She hoped through his unearthly abilities he would guide her to the rapist, but instead he took her to other places. Kate found herself almost every afternoon being led to the public library. She followed her benefactor's large, dark frame, not just to the doors of John Jacob Astor public library, but also down the aisles where Mr. Pipps would direct her to certain books, magazines, and other documents. The dark figure was operating without hand signals or mental communication, and Kate simply went where he lead her. Almost daily, she read books, newspaper articles, and everything else about the U.S. train system, and simple, country living. Over time she began to understand business from a commerce perspective and formed knowledge of the Christian traditions and values of those living in the central states of the growing country. She saw newspaper clipping of the clothing styles of simple women working alongside their husbands in the fields. Most of the pictures disgusted her. The women depicted seemed like slaves more than frontier pioneers as the newspaper descriptions often portrayed them. She had no desire to break her back hauling wood to the fire to make endless meals for an unruly horde of children. Yet, even though she did not know the full purpose of what she was learning, she understood enough to know a lifetime of servitude on the edge of complete poverty was not the purpose of the knowledge she was gaining. No, Mr. Pipps had something much more grandiose in mind. She read, she studied and she learned about a world far from New York.

It was hard to say just when the straight razor started to show up. It just seemed one day it was there. She first noticed it in her dress pocket and then again in her purse. Kate assumed that she must be transitioning the old four inch blade, which retracted into an old brown cover from place to place without thinking about it. Could she have grabbed it from the medicine cabinet in their small apartment? It might have been some miscellaneous leftovers from the myriad of men who had passed through the home during Ma's gold digging days. She often ran her thumb over the time worn insignia on the blade's cover. It was unreadable now and she knew that but when she squinted really hard, the letters it almost looked like R.C.P III but she knew better. Those letters in her mind being the initials of Raul Cladios Pipperstein III. It was just a silly thought that seemed to come to her repeatedly. Mr. Pipps had never been in her home and he had never given her a blade. Violence had never been in his nature, at least in his first life. Now, Mr. Pipps and she too, if Kate believed the feelings in her gut, where about to transcend their old lives into something very different. In any event, and for whatever importance it might have, the straight blade never seemed to leave Kate's side. After a month the girl's body had physically healed. She felt her strength return and her mind was no longer clouded from the drugs of the hospital or the cloud of depression that had been inside her brain. She was now on a mission, and it gave her purpose. Kate began to practice her art of seduction along with a new skill, the ability to kill. For hours, in private, she used a pocket mirror and perfected her smile and facial expressions. In the past, she had simply gauged her ability to woo men by the look on their faces, and the language of their bodies. Now, with the rapist Horace Jones to kill, she would take the art of manipulation and seduction to a new level. It would become her science. Each smile, wink, and eye movement was practiced and recorded in her mind. She knew how to make her body move in ways that attracted men but now she also practiced using mannerism and body language to do the same which were elusive. That is, subtle body movements that could be construed as normal but that still would elicit desire, but in only certain men. Men that is, with an eye for a dark, back alley rendezvous.

Finally, the night came. Kate had been preparing to leave the apartment having had another argument with Ma. Her mother might have been content to give her a month from the hospital to mend but now she was angry her daughter was not bringing in more of a regular income.

"Get back on the horse!" were the words Ma shouted nightly as her daughter left the apartment to return with only loose change.

Kate knew her mother could never understand her contract with Mr. Pipps and she had no inclination to try to share that knowledge. Truth be told, she coveted their special bond and would not have wanted Ma, with her limited mind and angry disposition, to be a part of what she had with Mr. Pipps, even if the old woman would have embraced it. When it came to Mr. Pipps, Kate was all in, well, almost all in. There was the little matter of whether or not he was a figment of her damaged imagination. Kate smiled a bit as the thought ran through her brain. Her mind had to be damaged to some extent, right? With all she had seen and suffered, the term normal, whatever that word really meant, could never fully apply to her again. Now the word crazy, was really the word in question, wasn't it?

As soon as Kate had descended the stone steps of her apartment there stood Horace Jones in a finely dressed suit walking towards her on the sidewalk. His strong frame bounced along, exuding power and confidence. He moved like a man without a care in the world. Even within the evening's dim street lights, his ocean blue eyes beamed, and his pearl white teeth glittered. It appeared as if life was being very good to the man. Kate's heart began to pound in her chest and her breathing became rapid. This was not how she had perceived events would occur. She thought she would stalk the man, watch his comings and goings and on terms of her own, would strike and kill him. Oh hell, she didn't know exactly how it would transpire, but nothing like this. For a moment Kate thought she might pass out in fear but then she saw Mr. Pipps, and her power came back to her. Unlike her, Mr. Pipps knew exactly where Horace Jones would be and somehow, he had placed them together. Again the straight razor flashed in her mind and she felt for it. The blade was in her dress pocket and its presence made her tingle all over. A smile crossed her face as she looked at Mr. Pipps, who was casually leaning against a black iron fence across the street. His burning eyes looked to the approaching rapist, to her, and then to the top of the apartment's roof. She knew exactly what she had to do. She would lure Jones to the privacy of the apartment's rooftop and slit his throat.

Making sure she did not appear too eager, she strolled down the steps of the apartment and bumped into the man as if by accident.

"Pardon me, my lady," his voice was soft and non-threatening. Kate smiled at the man and placed her hand innocently on his shoulder.

"Sorry, kind sir. I'm so clumsy." As she spoke the words she smiled and made eye contact, which lingered just a few moments longer than what was necessary. He responded with a pleasant smile.

"How pleasant the fates must be that I should meet such a beautiful and clumsy young lady all in the same evening," he said as his eyes wondered across her body.

Kate knew what to do. Her eyes slowly walked across his strong frame, and the beginnings of an oral contract for sex began. He inquired about her plans for the evening and she responded she had none. In the delicate ways it is always discussed, her role as sex giver and his as payee were traversed and confirmed. All the while Kate watched the man's eyes and facial expressions to see if he would remember her, to see if there would be a moment when he would realize she was the woman he had beaten and battered in the most heinous of ways that night at the hotel. The man showed no signs of a recollection. This both pleased and angered her. Of course, he would be easier to kill if he did not expect an attack was coming, but that also meant what he had done to her had meant absolutely nothing to him. She pushed back her anger and continued with her plan.

Except in cases where the men were too drunk or daft to pick a location for the deed, prostitutes usually allowed the men to choose the spot in which they would earn their money. Kate knew that Jones, who smelled of a sweet cologne and shaving cream, as he had in their last meeting, would attempt to take her to a location suited for his needs. Instead, she told him she had misspoke and she was indeed committed to another appointment in thirty minutes, but he was such a looker she could not help herself. Promising him privacy and some very personalized, special treatment, she convinced the man to follow her to the apartment's rooftop. Mr. Pipps was no longer leaning against the railing across the street and despite wishing to see his face, the girl made sure not to stare in that location for too long. It might place Jones on edge, because even rapists could get robbed by hustlers in the night. As they made their way up the winding, wooden stairway to the third floor she could hear Jones's breathing begin to labor. The man was twenty-five, maybe thirty years of age and in far too good of shape to be out of breath from exertion. He was sexually excited; he was ready to take her and probably would the moment they reached rooftop. Her hand felt for the straight blade in her dress pocket. It was there; she was ready. As soon as they entered the rooftop she would extend the blade and move in without hesitation. Lust would be clouding his mind and the steel would be on his throat before he could register he was in danger. She would step back and watch him stumble back and forth as he fought for air and struggled for life. Sweat began to run from her forehead and she, too, began to breathe in ragged gasps. She was in full anticipation of the kill.

As her hand was turning the doorknob, which gave access to the rooftop, the man placed an arm around her waist and began to lift up her dress. "I can't wait, my dear," he said as he kissed her neck. Kate had been with many repulsive men, in fact, the richer they were often the less desirable they could be. This man sickened every fiber of her being. She smiled and continued turning the door's knob. In moments he would be dead and she would truly be alive. *"Just a few more seconds,"* she told herself. His cologne once so pleasant to smell was a now a poison in her nostrils. His tongue danced across her cheek and sought out her breasts. The door latch clicked and they spilled onto the rooftop. Finally, he was in the kill zone and her hands, which had been slowing his groping pursuit now went to secure the blade.

"Let him have his way for the last few seconds of his rotten life," she thought as she reached for the straight razor. His breath was so hot it felt like a burning fog enveloping her body. He could barely speak and when he did his voice was animalistic, like a mongrel, which was in the progress of ripping gristle from a bone. "It's so seldom I get to enter the same honey pot twice."

The words made her body freeze. Their eyes locked and she could see it now in his face. He did remember her. Within his wild gaze she saw not only recollection but a desire to rip her to shreds. Unless she did something quickly he would tear her into so many pieces she could never be put back together again. Her hand shot to the blade in her dress pocket, but he was faster. He grabbed her wrist and laughed in a way that sounded more like a growl.

"Gotta little surprise for me down there? Do ya, my dear? Well I've got one for you too," he said as his hand clamped around her throat. Immediately, she was without air and began to see dancing lights in front of her eyes. She knew his free hand was pulling at her dress and she could only pray she passed out before what was no doubt going to happen next. With sadness, she knew he would most likely not allow that to happen.

As her consciousness was fading to black, she saw the man's body suddenly raise three feet in the air and then come crashing down to the rooftop's floor. Hovering above the rapist for several seconds was Mr. Pipps. The man started to get up but a powerful blow to his back delivered by her benefactor sent him crashing down again. She was speechless. Even when Mr. Pipps picked her up and carried her to the entrance door, she said nothing. It wasn't until she understood the door was being closed, that she was being shut out from the rooftop, that Kate began to argue the point.

"What are you doing, Mr. Pipps? This business is mine to conclude!" The door locked against her protest. She screamed and struck at the door for several moments while Horace Jones wailed in pain as blows struck his body. After a while there was nothing but silence. When Kate was certain access was not going to be granted, she slowly walked outside the apartment. Tears still ran down her cheeks as she made her way to the stone steps, which she had spent so many hours with her friend in their former lives. How could he have betrayed her? The kill was hers, and she had been denied vengeance. What was she to do now?

Kate did not know if she heard movement from the rooftop, or what drew her attention but she looked up as Jones's falling body was about six feet from hitting the pavement. He actually bounced. The sound his body made upon impact was like smashing fruit. Kate looked in all directions and saw the streets were empty. She ran to the body and to her surprise, despite protruding broken bones and blood that ran from his ears, Jones was alive and conscious.

"Wa...wa...wa" were the only sounds his mouth could generate but his eyes followed her as she knelt over him. It was impossible to tell which injuries he had suffered on the rooftop and which from the fall. Mr. Pipps must have wanted it that way. In fact, to her dazed shock her benefactor now stood only feet away, his arms folded as if he were now nothing more than an observer. The man's eyes began to roll into the back of his head and Kate slapped his face to orient him back to her.

She drew the straight razor slowly from her dress pocket and extended the blade until it shined under the street lamps. Jones was alive enough to see it and understand what was about to happen. He managed to lift his hand toward her. Several of his fingers were broken and they jetted out in different directions.

She gently pushed his hand away and said with a quiet smile, "It's time for you to die, my dear. It's time for the whole world to die, and for me to finally live." She pulled the blade slowly across his throat. Blood arched from his carotid artery and sent a stream of crimson across her face. The warm liquid felt like pure energy running through her body. The man jerked once, and Kate pinned him back to the Earth with her hand on his forehead. With her fingers she forced his eyes open and smiled as the fire of life left his body. Horace Jones the rapist was dead, but for Kate things were just beginning. Mr. Pipps was real and she knew he had been preparing her to leave New York. Now she was ready to follow him. Everything was going to change.

7 PRESENT DAY: THE TREK *TO ISLA DE LA MUERTE*

The "Colony" was code for a bandit stronghold in
south Texas. Specifically, or as specific as a myth can get,
the colony was referred to most often as the Isla de la
Muerte, or the "Island of Death." It was believed to be
located somewhere within the brutal and lawless terrain of
Zapata County Texas. Zapata County ran up against the
Mexico border. It was a poor county, and except for dirty
watering holes such De Las Ovejas, San Ignacio, Clareno,
and San Bartolo Carrizio was nothing more than rocky
farm land and burning hot prairie. Zapata County had only
one official lawman, Sheriff Miguel Sangrada Chimingez.
His palatial home was in the town of Alberea, which,
ironically, was not even located in Zapata County, but in
Encinal County to the north. For days Johnson went

south, switching railway lines when necessary, and collecting information from his agency about his final destination at the teletype offices when possible. The Island of Death was believed to have been established decades ago by Mexican bandits, who had fled across the hotly contested American border to escape capture from their own authorities. Over time American criminals with no place else to go, fled south, and like birds of a feather, they found safety in numbers. Someday, the Texas and Pacific railroad line, the line Johnson now traveled would run through Zapata County, and the area would get modernized for trade and commercial use. In short, the criminals would lose their place of safe haven. For now, the railroad stopped short of Zapata County, three hundred miles north in Duval County. In the town of Loma Chala, Johnson unloaded his horse from the train and prepared for the long journey to the *Isle de la Muerte*. As it stood he was simply heading on a southwest bearing and that wasn't good enough. The county was hundreds of miles of burning desert-like prairie, and finding the bandits hideout without specific directions would be like looking for a needle in a hay stack, which was on fire.

Against Johnson's instincts his employer, Clint Parker, had wired a sizeable contribution to Sheriff Miguel Sangrada Chimingez and arranged for the detective to

119

meet the man at his home. It was an expansive villa, almost a small town in itself, with tall white pillars and expansive iron fencing. Armed guards, given the title of "deputies" walked the grounds, and kept watch over the expansive estate from the rooftops at every location. A staff of at least forty butlers, cleaners, and cooks worked diligently in the way those employed by tyrants always do. A tall black man in a tailored suit escorted Johnson from the stables to the main house where he was shown to his room and told his host would meet him for dinner.

"Now you'll be collected in about an hour so clean that prairie dust off ya right now sir." It was clear the detective was meant to stay the night at the villa. His room was large and contained an oversized bed, dresser, and a long mirror was mounted across the entire length of the ceiling. Johnson walked several feet, watching his reflection until the action started to make him dizzy. His attention was drawn to a movement in the large room. In a corner was a large metal tub. Hot steam rose from within the tub and beside it was a young Mexican girl of twenty-years of age. She stood naked before him. She held a scrubbing brush and a large bar of soap. Her eyes looked to the ground, but she sensed his approach and curtsied as she spoke, "The Honorable Sheriff Miguel Sangrada Chimingez says you are to be cleaned and made

120

presentable." Johnson knew at once the girl was meant to accommodate him far beyond scrubbing his backside. The woman was beautiful, and the detective found her immediately attractive. However, this wasn't his mission and availing himself of the sherriff's prostitute would get him no closer to catching the murdering Benders.

Johnson knew he would not sexually gratify himself with the young woman, but he would also not send her away. That would be seen as a slight to Chimingez, who meant to return the favor he had received in the monetary bribe from the detective agency. Also, if the girl was seen to have failed to satisfy the detective she would be beaten, and that did not sit well with the detective. So, with little hesitation, Johnson stripped and entered the tub. With the assistance of the girl he was meticulously cleaned. Water sloshed over the sides of the metal tub and they both laughed as the detective repetitiously dipped his head under the hot water. All these sounds of frolic, as the detective knew, would be heard by the guards outside the door. Fresh clothes sat upon the dresser, but he was not expected to avail himself of these items yet. After he was towel dried they both walked to the bed and climbed in. Johnson made sure the bed springs sang loudly as they made their way under the covers. Then, as the young girl coiled herself around him like a snake, he spoke quietly in her ear, "You have made my time here very pleasant, and I shall report this to the Honorable Sheriff Miguel Sangrada Chimingez." He could sense her hand moving toward his manhood and he stopped her and continued. "However, I do not require this." The look on her face was both fear and relief. Johnson felt her body tense and he spoke quickly. "You may tell anyone who asks we did indeed do what was expected to have transpired here. For me, it would be my deepest pleasure to simply talk for a bit."

Over the next few minutes the girl's body relaxed. She seemed to understand she was not being tricked and that she would be rewarded for completing her task without having to relinquish her body to another of the sheriff's associates. Even more to her liking was that the gringo was kind and gentle, and soon she feared him not. Johnson followed his training and began collecting information from the girl. The numbers of guards on the estate, the visitors to and from the villa, and every detail about Sheriff Miguel Sangrada Chimingez was queried.

One thing the detective knew was the hired help of the rich were often privy to sensitive information. Furthermore, prostitutes often found themselves hearing more than most. The girl's name was Dominque, and she knew much. She knew about the quest to find the Benders family, although they had never actually been to the villa. She knew that Colonel York and his men had arrived nine days previous, and that the colonel and the sheriff had had many harsh words. The posse had arrived baring only threats, which did not sit well with Chimingez. The girl expected the sheriff may not have given these men accurate information as there was no profit in it for him to do so. Johnson smiled at the girl and thanked her for the information.

Placing her hand on his strong chest she looked deep into his eyes and whispered, "Senior Johnson, leave this place as fast you can. The sheriff is a bad man, and everything he tells you will be a lie. If these killers from Kansas do exist, he has probably already taken money to protect them or money from others at the Isla de la Muerte. Believe nothing he says." As soon as the words had crossed her lips there was knock at the door. It was the black butler who spoke. "Now sir, you be finishing up what ya got going on in there. Fifteen minutes till dinner."

As the girl exited through a servant's door, Johnson followed the butler to a large dining room. A long oak table was heavily laden with all manner of food. In the center was a freshly roasted pig. Large, gray, stone bowls held heaping portions of mashed potatoes, green beans, and yellow squash. There were mounds of apples and peaches and other fruits, which were not indigenous to the area. Steam rose from every direction, and all the windows were open to allow the evening wind to cool the room. Servants stood in white uniforms with small fans, which were used to cool those who would be eating, and run any flies away, which might wish to partake of the grandiose meal.

Within moments the Honorable Sheriff Miguel Sangrada Chimingez walked into the room flanked on all sides by large Mexican men carrying rifles. The man's voice was loud and he moved in fast to embrace Detective Johnson, "*Mi amigo!* Welcome to my humble home!" The embrace broke free into a handshake and reverted back into a second embrace. Chimingez was a large man of obvious Mexican heritage. His black hair was long and braided in the back. His brown skin glistened with a light sheen of sweat, which ran from his neck to his large stomach. His face seemed locked in a permanent smile. "Did Dominque get you clean, my friend?" Chimingez said as he offered the detective a seat in one of the large, oak chairs. He chuckled at the question. Johnson smiled and responded, "She is an amazing girl. Thank you for your hospitality." The detective gave the sheriff what he had coined as the "insider smile." That is, the smile that portrays a double meaning. All the men including the sheriff burst out in laughter as the message of his facial expression struck home. The men ate and drank as if they had been starved for a week. Chimingez loved to talk, and Johnson was smart enough to listen. Most of the conversation was centered on the sheriff downplaying his unexplainable, lavish lifestyle for a man who claimed to be nothing more than a county law enforcer. The man claimed no knowledge of the Bender family traveling into Zapata County or even the state of Texas. He further denied any contact with other bounty hunters of any kind. When it came to the location of the *Isle de la Muerte*, the sheriff was nonchalant in his answer. While he admitted that while stories ran wild in this area about a criminal hideout, all of his contacts had no real information of the actual existence of such a place.

"Surely you have ghost stories in Kansas of the same quality? We have banditos on both sides of the border, and they are evil men. Those that fall prey to their depravity make up stories of dark places from which these evil criminals hide from justice. They are nothing more than ghost stories." The sheriff watched Johnson's face intently to gauge whether or not his words were being believed. The detective showed no reaction and simply nodded. He did though come to a conclusion about any intelligence gathering from the sheriff. In short, Dominque had been correct. The Honorable Miguel Sangrada Chimingez was in fact a bald-faced liar. Nothing of value was going to be collected here. However, things could be lost. As the evening wore on the sheriff began to push Johnson for information.

"It seems your agency is bent on the capture of these criminal from Kansas. Please tell me all you know so I may be able to help you if information comes my way." Chimingez smiled even wider and moved in close and touched Johnson's shoulder as he spoke. Johnson mentally walked through his options and responded with a smile of his own and a shrug of his shoulders.

"Well I have to tell you, I think this whole trip to Texas is a wild goose chase. I go where they send me but I have observed nothing that leads me to believe the Bender family is in these parts." Johnson drank deep from a tall glass of whiskey and then exhaled hard. The men laughed again and his glass was quickly refilled. After several minutes, in which Johnson drank three more glasses of whiskey and complained about a lack information and evidence in the case, he managed to excuse himself to bed. He had evaded giving any information to the sheriff on the investigation. This time his room was empty of prostitutes and he slept until morning when again, the butler woke him with a light knocking on the door at 5:00 a.m.

They say in Texas that in summer it is as hot by 9:00 am. as it will be all day, so the best work is done before the sun really wakes up. Johnson was ready to leave but he was told the sheriff would not let him leave without a proper breakfast. Just as it had been with dinner, the breakfast meal was a banquet table of meats, eggs, fruit, and strong coffee. Chimingez seemed none the worse off for his excessive night of drinking. Again the questions came. The sheriff wanted to know where he would be going next and the amount of time he planned to be in his state.

"Well I have to at least travel into Zapata County. My employer expects that much." Johnson continued to act non-enthusiastic as he sipped his coffee. He continued, "I'll stay at least two to three days and make my way to the Texas & Pacific Railroad line and sleep the entire way north. I hate to say it, but Texas is just too damn hot!" This brought another round of laughter from the sheriff's men. After they had finished breakfast Johnson loaded his horse and prepared to leave. At the gate of the villa he was stopped and Chimingez and two other rough looking men, wearing sombreros, on horseback, rode up to him. The sheriff's smile was as strong as ever.

As he shook hands with the detective, he spoke. "It has been my pleasure to meet a fine man, and detective, from Kansas." Johnson attempted to speak but was cut off by the sheriff who continued, "Even though your time in Zapata County will be short, I wish it to be a safe journey for you." He motion to the other men on horseback who rode up alongside the detective. "That is why I am sending my personal men to escort and assist you while you are in my county."

Johnson shook his head. "That is not necessary. Detectives usually travel alone and I operate better that way."

The smile disappeared for the first time from the Honorable Miguel Sangrada Chimingez's face. "Oh but it *is* necessary, my friend. Where you go, they will go." With that, the sheriff snapped his fingers and the iron gate to the villa opened. Johnson and his escorts exited and started south into Zapata County.

8 JANUARY 1871: BITTERNESS, INFILTRATION, & REUNIONS

The winds were bitter cold as the New Year progressed. Another blizzard, this one much shorter in duration than the one Pa and John Jr. had endured previously, hit the plains and forced people to stay in their homes. It was during the days of strong winds and zero visibility that a feeling of the isolation of the Kansas prairie was brought home to Kate. There was little doubt why Mr. Pipps had picked this place. The Osage Trail had made this area a heavily travelled artery of strangers and when not in one of the few small settlements scattered throughout the state, people on the road where at the mercy of nature. It was a perfect place for people to disappear.

It had been three months with Kate and Ma at the Bender Inn, and still they had not made their first kill. And as important, they had collected no money. On the other hand, their expenses continued. Under Kate's direction, they had purchased twelve new chickens and built an expanded chicken coop. Purchases were made for additional seed for the garden lookout position, which John Jr. would man during most parts of the day in the warmer months, and more seed was bought for the apple orchard. Despite both Ma and Pa's grumbling when well-to-do appearing men would come to the inn, eat their meals, and leave unmolested, she was adamant that the time was still not right. Kate's ability in the past to bring in money for the gang, and keep them from the clutches of the law was holding the group together for now. With that said, every day the girl looked with great anticipation for her benefactor's return. Mr. Pipps had to show up soon. Kate was a better than the average observer of people, but it was Mr. Pipps's super natural ability to pick who should be placed under the blade, which had really kept them all alive. It was also his mystical ability to know who was carrying large amounts of money and those who weren't. He also seemed to select those who could die without bringing suspicion upon the gang. After her incident with the rapist Jones, she knew she had to wait for his signal when it came to these important matters. Still, as days passed without his dark presence near her, she asked more and more, "Where are you, Mr. Pipps? Please arrive soon!"

Kate took several trips into Cherryvale. The small town was just being incorporated but it was a bustling place. Two separate train lines brought in travelers and stock twice daily. The town had a doctor and two opera houses, which had multiple shows running every week. On several occasions John Jr. would take both the women into town to buy fabric for dress making. There were also three general stores and a barber shop, which doubled as a dentist's office. In the center of town was a post office with a teletype, which collected and sent message across the country.

Despite Ma being against it, Kate took a waitressing job at the Cherryvale Hotel restaurant near the railway station. For the girl it was an easy decision. Even though she had no desire to serve strangers food for a pittance when far more money awaited them at the inn, the restaurant was the perfect place to establish the Bender back story with the locals. So far, all the people in town who had a care to know had a limited reference point for the family. It came mostly from Pa's gruff and unfriendly interactions for the few necessary purchases they made for the farm and inn. Kate would use her people skills to subtly place a warmer and more average feel for the family

131

in the public eye. At the restaurant she smiled and laughed with travelers and locals alike. Her boss, Mr. Stanley, a sixty-five-year-old man and his wife, Eleanor, of the same age, were the first to be told the Benders' Kansas cover story. The Bender family were German immigrants who had lived most of their lives on the fishing lakes of the north. Kate could spin detailed stories of growing up near Watertown as a girl, and their decision to move south to Kansas with the national advertisement of land tracks to be acquired. She was a master of information dissemination. Never too many details, but always what was necessary to frame the desired message. To the people she wanted to know, the Benders were described as self-sufficient but not rich. They were hard working farmers and ranchers, but not so much to miss church. Kate and her brother, John Jr., attended church every Sunday with Ma and Pa in tow every other Sunday. Like so many others in the area, she made it known that the Benders had a small inn where travelers could get a bite to eat. There were many other inns like this in the county.

She poured coffee, and served plates of food smiling, laughing, and mostly listening. The restaurant was a hub of information. Cherryvale had a town marshal who served as one of the few law men in the immediate area. In time, she poured him coffee as well. George Majors would eat his

eggs and bacon, drink two cups of coffee, and read his
morning paper. He left his table every morning without
more than a smile. Kate noticed the older man's eyes did
not scan her body as did those of most other men. He was
either quietly dithering away his last years with a badge as
the friendly constable, or he was the quiet, serious type.
Kate had not made up her mind on which it was yet. One
whose motives she did sum up quickly was that of the
newspaper editor and reporter for the *Thayor Headlight,* in
Marty B. Laploom. The skinny man drank three cups of
coffee every morning alongside an oversized pastry. In
New York, he would have been called a dandy, but on the
plains of Kansas Kate did not yet know the equivalent
term. The man wore a different suit every day, and his
black, pencil-thin mustache seemed to catch one's
attention, or at least draw attention away from his balding
head. Laploom had what Kate had always termed, "The
liar's smile." It was a smile that never stopped, or even
faded in any situation. The reporter always smiled and
always asked probing questions.

"So, my dear, what are your thoughts on our little
town so far?" Laploom asked as one of his white bony
fingers tapped on a black, leather-bound note pad the man
always carried.

"It's a very pleasant place, sir. We are so blessed to be here," Kate responded, keeping her eyes down in an appearance of meekness.

"Any surprises since you have arrived, maybe a boy, maybe two? Surely they have been attracted to a darling like yourself." The reporter's eye's studied her body's reaction, as well as her face for a noticeable response.

Kate had seen the man fish out answers of an intimate nature from others, even when those giving the answers didn't know they were doing so. However, she was a master of deception and instead of freezing or allowing her herself to stutter in indecision, she continued to clean the table top in front of her and replied as if it were of little consequence, "I'm afraid my days are full of work and little else."

A frown formed on the reporter's face, and he began to seek out others of interest. Yes, it was his profession to be curious, but Kate could see it in his darting eyes, there was a dark twist to this fellow beyond what was obvious. The reporter, if he became curious, could be a real danger to their operation, and she would do her utmost to keep her acquired family at a distance from him.

The suiters flocked immediately, which was also fitting to Kate's overall plan. Rudolph Brockman and his younger brother Ern, who owned the Big Hill trading post near the Bender Inn, were both smitten with the girl. The spoiled John Lockheart, whose father owned the town's lumberyard, asked Kate for a date the second time they met. There was also Johan Smith, a burly man some sixteen years her senior, who owned the butcher shop, who made clear advancements toward her, which usually came with offerings of steak and stew meat. As had been the case since leaving New York years prior, her cultural studies allowed her to publicly reproach the men while drawing them in. She would socialize with them all privately, and within the underground social clubs of the town. In public however, the girl appeared a very upstanding, moral young lady.

She had read about the upsurge in spiritualism, which was sweeping the nation. The topic seemed to find its way into conversation often and it was moreover well received. The spiritualists believed the dead spoke to the living and they had with them important information to impart to those who had the ability to receive their messages. Kate listened as travelers and prominent residents spoke of conversations they had had with the dearly departed while in the presence of "spirit guides."

Spiritualism was both denied and embraced by the locals. It was an accepted indulgence for many, and soon Kate claimed she and her mother were long time members to this ritualistic belief system. This was a calculated move on her part. She was aware of four other new immigrant families to the area who identified themselves as believers. Two of the families were also German. In a way, this made the Bender family seem in tune with the times. More importantly, the novelty had great potential for money schemes and forming local alliances she wanted to explore. This could be a great opportunity to enlist Ma's ability to create elixirs and other potions. There were reports that the Garland Opera House in town carried spiritualist performances, which took place twice weekly. She would have to view one soon. There was money to be made here. A chuckle escaped her lips as she thought about the irony of the spiritualist fad. When she heard the stories from the patrons about disembodied voices shouting from the ceilings during séances or ghost husbands telling grieving wives not to remarry, they all seemed so farfetched if not completely ludicrous. Then she thought of Mr. Pipps and the stories didn't seem so unbelievable.

For three months Kate waited tables, washed dishes, collected information, and spread the Bender cover story. Over time, the locals started looking at her as a part of the community. The girl's ability to appear at ease in any situation, along with her perfect English and seductive beauty made it easy for her to make friends and gain their confidence. After two months, the owners gave her a key to the hotel restaurant and their complete trust.

Most days John Jr. would pick her up and they would make the five mile trip back to the inn. Kate did, on occasion, walk the distance but she seldom had to make the full distance on foot. After making her way down the hill, she would most likely encounter a farmer travelling by way of wagon that would take her into town. The rides helped to familiarize the girl and the family to the community and it allowed the girl to know the regular activities of the neighbors in the area. On this day she was ending her work day around 3:00 p.m. John Jr. was waiting as she exited the establishment. They chatted about nothing as they always did on these short rides. Kate immensely enjoyed John Jr. because he had no agenda, and despite his simple mind, what he said was always honest. On this day when they entered the Bender property Kate had a sudden feeling that was not usual. She jumped from the wagon as her brother took the team out to the barn. After three steps she froze. This time the feeling was overwhelming and she knew what it was. Slowly she turned in a circle and focused her eyes. Soon, her eyes found their target. Over two-hundred yards away, sitting on the neighbor's fence row was Mr. Pipps. Her benefactor's strong frame was relaxed and one leather-gloved hand rested on a fence post. As was usual, most of his face was obscured by his long, black brimmed hat, except for his red burning eyes. His face seemed a blur, but Kate imagined he was smiling.

Kate was overjoyed and began to approach the figure sitting on the fence. She knew that Mr. Pipps did not like to be approached. It was he who decided how close anyone, including her, was allowed to get, but she didn't care. She wanted to hug him, maybe kiss him even though she knew better. He would never allow that now as in his second life he was not tethered to an earthly frame as before. Kate also wanted to chastise her friend for leaving her alone for so long with a group he had selected and put her with. Yes, it had been Mr. Pipps who had guided her to the sanitarium where John Jr. was collected using nothing more than a few dollars and a forged signature. Pa had been arrested on the same night her benefactor had guided her to the New York constable who accepted a bribe for his release. Despite being almost completely broke at the time, over five-thousand dollars was pulled from the dead body of the rapist Jones which financed the group's exodus from New York and their travel to Ohio.

Since then they had made a fortune and they would make much more in Kansas.

Kate was about to break into a full run when her benefactor jumped from the fence and pointed to the east side of the road. The girl froze as she knew what the signal meant. Mr. Pipps had made a selection. Someone was about to die.

9 THE KILLING OF NATHANIEL FLINT
II

There was no question about it. Mr. Pipps pointed to the west, and as quickly as Kate's eyes went to that direction, a team of horses pulling a wagon came into view. A solitary man guided the wagon eastward along the Osage Trail. Kate signaled John Jr., who was walking back from the barn. He in turn emitted a loud, high piercing whistle, which alerted Pa, who was feeding the cattle a short distance away. Kate didn't know if the man would stop of his own volition, but he did. As if following an unseen script, which would end in his death, the man brought the team onto the property and alongside a hitching post near the house. The man looked tired, and his eyes never veered in the direction of Mr. Pipps, who now stood alongside the neighbor's fence line.

Kate went quickly into the house where Ma was already bringing out the dishes for the man's last meal. As they had practiced for months, a prepared meal of cabbage soup and cooked ham was on the stove, ready. John Jr. greeted the man, who could smell the food, and after a quick exchange of words, the two walked inside.

Nathaniel Flint II was a tall man of six feet five inches and had a strong build. His long white hair and long mustache of the same color placed him somewhere in his fifties. His clothes were dust colored but of fine quality, and his brown leather boots looked maybe a month old. From his first words those who understood the accent would know him as a Texan.

"Tarnations it's been a go for me. I could eat something that was still on the move!" These were the words that escaped from his smiling face.

Ma smiled back and began a conversation with the man. "So where are you traveling to, kind stranger?"

"Well, ma'am, I am heading to Dellbrooke Wisconsin to precede a cattle drive for my company." Kate took a seat near the man at the table as Ma placed a large plate of food in front of the Texan. The man removed his wide, gray cowboy hat and nodded his head to the girl. Kate smiled and nodded back, and Ma introduced her.

"This is my daughter, Kate. She always enjoys hearing stories from other states in this vast new country of ours."

As the man's eye's slowing walked across the girl's cleavage he responded, "Yes, yes it is indeed a vast country we have here. None more robust than my home state of Texas."

The cabbage soup was laden with beef and the man ate two platefuls along with the plate of ham and fried potatoes. He gulped two large glasses of cool lemonade while speaking to both women about the thrills of the trail and the cattle businesses. As was the usual ritual, after the food had been consumed, Ma would make her exit, and the traveler, to his knowledge, would be left alone with the pretty young girl. With a full belly, the man would relax, and his head would start resting on the sheet partition.

Kate was pleasant and alluring as always, but inside, her heart raced and her breathing was shallow. It had been a long while since they had taken a life and she felt the jitters of being out of practice. She had seen the beads of sweet on Ma's face, sweat, which that could have been attributed to her work at the stove, but wasn't. The older woman was as nervous as she. For both it wasn't fear that drove their feelings of anxiousness, it was adrenaline-fueled anticipation. For Ma it was the expectation of riches, but for Kate, it was different. The girl's biggest desire was to continue her communion with her benefactor, Mr. Pipps. It was a communion that was now laced with blood and full of violence. She knew that from somewhere, he was watching her now. She smiled when she thought of this.

The Texan finished a story, of which the content the girl had not even heard, and he laughed out loud at some clever finish he had given it. His head went back deep into the cloth sheet and a hammer wielded by Pa struck the back of his skull with terrific force. The Texan partially stood up as the momentum of the blow sent his body onto the table. The table itself, not built for the weight of the man's crashing body, broke, sending food in all directions.

Blood spurted from the back of Nathaniel Flint II's skull. His tongue flopped lazily outside his mouth like a dog's, and his eyes twitched in the back of his skull. Even so, the big man rolled over to his back as Kate sat down on his chest.

W, what? was the single word that fell from his mouth as Kate's straight blade open his throat. For a precious, few seconds his body twitched and the girl looked like a rodeo cowboy on a feisty bronco, but as quickly as it had started, the man's body went limp. An arc of blood had made its way to Kate's dress, but she knew nothing of it. The girl was in her own world. Waves of energy ran through her body and it made her powerful, alert, and, more importantly, alive.

"Find the money! Everyone do your job!" Kate said through a twisted smile they had all seen before. They moved like ants, silent, quick, and with absolute purpose. Pa, took the horses and wagon into the barn. Ma watched for visitors from the front porch while John Jr. stripped the body of all valuables. Just as the stories of the Indians leaving nothing to waste from the buffalo, the Benders left nothing that was sellable on their victims. From the Texan's body was collected a silver pocket watch, his traveling papers, and three dollars in change. Three gold teeth were removed along with a silver ring. His boots, which might bring three dollars, were removed. From inside his left boot was found twenty-dollars. The big haul was two-thousand dollars taken from a leather wallet inside the man's left breast pocket. A worn deck of playing cards rounded out his personal possessions. In the wagon a pistol, shotgun, and larger than normal cache of ammunition were located. When it was fully dark, Pa and John Jr. would start their journey with the man's wagon and team to South Coffeyville. They would get maybe two or three-hundred dollars for everything. It was a good haul, and everyone knew it. Kate stripped in the kitchen and from two large bowls full of water began to wash her body. This was done in haste as she had to be ready should another traveler arrive. Even Pa's lustful eyes did not wonder near her naked body. They were all in work mode and to stray from their errands could destroy everything.

The Texan's body was placed under a tarp in the back of the Bender wagon. After Pa and John Jr. had washed the kitchen clean and were examined to make sure their cloths and bodies were blood-free, the men left the inn to transport the man's body to John Jr.'s property to be buried in the apple orchard. They left with the last rays of sunlight.

The first kill had been a bit sloppy. Pa had struck the man with more force than was necessary, and a new kitchen table would be required. Though their process was much the same as it was in Indiana, they still needed to continue to practice. With that said, the Bender Inn had been successfully christened with blood, and most importantly to Kate, Mr. Pipps was back at the helm.

Over the next six months the Benders killed fifteen men. Unbeknownst to everyone in the gang but Kate, it was Mr. Pipps who picked who lived and who died. All the travelers who were slain were heavily laden with cash for land purchases outside the state and their disappearances were very hard to pinpoint along the thousands of miles of trail throughout the country. Kansas was turning out to be the perfect location for killing for profit. Still, there were complications.

As more and more were murdered, Kate began to become concerned that their fairly regular evening trips to John Jr.'s section of land might start becoming suspicious to the neighbors. They could plant crops on the ground or place cattle in the pasture but John Jr.'s land did not have the tactical advantage of the high ground the inn enjoyed. In short, it became apparent to Kate that sooner or later they would have to change how they disposed of the bodies of their victims. Little did she know how quickly they would find themselves in a fix, and how dangerous that fix would be.

10 JULY 1871: MYSRICS, LOVERS, AND THE BODY COLLECTOR

The evening air in Cherryvale was pleasant for early July. The coolness brought out more people than usual, and the growing town had a burgeoning nightlife, both legitimate and otherwise. For two months Kate and her mother had performed a once a week, forty-five minute show at the Zorn Opera House right on Main Street. They were one of seven performances that started at 5:00 p.m. and ended at the adulterous hour of midnight. The town's curfew was 10:00 p.m., and the temperance society would be in arms over stragglers out after that, except for the opera houses, which seemed to get a pass. Constable Majors seemed to be reliably tied up with other affairs at the closing hour when patrons would stumble, scurry, and generally shuffle out and hurry down back

alleys to their private homes. Kate went by the title,
Professor Miss Kate Bender. In her performance, Kate
would seek out the spirits, which were connected to a
patron in the crowd. A small but talented musical band
employed by the opera house would play mood music and
add to the overall performance. Kate was a quick favorite
as she was beautiful and added a sense of sexuality to her
performances as she usually selected men from the crowd
to talk with the spirits. It was the girl's ability to read
people, which had allowed to asked questions as an
emissary of those from the great beyond with uncanny
ability.

"You, sir, have just suffered a great loss, and there is
someone here, from the beyond, with a message for you!"
Statements such as these were later borne out when Kate
would ask and answer questions from the patrons in ways
only a true seer could. Some of the women present were
put off by the girl's ability to mesmerize the men, some of
them were their husbands after all, but overall she a was
quick opera house favorite.

Within a short time she was on the main ticket for
Saturday nights. This had several financial advantages. Not
only did Kate receive top performance pay, which would
have been at least two days' pay for a man in the factory,
but also, she and her mother were allowed to set up a table

in the main lobby and sell their elixirs the entire evening. It was here Ma's alchemy experience was utilized. They had potions and creams for everything from slow-wittedness to husband's malaise. Because the crowd that frequented the opera were people inclined to such purchases, combined with Kate's riveting performances, they would make three times as much selling potions and healing creams as was made on the stage. It was not the kind of haul that were made at the inn with the mallet and straight razor, but it was considerable. To Kate, the night performances kept her in the know about the happenings in the area. The Bender women soon knew more about what was happening in the county then Constable Majors.

What information could not be collected from the loose lips of the crowd at the opera house, Kate collected from her cadre of boyfriends. Her most aggressive suiter was Rudolph Brokman who operated the trading post nearest the inn. Kate felt it important to keep him close as he could be privy to any gossip that would pertain to them. She had picked Rudolph to date over his brother, Ern, because the older boy was definitely the leader and, frankly, he was much more handsome. More importantly, Ern would have adored her but Rudolph would die, maybe kill for her. That was the kind of loyalty she could use if things ever got precarious for their operation. She did regret having sex with the twenty-five-year-old so soon. Rudolph was now ready to marry her, and that was not on the agenda. Kate never allowed the lumber yard owner's son, John Lockheart, to become disinterested in her. To achieve this state she perpetually promised sex to the young man only to deny him due to technicalities.

"It's just too damp out today." "I feel the stars are aligned wrong for such a union tonight." "You have just vexed me to the point I simply could not enjoy the rapture of coupling with you." These and other statements would be said amongst heavy touching, which always kept the lumberyard owner's son coming back for more. Kate knew this to be overly mean, but it was necessary. Lockheart hated Rudolph Brokman, and should she find herself in a position where she had to sever ties with the trading post owner, she would use the spoiled lumber yard owner's son as the protagonist.

Ironically, it was the butcher who often brought her the most sensitive information. Johan Smith with his balding head, round stomach, and penchant for always smelling like sausage, had intimate ties with the law enforcement community. There was just something about the buying and selling of meat that seemed to open people up to talking. Smith bought, sold, and butchered meat for Constable Majors, the county sheriff, and Judge Holt, who ran the county court house. A few kisses and a warm embrace every other week was all it took for Smith tell the most intimate of secrets.

So far the Bender operation had garnered no attention by local law enforcement. The same could not be said for the pesky reporter, Marty B. Laploom. Column after column he wrote about disappearances of travelers in the surrounding counties. Some were not related to the Benders and some were, but the reporter always hinted that the numbers of the missing were growing, and fowl play may be afoot. It was hard to know if the man was simply trying to sell papers or if he knew something others did not.

At the inn the money rolled in with each murder. Kate was attributed with her mastery of selection when it came to the victims. And for what was rapidly moving toward a year, her authority reigned without question. The once weekly trips to the barn to satisfy Pa were reduced to once a month, and he was satiated monetarily, which reduced his other urges. It took as much as a week for all the proceeds from a kill to be collected. The cash be it coin or paper was placed into a suitcase of its own distinction. However, there were always additional funds from the sales of the horses, wagons, firearms, jewelry, and other items, which had to be transported, sold, and funds collected before they made their weekly split of the final profits. Most of the fence sales happened in South Coffeyville and Parsons. However, as more property was confiscated, more exotic items required specialists in the criminal underground. A rather foreboding man, a Dr. Author Kegan, in the countryside near Independence, paid top dollar for items of unique design. Kegan was independently wealthy and owned a building in the city of Independence proper called the Health Office of General Care. Here he served as one of many who practiced as a family practitioner, dentist, and optometrist. He was well respected and had many employees who worked as receptionists at his place of business, and servants at his large home located just outside of town. Privately, Kegan was a transporter of stolen goods and a master of things much darker. For the Benders, the doctor purchased stolen dentist equipment, and medical supplies, women's braziers and strange trinkets taken from the wagons of slain salesmen. Sellers of oddities were common on the Osage Trails as these merchants would frequent towns during community festivals to sell the "seldom seen products." Unfortunately, the common fences avoided such items but they were always favorites of Dr. Kegan. Kegan was an educated man and probably had acquired through study at least one, if not more of the degrees for which he gave professional service. Kate assumed the man to be in his early fifties, but he was in such good physical shape he could have been ten years younger. He was amazingly clever and an instant judge of character. Kegan had an affinity for Kate and requested she accompany every shipment of property that was brought to his private home. While Pa and John Jr. ate cold ham sandwiches in the servant's kitchen, Kate and the Doctor dined on Quail's eggs, roasted pig, caviar, and other delicacies.

Their conversations were a surreal culmination of treachery and honesty. It was as if their mutual participation in criminal affairs had opened a door to speak freely about acts that are never discussed, at least to speak more freely than Kate had ever done before. It turned out Kegan had his own trade routes of criminal wares being transported across the country. His servants, who were well paid and fanatically loyal, maintained his anonymity at all costs.

"Of course, my dear Katherine, this is all just a means to an end, as I know it is for you," he said as the two sat in his elaborate library after another fine meal.

Kate smiled as she responded, "What do you mean, my dear doctor?" She watched his face and body for indications that might run counter to his words.

The doctor's voice was both forceful and soothing at the same time. His movements were both graceful and purposeful. As opposed to most people whose bodies were in constant conflict, the mouth saying lies, which the body signaled immediately. Dr. Kegan either believed everything he said or was a master of controlling the physical tell-tale signs of deception. With ease the doctor continued, "You and I take what we need from this life, and to do so forces us to lead a double life. With that said, we do not plan to continue either our public or nocturnal careers indefinitely. We aspire for a higher plain of existence."

Kate smiled back as she processed the man's statement. The doctor was a master of words, but it appeared he was absolutely right, or was he? She brought forward her wine glass and the doctor refilled it. Batting her eyelashes seductively she inquired, "What higher plain do I desire, dear doctor?"

The doctor laughed and responded, "Katherine, my dear, please do not misunderstand my intentions. Yes, I desire you. I desire you very much, but not in a cheap, fleeting, carnal fashion. I desire you as one does a kindred spirit. A person who has, for some reason, stepped beyond the mortal coils that hinder so many, you now walk with a new reality of this world." The doctor stared longingly at her and continued, "There is no doubt about that. To one who can see it, it is ever present in your eyes." The doctor set down his glass and contemplated for a moment before continuing, "You're higher plain? Well most certainly it is to be spent with a person you love above all others. A very special person who has also taken that step beyond the common normality, let's say you are the Lilith to the Nephilim fallen angel."

When the girl looked confused the doctor laughed and raised his hands to the twelve foot high rows of book shelves and stated humbly, "I apologize for my esoteric reference. I am afraid it is one of my many down-fallings. With that said, I would invite you read from my many volumes at will, including the Sumerian epic poems not the least of which is my favorite, "Gilgamesh and the Huluppu Tree. Enough of this talk. Let me show you what plain I aspire to."

The doctor extended his hand to the girl, who took it, and together they walked down a long high-ceilinged hallway full of animal antlers of every kind. At the end of the hall way was a red painted door, which looked to be wood, but to the touch was found to be made of steel. The doctor produced three different keys to open it, and inside Kate saw a long winding staircase, which seemed to go down forever. A chain railing was the only barrier on one side to stop what would most certainly be a life ending fall. On the other side was a stone wall. Securing her hand on his arm, the doctor took the railing side of the steps and led them down.

His voce echoed in the cavern as he spoke, "It's a bit eerie the first few times a person takes these steps, but I assure you we will be there soon."

"Be where?" Kate asked, only to see the doctor's shadowed smile in return.

After a lengthy decent, they entered a large room with a cement floor. The doctor turned on a series of gas lamps, and soon the room was fully illuminated. There were several gurneys in one corner of the room and a series of machines of a medical nature. Some of the devices were motionless while others moved and seemed to have a life of their own. In the center of the room were three large operating tables, of which Kate had only seen pictures of in books. Two of the tables were occupied by human bodies, which had been partially disassembled. On one table a man's leg had been removed, and the flesh had been rolled back to expose muscle and tissue. On the second table an adult woman had been cut down the center of her body and her organs had been separated and placed beside her body.

Along the walls hung surgical instruments, which ranged from the benign to the maniacal, but what caught Kate's attention were the rows of hands. On a silver, metal table about ten feet long set at least twenty hands. By the clean look of the cuts, the hands had been removed with a surgical instrument just before the wrist. The skin color of the hands varied and the distinction between the sexes of the owners were evident. Inserted into several of the hands were metal pins and wires, and Kate wondered if the fingers could be made to move by manipulating different wires.

On a large wooden table were heaped papers, all placed in neat stacks. Four chalk boards held notes of a medical nature along with illustrations of the physical body, most notably, the human brain. Kegan said nothing as he watched Kate walk through the laboratory taking it all in.

At the far end of the room there were shelves full of glass jars. The jars were full of a clear liquid and each jar housed a brain of a different size. Some of the brains most likely belonged to animals, but Kate knew many were human. The final oddity was the partial body of the man mounted on a metal table complete with rollers. It was mostly a torso and a head as the arms and legs had been removed. The back of the man skull had been detached, and a set of electric prongs hung from a rack. With Kate's attention obviously transfixed on the body and contraption, the doctor removed the set of prongs and touched them to the man's brain. An electrical current jumped from the prongs and the man's eyes opened. With a slight manipulation of the prongs the man became animated. Kate was fascinated and repulsed at the same time.

The smell of blood, tissue, and antiseptics was everywhere. A vision of the rapist Jones shot into her mind and was quickly rejected. This was a place a death, but she knew the doctor meant her no harm. Had that been the case, she would have most certainly have been brought to this location by a different route, most likely on one of those gurneys from a back entrance and not the staircase. No, the man wanted to show her, a kindred spirit as he called her, his darkest secrets and she was not going to obstruct the process.

Without fear or loathing she turned to the doctor and placed a hand on his shoulder, "Tell me of this place and its purpose."

Kegan smiled and took in a deep breath, "This is what I really do. This is my destiny and true love." He raised his hands and began to walk across the laboratory. All the proceeds from my criminal operations are placed here to fund my medical research. Inside this room I break down the walls of stupidity and speculations that restrain the medical community today. The body, mind, even the soul, I dissect, analyze, observe, and test." Kate was about to speak when the man ran to his operating table and placed a hand on the metal table and continued, "There's still years of work ahead of me, but when the time is right, I will impart the knowledge of the ages to man. It will be like humanity stepping from the darkness into the light."

The doctor caught his breath and slowly brought forward two chairs for them to sit in. His eyes followed Kate's every move. When he spoke again, his usual soothing tone had returned. "I said we are kindred spirits. I believe this to be true. While we most certainly are traveling different paths to our place of Nirvana, we are travelers of the same nature and we can and must help one another to our rewards."

"But we have a very beneficial partnership in place, do we not?" Kate questioned.

"The stolen property, yes. But it is small compared to what I will now propose," the doctor said as he slid his chair closer to the girl. "If discovered, my research here would be seen as criminal and I would be hanged in short order. Still my work must continue. I require human test subjects. Those who are alive benefit me the most." The doctor looked at Kate and as if reading her mind he continued, "Yes, it is true, you have not stated that you have the ability to deliver such a commodity, but I am not a fool. The property you have brought me is far too valuable to have been simply stolen. It has been relinquished from the hands of the dead. From what I read in the newspapers, or more aptly, from what I don't read, your group is doing a good job of covering your tracks. I simply wish to offer you a proposal that will tie up certain loose ends and increase your profit margin."

Kate nodded that she was willing to hear him out, and the doctor chuckled slightly as he continued. "My dear Katherine, I propose that you transport the bodies of those you shanghai, preferably alive, to me for the purpose of medical science. I will use and dispose of this evidence as we do the property you sell us. All ties to your operation will have now vanished from existence, thus securing our long and self-beneficial relationship. I have entrusted my deepest secret to you because I believe this expansion of our partnership can work!"

The girl wondered if this recent revelation did, in fact, account for the doctor's deepest secret, but for sure he did bring forth an interesting offer. Kate was guarded with her words.

"If in fact we had the product you are looking for, to transport it undiscovered and unmolested the distance required would place our operation at greater risk than the things we bring you now. What amount of compensation would you offer?"

The doctor laughed out loud, which caused an echo effect in the cavern. "My dearest Katherine, I will gladly give you the riches of Solomon!"

Kate made a promise to consider the offer and left with Pa and John Jr. Though having to wait a substantially longer time than usual, the men were happy when they departed as they were given twice the amount of money they usually collected for their haul. Kate knew the extra money was an enticement from the doctor to bring bodies to him for experimentation in the future. This knowledge she kept from the men and would be hers alone until the time she decided on the value of such an action whether it was worth the risk. Among men, Dr. Kegan was as exceptional as he was dangerous. Was he on par with Mr. Pipps? Most certainly her benefactor would not have liked the doctor. Why did she think that? These thoughts and others danced through her mind as their wagon moved slowly through the night under a Kansas moon.

11 THE KILLING OF CHAN CHIN AND THE TUNNEL

Summer gave way to fall and the Bender's finely oiled machinery of murder continued without a hitch. Over twenty-five bodies had been interred in the apple orchard of John Jr.'s property. A strong oak table now sat in the kitchen, and the Bender's had long since been accepted as new locals, but locals none the less. Then chaos erupted at the inn, which almost ended the entire criminal venture.

It started when a large, ornate, white colored carriage arrived at the inn. It was late afternoon and the

162

oversized horses, John Jr. called them Clydesdales as he had seen such a breed in parades in New York, entered the property. The beasts were black, and their muscles were massive. The animals clashed with the white carriage, which seemed to sparkle in the Kansas sun. On the side of the carriage in black letters were the words, "The Reese River Mining Company." The Benders had entertained, fed, and sold stock to pairs of passengers before. They had served families and caravans and all manner of groups. What they had not attempted to do was kill and rob two people at once. It added an element of risk that was unneeded for their work. What the Bender gang, with the exclusion of Kate, did not know was the dark figure, Mr. Pipps, that Kate believed she alone could see, was picking the prey. To the girl's shock, her benefactor appeared beside the well and pointed his gloved finger at the wagon. The Clydesdales, which appeared exhausted from their trip, whinnied and kicked dust at the presence of Mr. Pipps, but the young Asian male who held the reins and directed the horses, seem oblivious to his presence.

Kate stood frozen, watching the spectacle of the carriage enter the property, and being even more awe struck that her benefactor would choose these travelers. Present in back of the carriage was another Asian, this one much older and wearing a fine suit. Kate signaled the driver to take the wagon to the barn, but a few stern words from the back of the carriage had the driver doing otherwise. Instead, the carriage stopped alongside the house in time for John Jr. to arrive with two large pales of water for the horses. Kate gave the signal to her brother that these travelers were to be dispatched and without a word he whistled, and Ma and Pa began the process of preparation.

They were in foreign territory here. Her decision, or better put, Mr. Pipps's decision now placed them in a position where they would have to kill two people and do both while keeping it private, all in the afternoon sun. Problems started from the beginning. The owner of the carriage, a Mr. Chang Chin, refused to allow his driver to leave the conveyance.

"Driver stay with coach, have girl bring him food!" the short man shouted at John Jr. as he exited the carriage. The driver bowed as the man walked with the assistance of a white cane to the Bender Inn's front door. Pa watched as the short man entered the establishment. In a low voice he spoke to John Jr. "I don't know why the girl's picked this bunch. Them Chinamen are no more than slaves for the mining companies. They get half German's wage or less. That old man going in the house is a pit boss. Probably brokers the bodies in from China. What is strange is that Reese River Mining is not here in Kansas, so why is he here?"

The men improvised on the spot. John Jr. would strike the old man down in the kitchen while Pa would kill the driver and drag the body out of view of passersby. Inside the house Ma served the old man food while John Jr. took his position in the hall way with the mallet. Pa, who was ready to strike at the first opportunity, found himself being dissuaded from action as the trail suddenly became more active than usual. The Tolls passed by with thirty head of cattle followed shortly by Mr. and Mrs. Tykes's slow moving wagon. A load of iron rods sat in the back of their wagon, most likely bought at the lumber yard in Cherryvale. All the locals gazed at the strange carriage as they waved to Pa, who waved back. This was not good, too many eyes would be able to place the carriage here, and it was something one would not forget. Additionally, the driver, who identified himself as Mr. Li, was overly suspicious of Pa, who asked to sit alongside him in the coach seat.

Mr. Chang Chin was angry from the moment he entered the house. He was offended the women looked him in the eyes when they spoke. He did not like the food served him and refused to allow Kate to sit next to him while he ate. The girl was relieved at first when she heard the mallet strike his small, balding head. It made a distinct cracking sound and sent the man's wrinkled face hard into his plate of stew. To all's surprise the little man raised his head and despite his nose being broken and blood streaming from the back of his skull screamed in a painfully high piercing tone, *"Baohu!"* Kate grabbed the man by the loose strands of white hair on his head and ran the blade across his throat. A swift fist struck Kate in the face knocking her to the ground. Mr. Chin stood up and with one hand holding his gushing throat attempted to exit the back of the house. He made it three steps before being struck in the face with a frying pan wielded by Ma.

No more had the calamity in the kitchen died down then it started up outside.

"Go!" screamed Kate as she held her swollen face, and immediately John Jr. was running outside. As quickly as she could, Kate made it to the front door and saw the debacle taking place. The small Asian man was beating the living daylights out of Pa. With a series of rapid chops and punches, which were followed by a round-house kick, the big man toppled from the coach's seat-bench.

In an instant, the driver had the horses galloping back the way they had entered. John Jr. was closing the gap but would not make it in time before the carriage was back on the trail. All appeared lost until Mr. Pipps appeared and blocked the exit from the property. The giant horses could have easily trampled him but they did not. Instead, they stopped in their tracks and began to rear up in a panic. The driver looked in all directions, not understanding what had scared the horses. This distraction allowed John Jr. to make his way onto the carriage and tackle the man. The fight went to the ground, and John Jr. would also have been bested by the little man had Kate's blade not found his throat.

What took place next was a mad dash to avoid complete discovery. Mr. Pipps was gone, and the horses immediately were calm. Kate started shouting orders the second the Asian man's body went limp.

"John Jr.! Place this man in the carriage and drive it along the side of the house." Pa was standing up now and slowly shaking his head. Kate shouted in his direction, "You! Take charge of the body in the kitchen and place it alongside this one in the carriage and drive this team into the barn. Let's go!" Everyone moved without hesitation and soon Ma was whipping blood from the kitchen floor while Kate washed herself clean from the water basin.

For several hours they waited to see if anyone would converge on the inn. If what they had done in the view of all of Mother Nature had been seen by unwanted eyes was unknown. Nothing happened. A few travelers passed by and the birds sang as evening approached. It appeared they had been lucky but they weren't done yet. It was just pushing their luck too far to attempt to take the eye catching carriage out of town, even by nightfall. They would keep it hidden in the barn until Kate decided it was safe to move. The pummeling by the Asian had angered Pa greatly, and Kate had allowed the man several drinks of liquor to take the edge off. Even so, the big man's eyes glared at her when she eventually took the liquor bottle away from him.

"Pa, you and John Jr. still have work to do tonight and you need your wits about you!" she snapped at the man knowing he was at his limit. The men would take the bodies to the other property by the darkness of night. Moods lightened when five-thousand dollars was removed from the body of Chang Chin. It was a huge sum of money, but the risk they had taken today was far too big.

While the men were gone, Kate ate supper and had one of her seldom chats with Ma. The old woman rubbed an herbal suave on her daughter's cheek, which seemed to diminish the pain on contact.

"Daughter, you surprised me today with the selection of the Chinamen. Why them? Why now? We never take two travelers at a time. Explain this to me, please." Ma's tone was civil, if not almost sweet which made Kate suspicious.

She responded carefully, "A railroad transport might have payroll money or other currency. It seemed like a good chance to take." Ma had known her all of her life and she sensed that her daughter was holding back.

"Yes, that is true but you took an unnecessary chance and with all of our lives. What we need is a backup plan if something goes awry." Kate knew what she said was right and her eyes went to the kitchen floor as she contemplated the problem. Suddenly, an idea came to her and she jumped to her feet. Looking out the kitchen windows her gaze traveled from the house to the barn. Yes, it would be a lot of work but it could be done. A backup plan they would have.

The next day Kate told the group her idea. "We are going to build a tunnel!" she exclaimed. John Jr. smiled as he always did, but Pa was having none of it.

"What are you talking about, girl?" he said, still hungover from the the night's previous drinking.

Kate looked to her mother as she spoke. "It was Ma herself who stated the obvious. We need a plan to thwart our biggest liability. And what is that?" Kate continued, just in case anyone might add that the problem was that she had picked two travelers to kill when that was

169

not their method of operation. "I'll tell you. Our biggest liability is being seen with a dead body. We take someone down and a fresh traveler arrives, we are in a fix. We get caught moving a body from the house to the wagon, we are done." John Jr. was about to add something, but Kate continued. "I have even thought about the trips to John Jr.'s apple orchard and I have a better plan."

The room's silence told her she had intrigued them all. Step by step Kate walked the gang through her idea. They would create a tunnel under the kitchen that lead to the barn. If a traveler arrived after a kill, they simply moved the kitchen table and dropped the body under the floor. After placing the table back in its regular position, they would be ready to entertain a new traveler in moments. Then, in their own time, they could use the tunnel either by day or by night to transport the body to the security of the barn to take the person's belongings. Furthermore, Kate stated the bodies could be taken by darkness to their own apple orchard a mere couple hundred yards away from the house. There was some discussion here as Kate's original plan of keeping victims off the property had seemed a sound idea. But Kate countered they had no way of observing anyone who might poke around John Jr.'s property while they had constant observation of the inn. Furthermore, this plan would alleviate any potential concerns of neighbors seeing repetitious trips by Pa and John Jr. to a property not being farmed. A few questions were raised but in short order Kate won the discussion.

Work on the tunnel began almost immediately. The hardest part was to get the first ten feet of soil removed from under the kitchen. Makeshift barrels carried earth from the back of the house to the garden and the orchard. Making sure people did not see the dirt being transported was vital. A constant watch took place and both Ma and Kate took turns digging and hauling the dirt. The killings ceased for a month as the tunnel was dug, supported with timber and stone, and given a wooden floor. The floor took extra-long to construct and Pa and John Jr. often worked through the night to speed the process. Kate was forced to the barn twice to keep Pa working the hectic pace. As usual, Kate had a plan. She hoped to trade goods with Dr. Kegan for a gurney. With such a device, and the wooden floor, bodies, either dead or alive, could be transported from the house to the barn swiftly and with ease.

In just over six weeks the tunnel was completed. Oil lamps were placed the entire length of the shaft and several airs holes were dug and carefully hidden from observation topside. They now had a safe and efficient means with which to continue their work.

Amongst the several tasks Kate had to oversee during their hiatus from murder was the transport of the Clydesdales and the carriage. The horses, while huge, were black in color and almost invisible by night. On the first sliver moon they were taken by night to south Coffeyville where they fetched a fair price. The carriage was another matter. It was so garish in design and bright in color it practically glowed in the dark. Kate thought first of painting it black, but even that seemed not enough. Finally, after every option had been exhausted, a vote was taken and it was decided that they would disassemble the thing and burn it. That would settle the matter.

It was early February and the winter had been blessedly mild so far. Kate fed the chickens and was preparing to go back into the house after gathering an armful of wood. Ma was cooking eggs and bacon and the smell had made its way to her nose. Pa and John Jr. had been out since before first light breaking the carriage down and soon they, too, would be eating the morning meal. Kate paused for a moment by the wood pile and scanned the farm and then the roadway. As had been the case since work on the tunnel had commenced, Mr. Pipps was nowhere to be seen. Did he feel his presence was not needed when killing was not on the agenda? Kate hoped that was not the case in his thinking. She preferred to have him near all the time and she felt vulnerable when he was absent. Maybe vulnerable was not the right word, it was that she felt alone when his presence was not with her.

Those thoughts and others were ripped from her consciousness when she saw John Jr. running from the barn. His eyes were wide and a plume of hot vapor shot from his mouth as he exerted himself. Even more alarming was Pa who soon followed at the same hectic pace. Without thinking Kate ran to them both. As they met, John Jr. grabbed her by the shoulders and took a few moments to catch his breath. Pa did the same as he literally gasped for air.

"Slowly, John Jr., and don't shout, just tell me what it is." Kate's voice took on a motherly tone as John Jr. had a tendency to shout when excited.

Still breathing hard John Jr. spoke in short sentences, "Gold in the carriage! Lots of gold! More…more gold than you've ever seen in your life."

Kate looked to Pa, who was still completely winded and could not speak. Instead, the man nodded his head up and down that it was true. The Benders had struck gold.

12 PRESENT DAY: THE DRINKING GAME, LOST AND ALONE

The sound of the rattlesnake's warning echoed in Johnson's ear. The tell-tale rattle started out as nothing more than a faint ringing and it wasn't until he was at least partially awake that he recognized the danger he was in. Thankfully, the detective was smart enough to lay still, his head still resting on his saddle near the extinguished campfire where he and the two Mexican escorts of Sheriff Chimingez had slept under the stars of Texas. While often on the trail it was necessary to sleep outdoors, Johnson and the two men, who still snored near him had bypassed the warm beds of the last two towns for a specific reason. The first were that the men who accompanied him, one being Juan Mentargo, a man north of fifty, who passed gas more frequently than he breathed, and the other, Roberto Santago, who was twenty-eight and mostly spoke about his adventures with young prostitutes, were both raging alcoholics and were prone to violent acts of stupidity when in town. In the small community of De Las Ovejas, both men, after drinking copious amount of whiskey had started fights with locals at the nearby tavern. The Mexican escorts were quick to flash their badges as deputies of Zapata County when things started to get really bad. Even their status as law men would not have dissuaded an all-out brawl when Juan shot the bar owner's burro outside the establishment. Knowing he would have been strung up alongside his drunken escorts unless he interceded, Johnson paid the owner for his loss and bought a round of drinks for everyone and managed to get the two men to leave.

The dilemma for Johnson was he had to get rid of the escorts before he made contact with the outlaw hideout and the unruly Mexicans were not going to be easy to slip. Despite drinking to excess, they always kept a careful eye on the detective and his movements. Both were handy with a gun and shooting it out against the pair would be dangerous business. When they were sober, they incessantly inquired from the Detective where he was

ultimately going and his intentions when he got there.
There was little doubt Sheriff Chimingez had trained the
two for this trip and if Johnson were to elude them, there
would be bad repercussions. Still this was what he had to
do. If the three were together at the time Johnson found
the *Isla de la Muerte*, it was unknown what bad things might
befall the detective. Either the bandits there would kill
them all because of the presence of the Texas law men, or
Sheriff Chimingez's men, if they were paid to protect the
criminal hideout and its inhabitants, would join together
with the bandits to murder the detective. There wasn't a
good option for Johnson unless he was allowed to
infiltrate the hideout under his terms. Juan and Roberto
had to go, and the detective would make his move today.
That is, if he wasn't bitten in the face by a rattlesnake.

It was not uncommon for snakes to edge up near
a campfire for warmth at night. Johnson was not
unfamiliar with rattlers. He had seen them from time to
time on the prairie near Dodge and other parts of Kansas.
However, they were everywhere in Texas and their
boldness toward humans was, at times, amazing. The
detective kept his breathing regular and calmed his natural
instincts to attempt to flee the danger. After a few minutes
the snake slowly slithered from its position on top of his
saddle behind his head, and down the side of his face to

his chest. It paused for a moment and then slithered off his body, past the sleeping Mexicans and into the brush. It appeared the snake had a bead on some mice that were nearby but it knew he was there. Its natural senses allowed it to detect his body from a distance. The snake could have bitten him in the right situation but it preferred to save its venom for something it could eat. Slowly, Johnson got up and stretched his muscles, which seemed to have tightened all at once after the dangerous event. The escorts, as if on cue, awoke and began cooking coffee, bacon, and beans.

The day started as the last four had. Johnson traveled southwest and the Mexicans followed watching his moves and asking questions. As far as he could tell, the men had been paid to watch his progress and later report what the detective found, or probably to the sheriff's own desire, what he didn't find. Both Roberto and Juan had been present when he had attempted to show disinterest in finding the Benders in the state. Both men had heard him say he would leave for Kansas after a few days in Zapata County. It had been a few days and he was still there. He was still moving south, and Johnson could tell the men wished to be done with this assignment and would soon try more than strong conversation to try to persuade him to leave the state. Johnson placed his plan into action.

The three men rode for twelve hours under the sweltering Texas sun. They stopped only to water the horses. By evening they arrived tired and dirty in the town of San Ignacio. The town was poor and full of low brow types, but nothing that led the detective to believe they were near the *Isla de la Muerte*. Here the detective would spend a healthy amount of traveling money from the agency to get the locals to do his bidding. Once inside the tavern, Johnson started buying the drinks, something he had not done before. The premise he forwarded for the celebration was he had gone as far south as he was required to satiate his company's demand that he look into the reports that the Bender's had entered the state. Tomorrow, they would head north and, eventually, he would take a train ride the rest of the way home.

This news made both Roberto and Juan very happy, and diminished any suspicions they might have had when Johnson pushed them to start drinking before they had eaten or hydrated their bodies after the long hot ride. Even alcoholics as they were, they knew better, but the detective gave off such an innocent demeanor they were lulled into a false sense of security. Johnson knew the men expected him to celebrate, and if he did not drink with them, they would become concerned. So, he had to appear to be as drunk as the Mexicans who were watching him.

Fortunately, he had prepared for this. Over their last few stops Johnson had drank Vodka in the presence of the men. Not enough to get drunk but enough to understand the men hated the drink and stayed primarily with tequila and rot gut whiskey. After consuming a few shots with the men, Johnson started quietly passing his money out to the locals who were more than happy to take it, under the guise he was going to play a few tricks on his friends. First, he paid full price for a Vodka bottle full of water. There was little chance the Mexicans would ever drink from his bottle, as they had an overabundance of Tequila being served to them by three young girls, who never stopped laughing and smiling. The girls had been paid on the side to show the two men a good time. To earn their wages they were to do one thing, keep the men drinking until they went to sleep. If it took sex to get that done, there were a few extra dollars in it for them. The girls were effective at their jobs. Through dancing, hugs, and kisses, they kept the men drinking, urging them to consume more and more. Johnson played alongside them acting as intoxicated as the two as he waited for the men to go unconscious.

To their credit, it took the two Mexicans five hours of intense drinking to lose all motor functions and turn comatose. During that time, Johnson spent more than two-hundred dollars on liquor, keeping the girls motivated, and several quite payoffs to men who were present and became fed up with the two deputies' antics. Juan broke two bar stools and Roberto permanently damaged the tavern's piano when he attempted jump off the top of the musical instrument. Next, and almost as if it were fated, one of the two men shot a horse at the watering trough. The money flowed from Johnson's hand to almost everyone present, and, finally, the men fell into a deep, alcohol-induced sleep.

Both men were taken to the local hotel where their boots and guns were held at the front office. Despite being up all night, Johnson went to the general store and loaded his horse with food, water, and ammunition. With luck he could get a full day's ride ahead of the men before they woke, and it would take another day before their heads would stop ringing. A last round of payoffs guaranteed the Honorable Sheriff Miguel Sangrada Chimingez's men would all be given false directions of travel when they inquired about the gringo's departure.

Johnson wasn't the kind of man who would kill the Mexican escorts to keep them off his trail. That would have made him like the Benders, or maybe a lesser version. Unfortunately, there were problems with having ethics on the hot plains. Roberto and Juan would have to report to

180

the sheriff and either they or others under his employ would trek after him at some point, and if they found him, violence was guaranteed. Worse yet could be if he evaded the sheriff's men. After all, he was seeking the Island of Death and the worst serial killers the nation had ever beheld. Danger was on every side of him.

13 DON'T FENCE ME IN

"Move out of there!" Pa shouted at John Jr., who stood between and angry sow and her piglets. The two men had been doing chores all afternoon and the young man had gotten lazy with the last job of the day, feeding the pigs. The pigs had prospered over the last year and what had started with three sows and two boars had now grown to a full pen of pigs of various ages. The pregnancy cycle of the pigs was dependable and constant. Every 114 days the mothers gave birth, or as John Jr. coined it, "the three three's." Each sow, almost to the day, gave birth every three months and three weeks, plus or minus an additional three days. Each sow had a litter between eight and ten pigs. Normally, litters suffered one to two loses, but not on the Bender farm. In a place where humans died at an alarming rate, pigs prospered.

John Jr. gave special attention to the pigs, making sure the runts got bottle fed if necessary and that the pens were constantly enlarged to avoid cramping the animals where mothers were prone to accidently smother the newborns. In all, through multiple births, only three piglets had succumbed to the elements of fate. John Jr. wept over all the deaths, even though being chastised by Pa for his silliness. Despite his father-like attention and love for the pigs, John Jr. also handled all the slaughtering of the swine. He did this without remorse or any notion of sadness. Kate had watched the process with fascination. At first she thought the young man would be placed in a situation of turmoil over having to kill the animals he so lovingly took care of. It may have been that the pigs slated for slaughter were now adults and had transcended all their baby-like qualities. For whatever reason, John Jr. brought the hammer to the pigs' skulls with blunt force, and without a trace of emotion. The blade next went to the pigs' throats, and the animals were hoisted up and tied to a metal bar where they would hang by their haunches. The pigs would kick, and blood often sprayed everywhere. John Jr. watched it all expressionlessly. It appeared that whatever love he had had for the piglets had been removed and replaced with a utilitarian desire for sustenance. The girl wondered if he felt that same detachment when his mallet crushed the skull of a man.

Kate had never been able to watch the boy during his part of the process of killing people as she was always consumed with her part, the cutting of the throats, and the spilling of the blood. For her, killing people brought about a mixture of emotions. Hatred was wrapped in desire and those emotions were covered, as if in a blanket of power, as her blade opened the throat, and the blood began to flow. The crimson flow from swine seemed almost dirty when compared to the blood of a human. As a man blead out, Kate could feel his power flow into her. She always felt an urge to swim in the lake of red that would flow across the kitchen floor. No, she and John Jr. did not have the same experience when they took life, be it animal or human. She felt good that John Jr. did not experience the same feelings she did during the kill and, ironically, she felt a bit bad for feeling so good, but so be it. Kate coveted the experience as something that was hers alone and despite her feelings of kinship for John Jr., she didn't want to share it.

Periodically, the pigs were transferred from their main pen into a temporary pen. This was done to allow for repairs to be made and for the filling of the water and food troughs. The pigs were uncommonly intelligent and for the most part they seemed to understand what was taking place when they were called upon to make the temporary relocation. The sows and the boars would move along with only the slightest suggestion and the piglets would follow the adults without question. The only time issues arose was when the pigs were moved right after a birthing when the sows were most temperamental and overly protective of their young. Pa had been charged twice by angry sows and the men quickly understood to give the new mothers a wide berth for a few weeks after the births and never to get between the mothers and their litters.

Today's work was a standard affair, except for the oversight of the top latch failing to be secured on the gate, which divided the two pens. Unfortunately, the normal jostling of the animals knocked the gate open, and then a new birthing sow saw John Jr. near her resting area and her maternal instincts kicked in. The animal weighed nearly 400 pounds and when she charged it was with the force of a wagon rolling downhill. Pa's warning saved John Jr.'s life, as he looked up in time to side step being hit straight on. However, even the glancing impact sent the young man flying headlong into the wooden fence. The fence did not give and there was a loud snapping sound that instantly made Pa's eyes widen. Worse yet, the impact knocked John

Jr. unconscious and the sow was circling around for another charge.

Without thinking about the danger, Pa jumped into the pen and lifted John Jr. up and dropped him on the other side of the fence and out of immediate danger. The sow was on the man immediately but Pa was ready and he rolled with the blow of the large animal's head to his hip. As soon as the sow was past him he was back on his feet and climbing over the fence.

"Wake up, boy! Come on! Wake up!" Pa slapped gently upon the boy's face. There was no reaction from John Jr., and his face was turning pale. Chances were high he was bleeding inside or something equally as life threatening.

Pa carried the young man to the house where the women assessed the injuries. Ma placed a set of herbs under John Jr.'s nose. After a few moments he began to stir, then, he came to full consciousness. When John Jr. awoke, he was in great pain and began to scream uncontrollably. After several minutes of ear piercing screams, followed by spasms and wailing, he fell unconscious again. Ma stated he had to be brought to a doctor immediately. No one argued the point though it was an action of last resort. The gang did not wish to have the entanglements of a paper trail for medical help or to field personal questions a doctor might place before them. This exact situation made regular concerns worse. What were they to do if John Jr., in the fit brought about by his injuries, began to scream confessions of murder and robbery? Did they run? Were they to kill everyone present to silence witnesses? What would be the ramifications of that?

The journey to the doctor was slow and arduous in the wagon, as each bump they hit caused John Jr. to twist and moan. Furthermore, they could not stop in Cherryvale which was only six miles away as the town's only practitioner, Dr. Jim B. Long had recently died after falling down a flight of stairs, that lead to his office above one of the town's more active saloons. Their only choice was the longer trip to Independence. Three quarters of the way to the town, blood began to trickles from John Jr.'s eyes and ears. What they presumed to be a bad situation with the young man's health had taken a turn for the worse. Kate patted his hand and spoke to him in a soft voice.

"Everything will be fine, John Jr., you just don't worry about nothing." Kate had so internalized her role within the fictitious family that for her it truly was her real brother clinging to the edge of life.

Independence was a hustling and bustling town and they had four official doctor's offices along with the local healers which were used at about the same frequency. Of the four official medical practitioners in town, was their compatriot in stolen goods, Dr. Author Kegan. Kate mulled over the idea of taking the injured member of the gang to Kegan. There was logic to such a decision. Kegan would never share anything criminal that might spill from the lips of her injured brother; after all, the doctor was culpable of the same and maybe worse.

As her mind weighed all the possible outcomes of their next action, she decided not to use Kegan's assistance at this time. He was just too dangerous a man to their anonymity if they were to place themselves together in the public eye. She had no idea when and if his chambers of deadly secrets would be discovered, but if they ever were, she did not want any public ties to the man, even if it was as a regular client. No, they would pick the first available doctor and avoid the public entanglements of Kegan. As luck would have it, be it good luck or bad, the first doctor's office was a sturdy, stand-alone, wooden building with a large, white sign out front that said, "Dr. William York- Family Practitioner for all Ailments of the Body and Mind."

The doctor's office was large and had a clean appearance. A recent coat of white paint was on the walls and the nurses, three of them wore clean uniforms. As soon as they pulled in front of the building a nurse was summoned, and John Jr. was placed on a gurney and wheeled inside the building. He was quickly taken past the less injured and sick, who waited in the large waiting room, and taken to room where he was placed on a metal examining table, which was similar to those found in Kegan's underground laboratory. Kate was certain the work done on this table was different from what she had seen previously. The room had a strong smell of alcohol, and a nurse did an initial assessment of John Jr. while the family was ushered to the waiting room.

For three hours, they waited as more patients arrived and others left. They had not even had a glimpse of the doctor and their inquiries on the state of John Jr. were simply deflected by the nurses, who said they would have to wait to speak to Dr. York.

After five hours, Pa started to get unruly.

"Who do these people think they are? You! Woman! Get in here and answer me what is the condition of my boy!" Pa's voice was like a bear's growl, and even the sickest in the room looked in his direction.

A nurse of about thirty years approached Pa and said in a stern voice, "Quiet yourself, sir! Such loudness will not be tolerated in Dr. York's office. Do you understand me?" She glared at Pa who glared back. The big man was mad enough to slap the woman down, and had it not been for Kate, who caught his glance, violence might have ensued. As it was, the woman gave a half-smile of superiority and motioned for the group to follow her. "Now, Dr. York is ready to visit with you and if you will all quietly come with me. We will get you reunited with your loved one."

"Reunited with your loved one," Kate thought to herself. It had a tone of finality to it, and she could not shake it out of her mind that it sounded like a subtle statement of death. Were they being led to see the deceased body of John Jr.? Was their next stop the funeral home? She would never allow his body to be buried at the inn; not like the others. John Jr. would get a city burial with a fancy grave stone. She owed him that much and more. Thoughts of death and John Jr. shot through her mind when they entered the examining room and saw the member of their gang, alive, awake, and sitting on the metal table.

A man in his midsixties with thick, white hair stood in front of the young man and gazed intently into his eyes. John Jr.'s head was wrapped in bandages as were his ears. There was a nasty bruise, which ran down the side of his neck, but he was alive. The entire group was both relieved and amazed.

A couple of moments passed as the doctor spoke quietly to John Jr., his lips close to one of the boy's bandaged ears. When this was done, the man moved with surprising quickness to the group, shaking Pa's hand first, then Ma's, stopping longer with Kate.

"You must be the sister, Kate, I presume." The man's brown eyes studied her carefully.

Kate curtsied, as was proper, and the action replaced any need for a verbal response. Dr. York paused for a moment, and when words from the girl were not forth coming he stepped back a pace and engaged the group.

"The boy's head has been concussed and he should be kept awake for the next fifteen-hours. There's a couple lacerations on his noggin, which will need to be cleaned and bandaged over the next several days. He can eat and drink, but not to excess, and no alcohol for a week. He will have a hell of a headache for some time. If it impedes his sleep, he can chew on a piece of willow bark and drink warm chamomile tea." The man's face was smooth shaven and it seemed to draw attention to his sharp eyes, which looked the group over intently. "Most doctors would send him off with a bottle of laudanum, but not me. The stuff is too damn addictive." The white haired man gently touched the boy's head twice more, inspecting that the bandages were ready for travel and then final instructions were given.

The medical bill was paid on the spot with a ten percent appreciation fee, not unlike a tip. It was fashionable for the times but almost excessive. The doctor became busy as he was immediately called to see another patient. The Benders left through the back door and were soon on their way home. Considering the situation, it appeared that things had gone well. After all, if each were to be honest, they expected to lose John Jr., and he was now awake and talking. The doctor was competent and there was no reason to question his prognosis that the young man would fully recover in time.

As the wagon made its way east toward the Bender Inn, Kate's mind scrutinized every event that had taken place. John Jr. being left alone with the doctor for five hours was a dangerous situation. She had studied the doctor's body language, tone of voice, and his eyes. Men like to lie but their bodies usually give them away. Dr. York was still a mystery to her. If anything had been said to him by John Jr. that was a threat to the gang, she could not directly discern it. What bothered her as their wagon made its gentle journey home was that she could recognize Dr. York was a complex and intelligent man. A man like that would have control, would be able to restrain himself even if he heard the most villainous of statements being spouted from the lips of a half unconscious boy. In fact, a man like that might simply store the information until one day, when something else popped up in his consciousness, would cause him to put it all together. This was a danger they would have to face when and if it came to pass.

14 JUNE 1872: GOLD RUSH, MURDER IN PRINT

Over the months the travelers continued to stop, and Mr. Pipps continued to point out a selected few. Their names—Ben Brown, W.F. McCrotty, Alonzo Zetris, Henry Mckenzie, Sam Franken, Willis T. Shone, and more, were simply words on documents, which were evaluated and, most often, buried with the bodies in the orchard. The victims had no special meaning to any of the gang except for one thing, they all carried large amounts of cash. To this endeavor, Kate appeared more than capable of being able to find the treasure that moved across the Osage Trail. Slowly, each member of the gang filled their own personal, large suitcase to its capacity, with their portion of the weekly cut and each added a second suitcase to hold their growing wealth. The trap door under the kitchen table, and the long underground tunnel, which led to barn, greatly decreased the chances of the Bender's bloody work being discovered. The process had been streamlined and the killings were now at full capacity.

The success of the gang was not without its own difficulties. After the killing of Mr. Chan Chin and his martial art wielding assistant, the Benders had come into custody of a huge amount of gold. 200, one-pound bags of gold sat in the heavy, metal lock box, which had been hidden inside the ornate, white carriage. This was a fortune, more than their combined wealth from all their work in Kansas. The market for gold in 1872 was $23.19 an ounce. There is sixteen ounces in a pound. Thus, one pound of gold was worth approximately, three hundred and seventy-one dollars and four cents. In total, the gang was now in possession of around seventy-four thousand, two hundred and eight dollars. Tremendous wealth was now in their hands, but they had precious few ways to turn it into paper currency. Yes, all the surrounding towns had a gold merchant. Settlers often brought in gold as a currency but Kansas was not known for its gold mining and there was no way for the group to use conventional gold vendors to convert their find. Even if they had taken small portions of the gold to every surrounding town it would have gathered immediate attention. Knowing the railroad would never give up a payday of this size without a lengthy and exhaustive investigation, they had to find a quiet means to liquidate their amazing wealth. It was contentious, but Kate managed to convince the group to bury the metal lock box in the barn. It was too dangerous to keep the gold in the house, and for now, it was their back-up plan to grab the lock box and run if they were to ever be robbed and their personal fortunes confiscated, or if the law came after them. Kate knew that besides John Jr., who never cared about money in the first place, the rest all lost a certain amount of sleep knowing the wealth of Alibaba was sitting four feet under the ground in the barn, along with the cattle feed.

Kate did, indeed, know of one way they could turn the gold into cash. They could take it to Dr. Kegan. He would have the means to send the gold to the four corners of the Earth. He would most certainly take a sizeable cut for his service, but that was going happen with any fence they dealt with. Kate kept quiet to the group about this because if she had told them they would have pressured her to make a deal. What she knew from her last private meeting with the doctor was he desired something much more than riches. He wanted bodies for his

laboratory and he would use their dilemma with the gold
to pressure her to deliver specimens to his operating
tables. Worse yet, the man had a mesmerizing nature about
him, and it would become all too easy for her to fall into
an agreement with the man for his laboratory to be
regularly filled with travelers from the Osage Trail. No
matter what the compensation, Kate knew this was a risk
not worth taking. She also felt that too much time around
Kegan might cause a rift between her and Mr. Pipps. The
two were like cosmic opposites, and to bring them
together could only spell disaster. It had been for this
concern, primarily, she had avoided any further visits with
the alluring doctor.

It was in June when they were faced with inquiries
tied to murder and the gold. It came from none other than
the weaselly reporter, Marty B. Laploom from the *Thayor
Headlight*. Kate had kept a wary eye on the reporter, always
from a distance and never attracting attention. Laploom
was a myriad of contradictions. For the most part he
stayed to the towns near his barber's, the coffee shops, and
places of where soft men dwelt. As long as the stories were
easy to collect, he did his job without bringing an ounce of
perspiration to his lotioned and powdered brow. However,
when news was scant, or if something caught his fancy, the
frail man could was capable of going to amazing lengths to

get a story. His readers loved the dirt he often exposed on political figures and the gossip he could stir with innuendo, which was constantly showered upon those he disliked. When Laploom's black carriage arrived at the Bender Inn in midafternoon on a June day, Kate's heart jumped in her chest.

Other than the white carriage, which had brought the two Chinamen from the railroad, only Laploom had such a conveyance. The reporter's carriage was smaller, black in color, and far less grandiose than the sparkling white model of Mr. Chang Chan's, but to the local dirt farmers and cattlemen it was something to see. It was certainly a transport befitting a dandy. Laploom's coachman was a grumpy old man by the name of Earl Trent. Trent was fifty plus years old and usually covered in at least three of different ages of dirt. Most locals gave Trent a pass on his perpetually foul mood, a byproduct of being under the paper's employment, and the thumb of Laploom. The reporter for the *Thayor Headlight* didn't always travel in the carriage and it seemed he used it when he was in his most arrogant and judgmental of moods. The carriage, and the weaselly reporter inside, stopping on Bender property was not a good sign.

Immediately, Kate signaled John Jr. who was in the yard. He ran to the house and alerted Ma. Pa was in the pasture checking on a couple of cows who were to give birth any day. There was no time to collect him. Kate would have to deal with the reporter directly. The girl made it to the carriage as Trent opened the door for his employer. Laploom exited with the speed only vermin possess. His beady eyes were sharp and they darted across the farm yard collecting information.

His thin mustache lengthened as he smiled, "Ah, my dear Katherine. How are you today, young lady?" His eyes scanned her quickly and then his focus went to the barn and the house. In his left hand was the notepad he was known to carry when he was "collecting the dirt." In his right hand was a pencil, the lead recently sharpened. Kate wanted to speak but was preempted by the reporter who spoke with an air of superiority. "I do so apologize for arriving without an invitation but I am investigating what I believe will be a magnificent story, and it has brought me here." Laploom bypassed the dirt path to the house and began to walk toward the barn. Kate moved quickly in an attempt to get a head of the man and learn what he was after.

"Pray tell, sir, what is it we can do for you today?" Her words came out in a rush as the reporter was quick on his feet and she had to all but run to get a head of him and stop his advance.

The reporter eyes went again to the barn and then began to look over the pastureland. She could almost hear the gears turning in his head, and it sounded like workmen building a hangman's platform.

"Admit to a crime!" the words burst out of the reporter's mouth as his eyes locked on the girl. It was like lightening had struck her body, and Kate felt a burning sensation go through her from head to toe. Anyone else might have given themselves away, but not Kate Bender. She knew if the reporter had any real knowledge of what took place here, he would have been followed by an army of lawmen. No, the fidgety, thin man was simply digging, but that was almost as bad. She had seen Laploom use this accusation style of questioning. He often got confessions from people who were aggressively confronted. Others would lie with their mouths but their body language would give them away. Laploom had the same skills as Kate did when it came to reading body language. Today, as the reporter watched her intently, the girl appeared to not understand the question.

"I'm sorry, sir, what do you need?" She scratched her head as if the question had come to her in a foreign language.

Laploom frowned at her response and then momentarily dismissed her as his eyes continued to surveil the area. When he spoke it was in a long stream of rambled statements, as if he was talking only to himself.

"A courier for the Reese River Mining Company has disappeared. It was a two man traveling group in a white carriage of superb construction." Laploom turned back and looked at his carriage, which now stood in the hot afternoon sun.

"Would your driver like a drink of water?" Kate hoped to break the man's train of thought.

"He's inconsequential." The driver returned the reporter's look of disgust. Laploom opened his notepad and began to read from it. "The carriage was created by Henry H. Smith and Samuel B. Collins of the Collins Manufacturing company in Washington. It was pulled by two, black in color Clydesdale horses, of which there are no known breeds in this county. I weep inwardly that I was not present to see such a marvel!" The man brought a silk handkerchief from his pocket and dabbed at his eye in an overly dramatic fashion, and then continued. "The point here, my dear, and it is of paramount importance to finding the truth of this case, is these travelers could not be overlooked by the eyes of even the most common." Again, Laploom went back to his notepad and began flipping through pages until he found what he was looking for. "Here it is; in our local area, there are over fifteen sightings of the courier traveling east along the Osage Trail. The nearest sighting was only two miles from here. What can you add to the story? Surely you saw a white carriage being pulled by giant black horses. I can only assume it would have been a happy spectacle to your meager existence here on your little mountain." Laploom smiled as he spoke.

Kate knew that to hesitate would be as dangerous as to answer poorly. With eyes pointed to the ground in humbleness she answered, "Most certainly, sir. I did, indeed see the carriage you speak of. Even the months that have passed cannot dim my memory of that fine day."

Laploom shuffled through his notepad to a clean sheet and poised his pencil over the paper. "Tell me everything you remember, spare no detail." The tip of the man's tongue protruded from the right corner of his mouth as he wrote her account.

As if pulling it from her memory, Kate spoke. "The horses were black and giant. As they moved down the road it looked like there were tassels attached to their, you know, feet. The carriage sparkled and there was a Chinaman at the reins. Oh how I hoped they would stop so I could pet those horses." Sadness went across the girls face and she looked back to the trail before continuing, "But, they just kept on going east. I guess they weren't hungry or maybe those folks from China don't eat regular farm food. Is that right, Mr. Laploom? Kate looked at the reporter with an expression of genuine inquisitiveness.

The reporter stopped writing and looked at her. He wasn't satisfied, and it was obvious in his tone and demeanor.

"*Hmmm*, kept going east down the trail, you say?" After Kate nodded her head in the affirmative, he began to speak while slowly walking in the direction of the barn. "You see, this is the problem I have with that, little dearie. I have talked to every farmer east of here for ten miles, and not one of them saw the carriage that sparkled or the giant black horses with tassels on their feet. It's like they made it here and then disappeared from the face of the planet." This time Laploom pretended to be looking elsewhere but through the corner of his eyes he watched for a response from the girl.

Again Kate did not delay in her reply. Laughing out loud she said, "Not a real surprise, sir. It's because of the inn we kind of keep an eye on the road for folks who might want to get a bite and such, but most folks around here are working way too hard to keep up on who goes up and down the trail." This time she smiled big at the reporter, who mimicked the same back to her.

It was the perfect answer. Laploom could repeat her statement to every neighbor on the mound and none would challenge it, or feel malice against the Benders for having said it. Laploom had exhausted his inquiries with the girl but he wasn't done yet.

"I need to speak to the men, where are they?" Once more the reporter began to walk toward the barn.

There was no good direction for the reporter to go. The gold was buried in the barn, and the bodies were in the orchard. If they took the man in the house, the reporter was likely to smell the suitcases full of money, which were hidden in the makeshift attic. It was nothing but potential disaster in every direction. To make an almost untenable situation worse, Mr. Pipps became visible, and now one more explosive element was added to the mix. Kate's eyes widened as she saw the shadowy figure sitting on the roof-top of the inn. She averted her eyes immediately, as to not draw the attention of Laploom.

"Let's go inside. You can talk to John Jr. there." Against her desire, she took the man's bony arm and led him inside the inn.

Ma had been eavesdropping for some time, and Laploom's inquiries had soured her mood. The woman was snappish with the reporter, and for once Kate welcomed it. They needed a new tactic to get the man to leave, and rudeness might just be the trick. The older woman served the reporter burnt coffee, which he grimaced to get down his throat. Ma claimed her entire day was spent over the stove and said to have seen nothing. John Jr. asserted the same, but with a different alibi. He claimed to have been in the pasture with the cows helping to deliver a calf. It was something Laploom had no way to dispute, and he would not be able to come across evidence that would later refute it. The reporter insisted on talking to Pa. This was a concern to everyone because while the big man would claim to have seen nothing, his anger, if kindled, might cause him to speak out of turn. The reporter would push him hard. He had done this to John Jr., but the two were very different men. John Jr. hadn't even noticed Laploom was subtly accusing him of lying in the hopes of provoking different answers. Pa was likely to beat the man's face in. They couldn't kill this man in broad daylight. Laploom was well known locally, and most likely there were more than a few who knew he was at the Bender Inn. He had to leave this place both alive and clueless of the real activities on the mound.

Every moment he remained on their property decreased the chances both would happen. As they had entered the inn, Kate saw Mr. Pipps sitting inside the reporter's carriage and she wanted to scream but did not. Inside the house she just wanted it all to end.

"Your man outside with the horses looks absolutely parched; he must truly hate you for making him stand out there in the sun." Ma gave a false look of concern, which almost made Kate chuckle from both tension and the idea her mother cared about anyone. Had she seen Mr. Pipps and assumed it was the man's driver? This was all insane!

"Oh yes he hates me very much." Laploom stated absentmindedly as he eyes looked over their meager home. "When will Mr. Bender be home?" he asked for the third time.

"He will be out all night with the cows! Like I already told you, we have two pregnant heifers overdue!" Ma snarled at the man as she spoke.

Thankfully, a small family of travelers arrived in a worn-out wagon and began to unload in the front yard. By chance they were a German family, and within moments, everyone was talking in their native tongue, which further alienated Laploom from gathering information. Amongst the travelers, a ten-year-old boy wearing a straw hat and brown suspenders handed Laploom's driver a canteen full of water, which he gulped eagerly. Now, with everyone at the inn appearing happier than himself, Laploom jumped into the back of his carriage and screamed at the driver to leave.

Kate watched the carriage leave as the crisis had been averted. The problem was that it was far from being over. The reporter may have left empty handed but his curiosity had not been satiated. Chances were he would be back and she would have to decide how to handle him. That is, if Mr. Pipps did not make the decision for her. She looked in all directions for her benefactor and soon saw his dark figure at a distance in the apple orchard. Utilizing his unnatural abilities, he was jumping back and forth over great distances. This was a game he played, which Kate knew well. For whatever reason, her protector from between worlds found amusement in leaping from grave to grave of the victims. It was a dark variation of hop scotch, which he did at least once a week. As the number of shallow graves continued to grow, the girl had long lost knowledge of where every body lay. That was not the case for Mr. Pipps who not only knew the location of each unmarked grave, but could jump endlessly from grave to grave without a misstep. Kate found herself amused at his ability to do this but never understood why he seemed to enjoy the entire undertaking so much.

As the travelers began to eat supper, Pa finally arrived from the pasture. He walked no more than fifty feet from Mr. Pipps in the orchard, and as always, there was no acknowledgement of the dark figure by the big man. Without warning, Mr. Pipps's body sank into one of the graves until he was no longer visible. It was another of his games, which only a supernatural entity of his construction could manage. Kate wondered if he did this to converse with the rotting bodies of their victims, maybe give them a weather report from topside. Pa walked past her with his usual grunt, and Kate smiled. She smiled because for once the man had been where he needed to be at the right time. She smiled even more because she could see Mr. Pipps, and Pa couldn't.

It had passed her mind several times earlier that her benefactor could have given the signal the reporter was to be put down. At the time the thought had scared her because she knew the risks such an action could bring them. Then again, if Mr. Pipps had selected it to be done, wouldn't his otherworldly abilities have protected them? Secretly she had also thought for the first time about taking the reporter to Dr. Kegan for human testing. She thought herself capable of viewing, no that wasn't the word, she thought herself curious to see the doctor dissect, and tinker with the obnoxious reporter. The thought made her smile as she knew a great deal of his experiments would be done while Laploom was still alive. Maybe it was time to visit the doctor again and dine in his mansion and share in his stimulating conversation. She smiled again until at a distance she saw Mr. Pipps watching her intently. Even from afar, he seemed to know what was on her mind, and she knew he didn't approve. Immediately she turned and walked into the liveliness of the Bender Inn.

15 PRESENT DAY: BLOOD BATH ON THE ISLAND OF DEATH

Having abandoned his escorts, Johnson made his way into the open frontier of Texas. The air was thick and hot, and the grass in the pasture land was brown from lack of water. Despite being only a day or so ahead of the two, now angry Mexicans who would be pursuing him, Johnson still did not dare to push his horse and see it die in this burning dessert. A man without a horse in Texas, in this heat, was a goner.

The towns were few and far between and mostly full of Mexicans who moved slowly in the heat and stayed to whatever served as shade. One thing was for sure, no one knew, or would say, even for money, where the outlaw camp called "The Colony" or the "Isla de la Muerte" was located. For six days Johnson rode mostly by night and rested the horse and himself by day. It was a desert traveling tactic, and there were both rewards and dangers to doing this. For Johnson, it kept him and the horse hydrated. However, Roberto and Juan would certainly have others with them, and if they met again, they would kill him, or at least try.

After six days without shaving or bathing Johnson looked and smelled like any criminal on the run. After another four days of dust and sweat drying on his body, even his employer would not have recognized him.

On day eleven, Johnson found himself moving slowly along a rocky ridge. He had taken the high ground the previous day but found the descent off the ridge too dangerous to travel by nightfall. In addition, his tired horse needed an extra day to rest after having picked up a nasty thorn in its leg. It seemed everything that grew in this state had thorns, and both he and his steed had collected more than a few along the trip.

It was early morning as the two negotiated the descent. Johnson walked on foot while he led the horse down the steep decline to decrease any chances the animal would lose its balance. Both were fatigued despite the extra down time. The horse had not only carried the detective, but also his equivalent body weight in stored water for most of the journey. This had saved them both thus far, but they had not come across water in two days. They were down to only two full canteens, one of which Johnson had shared with the horse before they started that morning. It was an almost reckless use of their water reserves, but as with most things with the detective, it was strategic and it was placed toward achieving a goal. He needed at least ten miles out of the horse, no matter how hard those ten miles might be.

Upon reaching the high ground of the ridge the detective had seen it, or had he? The sun had been setting, and he couldn't trust it to wishful thinking. With the first rays of light this morning the detective had confirmed it. It was difficult, even though his customized John Browning French made binoculars, which Clint Parker had sworn him to never lose, to see with absolute clarity among the rippling waves of heat generated even in early morning, but they were there. Bodies in the dessert. Several, along with dead horses, were scattered across the dessert almost in a perfect line. To the detective's trained eye, even at a distance, there was purpose to this carnage. It was the bloody trail of a gunfight during a pursuit. He would investigate it and discover the details in time, but for now, it was the best lead he had come across.

At a distance, and from the heights of the ridge, it had been invisible, but as he made it to open ground the detective discovered a trail some two to three weeks old. Johnson studied the path, which snaked southward through the prairie, stopping every few miles to take notes. His tracking knowledge was extensive and he could reliably estimate the number of horses that had passed through recently and information far beyond that. For instance, he knew fifteen or more horses, two of them lame from injury, had come through, riding hard. The riders were pursued by at least three times as many all in hot pursuit.

"A posse," Johnson thought to himself as he looked down the trail. He continued on, looking for clues, and a mile down the trail he found rifle shell casings.

"They're in firing range now," he said out loud and he raised his arms as if holding his rifle and firing while still riding.

Three more miles further, Johnson found the first body. It was a young Mexican teenager and he had been killed by a rifle shot to the chest. Shell casings were everywhere and it was apparent the pursued group had made a short stand here before thinking better and riding on.

Here the two groups had been very close, and the shell casings of all variety of weapons littered the trail. It didn't take long until the area of the main firefight was located. Johnson stopped twenty yards away by a large rock, which gave decent shade for the horse. He gave the horse a couple full swallows of water and then stepped away while the animal gave him a look of dissatisfaction.

Johnson processed the crime scene meticulously. Two horse carcasses lay in the Texas sun. They had been partially consumed by buzzards by daylight, and coyotes by night. Upon close inspection it was clear the horses had been killed during the firefight. There were sixteen bodies in total and they were divided on two sides of a six foot long rock, which was about four feet tall. It appeared the group being pursued had lost a horse, and had decided to take a stand with the rock as their only cover. It was not great cover and Johnson presumed it was a battle brought on by necessity and not desire. Still, despite the numbers against them, the pursued group did quite well. Of the sixteen dead, twelve came from the pursuing group.

Despite the ravages of the Texas dessert, Johnson checked all the bodies. Only one of the dead here was a Mexican. The rest were white-skinned Americans of different ages. This was more than a rural dispute among locals.

The faces of the dead were bloated, torn, and in a horrible state of deterioration. Still, Johnson was able to identify one of the dead as Roy "White lace" Ballington. Ballington was an Oklahoma based train robber known for spending exorbitant amounts of money on prostitutes. The man was known to buy expensive lace stockings for the women of the brothels, and had done so in a string of towns in his state. The detective remembered reading in the papers that the Governor of Oklahoma said there would be more perfume at his hanging, alluding to his popularity with the brothel communities, than was present at one the of up-and-coming brothel run by Mattie Silks. Ballington had killed two train conductors and a deputy in Oklahoma City at least two years ago. Johnson knew his face from the wanted posters, but the outlaw had not been seen for over a year. Now his dead, bloated carcass was in south Texas as part of a brutal gun battle. But why? Had he been running to the fabled Isle de la Muerte? Had his pursuers been looking for the Benders?

There were no badges among the dead, but there was plenty of money in the pockets of the pursuers which confirmed to Johnson this was a formed and financed posse. Because the pockets of the bodies had not been gone though, it meant the pursuers not only gave immediate chase after the fleeing group, but also they had not come back by way of the same trail. That was weird. Johnson had seen lots of posses, and there were always a few bad eggs in the bunch. That fact that paid trackers didn't take a few minutes to lighten the monetary load of their dead comrades was odd for groups such as these. It also gave credence to the actual remoteness of the trail. No new travelers until himself had come across the bodies. This was truly a no-man's-land. Ten of the original fifteen pursued riders continued south, and whoever led the posse managed to keep riders chasing at a reckless pace. Could this be the work of the fanatical Colonel York? If so, the number of his group had been greatly diminished. Johnson left the bodies to the Texas wildlife and continued to follow the trail south.

It was late afternoon when the detective found himself along the roughest terrain yet. The temperature had gotten hotter by the hour, if that was possible, and the red dirt had turned to hard clay. Scorpions and horned toads chased red ants in the burning sun. Large sink holes and uneven ground made travel even slower. A wide canyon offered a momentary break from the sun and Johnson took the opportunity to stop. Together the detective and horse drank the last of the water. It was a quiet ceremony. Johnson's suffered from muscles spasms across his back and arms as a result of dehydration. His ears rang, and his vision was beginning to fail him.

The detective was shaken from his water deprived daze by the sound of gunfire. Within the canyon the sounds bounced off the walls and made in difficult to know where it was coming from. Johnson grabbed the horse's reigns and shook his head to clear his mind. There it was, a quarter of a mile away, a small settlement with maybe five small wooden shacks. The ancient looking dwellings were taking gunfire from over sixty men on horseback. In return, from every window and doorway of the old buildings, rifles could be seen firing back. It was a strange thing to watch, but Johnson had to get in closer. A series of naturally cut ravines ran in every direction toward the buildings and the detective decided to use them as cover to approach the battle unseen. The ravines were formed by erosion and most were six to ten feet deep. They offered great cover, but in several areas were too high for him to peek over to assess his advance. It also became somewhat confusing as crisscrossing ravine channels made it difficult for Johnson to know where he was in relation to the wooden buildings. Was this the fabled Island of the Dead? It was certainly in the middle of nowhere and it was certainly under attack. However, it didn't seem like an oasis from the law, it seemed more like a place to die.

The sound of gunfire grew, and the amount of ricocheting bullets bouncing off the walls of the ravine tunnels made it certain he was close to the main action. The detective ran forward, as it seemed to walk was just going to get him shot sooner. Dust began to fall into the ravine walls from the action above and soon the detective was running in growing dust and darkness. He choked on the dust and pulled his red bandana over his nose and mouth to help him breath. He hoped for a clear space where his eyes could assess the situation and where he could find better cover. This did not happen. In fact, things got much worse. All of a sudden, there seemed to be no earth below him. There was nothing but air and the sensation of fallen. The ground obviously had not disappeared, but a sharp decline had given him the sensation. Even more unnerving was the fact that the stray bullets that had been bouncing around from above him earlier now seemed to have purpose. There appeared to be bullets aimed at him. The dust was thicker than before, but as he fell hard to the Earth, Johnson saw the glimmer of open sky. He had blindly ran out of a cavern tunnel and into the main gun battle. On every side of him guns blazed. Johnson had entered the cavern tunnel with his rifle, but a bullet tearing through his left shoulder sent his preferred weapon spiraling into the ever growing cloud of dust. A man on horseback bore down on him and fired over his head. Though instinct, Johnson drew and shot the man from his steed.

The open ground surrounding the old building was now full of men fighting to the death. The number of men fighting the detective had observed earlier had now grown to at least 200 people, all fighting one another to the death. At that moment Johnson was no longer a detective for the Clint Parker Security Agency. Instead, he was back on the battlefield, in the grips of the bloodlust of war. Another bullet, this one grazing his cheek, went almost unnoticed as he grabbed his bowie knife and drove it deep into a man's chest who approached him at full speed, screaming. The man stopped in his tracks and grabbed at his chest with one hand as he raised his revolver with the other. Johnson fired first and saw the man's silhouette within the thick dust shake, and then fall to the ground. What he did not see was the glimmer of the man's badge as he fell to the Earth. The badge read "Deputy Sheriff -Wilson Co., Kansas."

16 DECEMBER 1872: THE KILLING OF GEORGE AND MARY ANN LOUNCHER

Everything changes. In the best of times or the worst, the inevitable conclusion of all things is that nothing stays the same. Kate knew the Bender Inn would not be her final destination. The gang she had formed and even the lifetime she had spent with her mother were just moments in time. They were all destined for something far beyond Kansas. Was it a long, lavish, retirement basking in the wealth they had accumulated or was it a short trip at the end of a hangman's rope?

Though they had managed to conceal their identities as the murderers of so many travelers, the Osage Trail started to become a place avoided by those moving through the country. People passing up and down the road were getting fewer and farther between as it simply became a place to be avoided. It became harder to pluck a person here or there amongst the many travelers with any anonymity. This must have been the case even for Mr. Pipps, with his supernatural abilities, but there was more to it.

For all the work Kate had put into keeping the family's public perception clean, knowing the news of the county, and denying scoundrels like the reporter Laploom from placing their secrets in print, somehow she had allowed herself to become distracted. It would have been easy to say her loss of focus came from the issue of the gold. The gang had grown tired of such tremendous wealth remaining buried in the barn and, thus, Kate began to parlay a deal with Dr. Kegan to exchange their find for cash. Truth be told, the girl invited the distraction, but it came at a heavy price.

Days turned to weeks and then months, in which Kate traveled regularly to the doctor's private home. There she allowed herself to be pampered by Kegan's private staff, who fed her extravagant meals full of foreign dishes only a man of great means could acquire. Together they traveled to Oklahoma and Missouri and took in operas and plays of the highest quality. In the solitude of his castle walls they consumed opiate blends of the doctor's own construction and their minds danced into new plains of existence. After repeated requests by Kate, the doctor acquiesced to physical congress, and the girl showed him another level of bliss.

Soon Kate started to stay over at Kegan's home. Almost every night the doctor would leave the warmth of the bed's silk sheets and quietly make his way to his underground laboratory where he would work for hours. Upon his return he was like a dog on the hunt, breathing heavily, and his desires for the flesh hot. Kate smiled as the man made his stealthy retreat from the bed as she knew what kind of man would soon return. Despite the pleasures of the Kegan castle it also meant Kate's presence and leadership at the inn was diminished. For longer stretches at a time victims were not selected and idle hands became bent for trouble.

Pa was jealous of Dr. Kegan's private interludes with Kate. The girl had not reneged on her obligations but the big man, who played the father role of the Bender family, was angry by nature and he soon burned with a hatred for the man in Independence. His anger also went to Kate for giving the doctor her time, amongst other things. The big man started drinking more and more throughout the day.

He had been on a strict drinking regimen since the women
had arrived at the inn, and the discovery of Pa's drunken
murders, which had almost cost them their entire
operation before it had had a chance to start. When Pa got
drunk, he got angry, and when he was angry, he seemed to
find an excuse to kill.

Ma had always been a reluctant participant to the
operation. She had never embraced her position of lesser
authority within the gang. It had been the money, and only
the money, which had kept her playing the part of
assistant, cook, and subservient helper. Ma and Pa hated
each other, and without Kate present to dispel quarrels
and keep them on task, they fought incessantly. The older
woman kept a poisonous blend of herbs in a small, square
green-colored tin. The tin was easy to conceal, and she had
used it on several occasions to begin the end of men she
no longer had use for. The tin contained a custom blend of
cooking herbs with minute additions of mandrake and
foxglove. The poison could easily be administered to food
without detection, and death was slow and bitter. The
victim would suffer from kidney and liver failure, along
with aching joints and night sweats. Most victims, if
poisoned over time, would stop eating and would die
appearing to have succumbed to natural causes. Now,

with almost every meal the old woman debated placing the poison in Pa's food.

John Jr. had never been the same since his head injury. His wounds had healed, but his demeanor had changed. He smiled and laughed less. There was a look of seriousness, which was now always on his face. He spent more and more time alone, even preferring less time with Kate, which he had always enjoyed. The boy was also less tolerant of Pa, who had always been abusive to him. On more than one occasion the two men had squared off as if to fight. Kate had been present and had separated the men. Even Pa had seen that John Jr. was different. The boy walked differently, and his voice sounded flat and dull. Mostly, there was something in his eyes that had changed, and the change was dark. Then, of course, there were his constant conversations with himself. More often than not, he spoke to himself while doing his chores and in his private time. He became very annoyed when these conversations were interrupted. Had Kate been spending more time at the inn she would have noticed John Jr.'s strange behavior and many other things that would have brought her concern. In the small ways that storms build up before unleashing their fury, the Bender Inn was quietly spinning out of control. In the middle of December it happened. The beginning of the end for the Benders began, and it began with the spilling of blood.

Kate was sitting in the front of Dr. Kegan's well-furnished wagon. A hired driver had the reigns, and the two sat on a high-dollar, padded, maroon bench seat, which absorbed every bump in the road. A thick blanket of the same color was draped across her lap to diminish the bite of the mild winter day. The driver, a sturdy man of forty years, was one of many the doctor employed. He carried a revolver around his waist and he was more than capable of handling any problems they might face during their journey from Independence and the inn. Kate had wondered if this man transported stolen goods across the country for the doctor. Would he be the one to take the Bender's gold to Independence? A deal had been struck, and soon the Benders would have more cash than they would ever need. Kate had made the decision that once their money was secured, they would leave this place and disband the group. Not only would she disband them but she would part with Ma forever. It was long overdue that she be free of that vile woman.

The deal for the gold had involved compromises Kate had originally stood firm on opposing. Kegan wanted human subjects, and the Benders would supply him ten adult males. In exchange for these live subjects, something that added extra risk to the gang, the doctor limited his commission to twenty-five percent. It was a fortune but better than what another fence might have charged, and in the case of the gold, there were no other fences.

The Benders had delivered seven men to the doctor thus far, and it had been a chore fraught with mishaps. Kegan did not want men with smashed skulls and so the hammers were abandoned and instead Ma devised a chloroform mixture that was applied to a rag and placed over the nose and mouth of the man until a state of unconsciousness was achieved. This usually involved violent battles between John Jr., Pa, and the victim all taking place within the Bender Inn. Next, the unconscious men were tied and placed in the Bender wagon under a tarp. By nightfall, the captives were taken to Independence. Though Ma was a master of dark chemistry, it still proved difficult to keep grown men of different ages and weights unconscious for the entire trip. Dr. Kegan's future laboratory subjects could, and did, often awaken suddenly during transport, and after several half escapes, which included ear piercing screams for help, which shot into the darkness of the countryside, both men together took the entire trip leaning over the victims with chloroform soaked rags. In such cases, Kate would steer the horses to their destination. The process was fraught with danger and opportunities for discovery for everyone in the gang. They would meet the doctor's quota none too soon.

On this mild winter's day Kate exited the wagon at the entrance of the inn. Neither Dr. Kegan nor his employees ever set foot on the property. This was by Kate's request as she wanted the doctor, and all that was tied to him, as far as possible from Mr. Pipps. This was an effort that was getting harder and harder to maintain, especially as her feelings for the doctor were growing. When the gang's criminal operation in Kansas was completed she would have to make a monumental decision. Leave with her mentor Mr. Pipps, or stay with Dr. Keagan. Deciding would be the hardest thing she had ever had to do.

A finely constructed wagon sat near the barn. The family was obviously entertaining travelers, and this would place a few coins in the inn's cash box. That was at least something. Kate's mind was still on the doctor when she heard Ma scream from inside the house. The scream was followed by a crashing sound. Before she started to run, Mr. Pipps's black, leather-clad figure flew over her head at great speed and in the direction of the inn. Kate gave chase. John Jr., who always watched the windows for traveler's opened the door for the girl who viewed the unwanted and unauthorized carnage within the Bender Inn. A man of around thirty years of age lay on the kitchen floor convulsing in a pool of his own blood. A blue and ivory pocket knife, which depicted horses at play, had fallen out of the man's pocket. Thick rivers of following crimson surrounded the knife on the kitchen floor as if it were a tiny boat on a raging, red river.

He had been struck in the back of head in addition to be being stabbed at least ten times. Blood poured out of the man in multiple water falls. Never had the Benders unleashed this much carnage on a single victim. The bloody mallet was on the floor.

Pa, still holding the blood-soaked knife, watched on with a killer's glint in his eye.

"What's going on? Why? Why is this man dead?" Kate shouted.

"He was a danger to us!" Pa said through slurred lips. The big man swayed slightly as he spoke.

"There's no truth in this drunkard! Ma shouted and continued, "We were just feeding these folks when he bashes this man's head in and starts tearing him to pieces!"

Kate's eyes widened as she realized her mother's words. The man was not alone. The realization came to her at the same moment she saw her. It was a girl, maybe eight years old. Her blond hair was tear-matted across her face. She wore a white dress with a purple flower print. The girl sat in the corner of the kitchen curled up on the floor in fear.

The sound of Mr. Pipps jumping across the inn's roof sounded like thunder in Kate's ears. He was angry and so was she. These people were not supposed to die and it was her fault it had happened. Had she been here, Pa's deadly tendencies could have been controlled. Now they were outside the supernatural protection of her benefactor's ability to pick safe kills. This situation specifically had an omen of badness attached to it. Kate looked at the child on the floor, not through the eyes of a killer, but through the eyes of a young street urchin of New York. She saw herself for a fleeting moment in the girl's pain and fear. Then it was over. Pa was moving in on the girl with the mallet.

"No witnesses." The smell of liquor from his breath filled the air.

Kate jumped in front of the big man and screamed, "No! You've done enough! Take care of this body Pa! I will deal with you soon enough." Her stern gaze was almost not enough to deter the intoxicated man, but he obeyed. Gently, she got the girl to her feet and covered her eyes as she led her out of the house. With a nod, she signaled for John Jr. to follow. He did so stopping at the barn to grab a shovel. He seemed to already know what she had planned. Pa stepped to the back steps of the house but seemed to know better than to follow. Mr. Pipps stood inches from the man's face and his eyes burned like hot coals. Things seemed to squirm across his shadowed face, and the heat of his anger was everywhere. Pa, who could not see the shadowy figure, was given the gift of not knowing the anger emanating everywhere like a wave of heat. Kate felt it, but she moved on with the girl, as she had more grizzly business to attend to.

"Why did this happen? I want my daddy!" the girl said between sobs.

Kate's voice was soft as she replied, "I don't know, dear. I really don't know." She looked to the orchard in the distance and selected a quiet spot where they soon stopped. John Jr. stood at a distance waiting for Kate's signal. The shovel was in his hand and his heart was beating fast.

In the shade of one of the trees they both sat down. There seemed to be little chill in the air or at least neither of them felt it. Kate began to comb the girls matted hair and sing gently to her. It was a song she had learned at the Harmony Grove church. The words had always been important when in the presence of the congregation, but here in the orchard, it was simply the gentle sounds that gave comfort. The girl had stopped talking and was lost in her own world, and Kate was about to send her to another. Mr. Pipps jumped frantically from grave to grave kicking dust as his boots struck the ground. He did not approve of the father's death and made several attempts to dissuade Kate from what she was about to do. Despite the dark figure jumping in front of Kate several times and almost touching the girl's arm on their trek to the orchard, which made the young girl flinch, Kate would not be stopped. They were past having options. As Pa had stated, there could be no witnesses, and while she would not let the girl be put down in the same way as the men, she would have to die.

Kate moved in front of the girl until their eye's met. A sweet smile formed on her face and she spoke in the same gentle tones she had been using. "Little girl, what's your name?"

Her ability to win people over was not limited to adults, and the girl soon smiled back and responded, "My name is Mary Ann Loncher, miss."

Kate smiled deeper and stroked the girls chin. "Mary, that's a beautiful name." The girl smiled back as a tear rolled down her cheek. Kate continued, "Mary, I want you to close your eyes, can you do that for me?" The girl nodded and did as she was told. Placing her hands on the girls shoulders, she eased the girl down until her entire body was lying on the ground. Kate's voice was soft and her hands gently caressed the girl's cheeks as she spoke. "Mary, I want you to keep your eyes closed and don't open them until I say." The girl nodded. Kate closed her eyes as well. "Mary, picture a summer day; the flowers are in bloom and the birds are singing. You and your father are riding in your wagon, and the smell of newly cooked bread is in the air. You're both happy, as you know soon you will be eating that hot bread with butter and honey. You know your father will hug you and kiss you many times on this day, and you will laugh and sing together. In the evening, you will curl up in bed and sleep in the warmth and happiness of each other's loving embrace, and all will be joyous for evermore."

Kate smiled at the image in her mind, hardly aware that her hands had gone to the girl's tender throat before the story had begun. Mary Ann Loncher had not struggled and the girl had passed gently if such a thing could be said. John Jr. was already digging the hole.

"Make it deep," she told him, and her fictitious brother did so, knowing she intended for the father and daughter to be buried together. Kate placed the little girl into the grave gently and then walked the pasture for several hours by herself. During that time the father was

232

placed in the grave and the bodies were covered with earth.

When Kate returned to the inn, it was late evening and the sun was about to set. As she entered the back of the barn she saw the burning embers of Mr. Pipps's eyes at a distance. She walked in his direction as her communion with her benefactor had been scant of late, and she would need his guidance now more than ever. His shadowed figure was in a seated position in the barn's corner and almost invisible to the eye. Kate slowed as she came nearer as something seemed out of place.

"Mr. Pipps we need to talk. I'm so sorry about today." She said in an apologetic voice. She knew their conversations were not with words but she needed his help if they were to avoid a bigger problem than what had already transpired today.

The shadowy figure shot to its feet and moved into the light of the setting sun. It was not Mr. Pipps but John Jr. As had been the case for a while, his innocent expression was gone and replaced by something else. When he spoke, a stranger's voice sprang forth.

"Your demon is unhappy with you and wishes to be left alone for the time being." His voice was laced with sarcasm. Kate was awestruck and fought to find her words.

"You can see Mr. Pipps?" She choked out.

"I see him and commune with him." John Jr. said in a flat tone. Before Kate could respond he spoke again. This time there was true anger in his words. "He loves me and cares for me. Something you used to do before your entanglement with Dr. Kegan." Kate stood silent. A twisted smile formed on John Jr.'s face and the gentle, happy boy she had known was now completely gone. "Oh yes, he knows about your lover in Independence. He sees things far and wide and he is quite unhappy about it. He blames you for what happened today, and yes, everything we have built here will now fall to pieces because of your treachery. Pray the dark one saves your backstabbing hide!"

"Please I must speak to him. I must make it right somehow!" Kate pleaded.

John Jr. leaped at her and grabbed her by the throat. He hissed as he spoke. "He doesn't speak to you anymore. If you wish to know his intentions, it will be through me you will inquire! Pray he doesn't send me to choke the life out of you like you did that little girl in the orchard."

"What has happened to you, John Jr.?" Kate asked in choking sobs.

He released her and began walking towards the inn. Over his shoulder he replied, "My eyes and mind have been opened to the unseen realm around us. I no longer

234

serve you and your whims. I now serve the master and he shall give me what is rightfully mine!"

Kate stood in the darkness of the Kansas winter night. She was now completely alone.

17 PRESENT DAY: SAVED BY AN OUTLAW

Slowly, Johnson registered he was awake. It came in stages and it was made all the harder by the low lighting of wherever he was now. When his senses were about him, he noticed he was lying in a makeshift bed in a large underground cavern. There were people everywhere, women and children milled about doing normal daily tasks. This was not the same place where the gun battle had taken place. There was a feeling of tranquility here, or maybe that was just in his head.

In the center of the room was a giant stone fireplace, which was open on two ends and was being used as a stove to cook food. Large kettles of soup bubbled on one side of the fireplace and women attentively stirred big black pots with long wooden ladles. The smells were delicious and despite the heat emanating from the fireplace, the room felt invitingly cool. Johnson's mind was still moving in slow motion but it came to him, he was underground. Possibly a cave, but he had never seen a cave of this size before. There were at least eight entrances to this large, cavernous space. He counted twenty women and sixteen children, who moved around him. There were long wooden tables surrounded by chairs, and preparation tables for the food, and an area where the children played in order to stay out from underfoot of the cooks. It was like a giant kitchen. He also noticed there were no men present. Where were they?

Slowly he sat up and immediately felt pain shoot through his body. He had been shot in the arm, but he knew that pain. What he did not understand was why the room began to move in strange ways. With his good arm he raised a hand to his head and felt thick bandages. White flashes shot across his eyes followed by a jolt of pain, which almost made him throw up. The detective closed his eyes until the pain passed.

"Lay back down, you blasted idiot! You're not even half-healed yet!" came a female voice. The yell was followed by several hands, which grabbed him and pushed him back on the bed. The hands were female, and despite a few more stern comments, the women were gentle with him.

When his mind settled, Johnson attempted to play back recent events to understand how he had gotten into this predicament.

There had been the gun battle by the wooden shacks. He had been on foot, having just emerged from the ravine tunnels. He thought at first it was just every man for himself, but that wasn't true. There were two sides at play in the raging gun battle. There were men in bandanas and most of them were on foot like him. They fought with a large number of men on horseback. Yes, he had shot at least four men on horseback and killed two on foot. The dust was so thick it was like fighting for your life when the enemy can't be seen until they are a few feet from you. He remembered a bullet grazing his cheek. He had been knocked off his feet at least three times by charging horses and then he took a bullet to the arm. The impact had sent him down hard and he would have most certainly have been trampled by horses had not a gloved hand reached down to him.

"Get up!" a voice had shouted to him above the sounds of battle. It was a man with a red bandanna across his face. He wore a gray hat, which covered most of his face, but his eyes were bright blue, and his voice was calm despite the chaos that was everywhere.

"Put your back to mine and kill anything coming at you on horseback!" The voice was strong and confident and Johnson complied without question. It worked. The two men covered each other's flank as the dust thickened. Each man shouted to the other when they were reloading and together they repelled several attacks. The detective remembered his difficulty reloading with his injured shoulder. By the third time his pistol went empty, his fingers started to betray him, and he remembered cursing as several of his bullets fell to the ground. Then that was it. Everything went black. He could only assume he had taken a shot to the head, and the man he had fought beside had brought him here. But where was here, and where was the man who had most likely saved him?

Several hours passed. Johnson went in and out of consciousness. During that time he thoughts he heard men's voices and though he could barely open his eyes without intense pain, he saw an influx of people in the large room. It was hard to tell what was real and what might have been a dream. However, two days later he awoke hungry and alert. With the assistance of a young woman in her early teens, the detective was helped to his feet and allowed to walk around the room.

This place was more amazing than his initial assessment. It was much more than a large underground cavern. It was an underground city. Though the tunnels he could see living quarters, work stations, even underground stables with livestock. This was a complete hidden world.

Slowly, he was taken to the bathroom. He was amazed to see the place had indoor plumbing. The girl offered to help him, which he refused and then immediately knew he had made the wrong decision when he almost passed out while making water. He had obviously been hydrated during his bed rest and most likely fed. Later, he carefully sat down at one of the wooden tables and was given two bowls of soup, which he ate ravenously. The women brought him food, water, and later drew him a bath. He accepted the help of two, older women with cleaning, and the experience was not as fun as his time with the young, Mexican prostitute. The last thing he needed now was to fall and crush his already damaged head. Especially, since the women, while helpful to his personal needs refused to answer any questions about this amazing place.

After a week underground Johnson was made privy to the men. At least 150 men came into the dining hall and ate. Each man wore a red bandanna across his face to hide his identity. Johnson could tell by the warm embraces of the women and children, which many of these individuals were here with their families.

A handful of men approached Johnson, all of them were covered with dust and they all wore guns with handles that were shiny. The detective knew this was a byproduct of recent usage. Had more killing taken place in his absence? A voice he knew made that question disappear in a flash.

"This dog is a lawman and he needs to die now!" The voice came from a large man who smelled uncannily like a dead skunk. To solidify his intentions to violence, the man withdrew his bandanna to expose his identity. Yes, it was the notorious outlaw John Kenny. The man's face was in a scowl and his hand was on his gun. A few voices of opposition sounded but were immediately drowned out by Kenny. "I don't care one iota what this tin star did up top! He killed Don Frange and a bunch of my men, not to mention bungling the robbery of the MK&T. Hell! I have killed men for much less than this. Step aside, boys!"

John Kenny pulled his revolver from his holster and pulled the hammer back in a single deliberate motion. There was nothing Johnson could do. His gun and holster had been missing since he woke, along with his boots. He had recovered a great deal over the days but no one out runs a bullet at this range. Only one thing stopped Kenny from pulling the trigger, an act he greatly desired to do. As he applied pressure to the trigger, the outlaw felt a gun barrel press firmly to his skull.

"John Kenny! You fight well but have major problems when it comes to listening." It was a younger man, who stood to the side of the Kenny, who spoke. His face, too, was covered but as before, Johnson recognized the voice. It was the man he had fought back-to-back with during the gunfight. The rest suddenly got behind this younger man, and there was no doubt they supported his play. This angered Kenny, who fought to hold his tongue.

"Mr. Howard, I did, in fact, listen to you earlier, but this here fella is a tin star, a law dog, I tell ya. He's just like the ones we was fighting up top. Also, I have history with him and a revenge to collect that was owed to me before you met him. I'll collect what's due me!" Kenny's voice lacked his usual authority as he finished his words. He feared the man who held the gun to his head.

When the man responded, his words were as calm as they had been during the gunfight. "John Kenny, I want to bring you to the realization of this moment. Please holster that shooter so we can talk like men. That is unless you just want me to blow your brains out of your head right now." The man pulled back the trigger of his revolver. Johnson saw the women and children place their hands over their ears. They certainly believed Mr. Howard would indeed pull the trigger, and inevitably John Kenny believed the same as he holstered his gun and faced the man.

Mr. Howard then continued, "If you say this man is with the law I will believe you. However, half the men in here have wanted posters with their faces on them, and half of that half were law men themselves at one time or another. That claim can be said for you, can it not John Kenny?" John Kenny snorted at the statement but said nothing. After placing his gun back in his holster the man continued, "What matters now is where a man stands when it's life and death." Pointing to the detective, he said slowly, "This man fought with me and killed many tin stars. If he was the law, he's not anymore, and more importantly, he saved me and now he is under my protection." The man pulled down his bandanna to expose his true identity and then continued, "And as everyone knows, I am a man of my word." Cheers rose from around the room. Kenny walked away, seeing he was clearly outnumbered and overruled.

The man extended a hand to Johnson who shook it. He introduced himself as Thomas Howard but Johnson knew the face as he had seen it on posters and in dime store novels. The man in front of him was a rising star in the criminal world, the man was Jesse James. The men that had stood behind him were no doubt Charlie and Robert Ford, among others. Like his pictures, James was a handsome man and very articulate. He also had very good manners, and the women smiled at him as he passed, even the married ones. Despite this, James was a killer wanted by the law in Missouri and other states, as well as being the fixation of Alan Pinkerton. Despite this, James seemed extremely open about the hideout. This was, in fact the fabled *Isla de la Muerte*. The wooden shacks the criminals had defended were unused distractions to misdirect the law. The hideout was not even near that spot, and James made it clear that the location to, and the entrance of, "The Colony" would not be information he would get.

"Yes, John Kenny is too quick to decide to kill, but there is always a need to keep this place secret. I do share that concern with him. Anyways, I do not believe a man employed by the Clint Parker Detective Agency, seeking the Benders from Kansas will suffer from not knowing the exact location of this hideaway." James smiled at Johnson's look of bewilderment. "It's not magic. We found your horse with your notes and communications. Kansas Governor Osborn's bounty for the Benders and all of it, I have kept private for your protection. You are much closer than you think to your bounty and it is one that not even John Kenny would stop you from collecting if he knew."

James signaled for Johnson to follow him, which he did. The detective was led through several rooms of amazing construction. As it was explained, the underground city had been constructed over one hundred years ago, and the work continued today. Air tunnels had been cut for ventilation along with irrigation passages, which brought precious water into the city from underground wells. The water from these wells also moved human and animal waste out of the city through an advanced plumbing system.

"Criminals are often smarter than you think," James said, as he showed Johnson an elaborate set of mirrors, which brought light throughout the underground city and reduced the need for candles. "That doesn't even account for our underground farming, but let's focus on the Benders." James said, as he motioned him to the living quarters.

The living quarters were massive, with family and single dwellings. Room after room had been cut into the stone walls of the caves. In the center was a medical station, James said that people came and left here on a regular basis. For some, this was a rest station, for others, this was home. With this being the case, at least three doctors were always available and they did most of their work here. While none of the doctors wanted to talk to Johnson about the Benders, James pointed to one of the large beds in the corner and spoke. "That's where they kept him. No one will even use that bed now."

"Who... what are you talking about?" Johnson made one of his first inquiries of the man.

"The one they call John Bender Jr." I read all your notes and I have to say, you're not a bad detective. If Pinkerton had you under his employ, I might really be in trouble." James laughed as he spoke but became serious again. "This was where the youngest male of the Bender gang stayed. I'm told he was sick when he arrived and sicker when they left. The doctor's say he's not long for this world." He could tell what the detective was going to ask and he raised a hand and spoke first. "They don't know what it is, but it's not a normal sickness. They watch for that down here. We're all too close together to let something bad run rampant. So, they checked for malaria, small pox, typhoid, and it was none of those things and it wasn't consumption either. Whatever it was it had a hold on his brain and he screamed about demons and all kinds of things unchristian. Then there was Kate." He said looking at the detective. "You all don't know anything about her, at least not from your notes. She's a crafty one. They were only here a short time, and still she was almost running the place. The women hated her and the men wanted her, and she knew what to do with both. Had it not been for that demon talk from her brother going all the time that scared folks, things might have been different. But, hearing that boy scream about it all the time, people started seeing that demon, and the Benders lost their welcome. They paid a few of the right people and they were on their way, all quiet like."

"How long ago?" Johnson asked, fearing the answer.

"Maybe three weeks, maybe less," James replied.

Johnson shook his head. All this work and he was no closer than before. James sensed his thoughts and placed his hand on the detective's undamaged shoulder.

"I have to ask you. Did these people kill all those folks, like it says in your papers?"

Johnson nodded to the affirmative.

"Then they have to go. I have stolen and I have killed but what these Benders have done is medieval. I can tell you where they are right now, and you can catch them if you ride hard." James looked at Johnson and then to the ground. When he spoke it was as if he was talking to himself. "The problem is, and I can see it in your eyes, you're going to try and take them back for a trial in front of a judge. These people were never meant for trial on Earth. You got to kill them all; send them straight to hell. Especially Kate Bender."

"You act like you saw a demon. Did you?" Johnson asked, half laughing.

James didn't answer but simply signaled him to follow. The detective was headed for a showdown with the Bloody Benders.

18 MARCH 1873: THE KILLING OF DR. YORK

Dr. William York sat in his kitchen drinking coffee and reading the *Thayer Headlight*. The city of Independence had its own newspaper, which ran by the title *The Reporter* and a fine publication it was. However, a great many of the doctor's patients, as of late, had been coming from east of the town since the death of the established doctor in Cherryvale. Truth be told, the doctor enjoyed the writings of the newspaper reporter and editor, Marty B. Laploom. He especially had followed the reporter's writings, almost a regular thing now, on the disappearances of travelers in the area. Laploom knew how to spin a yarn, and Dr. York was fascinated by the mysterious stories of disappearing travelers who seemed to just vanish straight from the face of the Earth. The reporter made wild speculations as to the motivations of whoever was making people disappear. In one of his columns, Laploom wrote about the notorious Boone Helm whose rampage of murder and even cannibalism ran from 1851-1864. During his execution Helms, known by then as the "Kentucky Cannibal," had told the authorities present, "Every man for his principles! Hurrah for Jeff Davis! Let 'er rip!" As Laploom had reported, Helms then thumped off the scaffolding of the hangman's platform, with the noose around his neck, before the trap door below his feet could be activated. It was another scary but entertaining article from the editor from Thayer.

Dr. York operated on a strict schedule. He was up every morning by 4:00 a.m. He took a bath, shaved, and ate breakfast all before five o'clock. For thirty minutes he and the wife drank coffee and read in silence. The bay window of their kitchen oversaw the street outside, and from time to time their attention was drawn to a passerby or the activities of the birds, but not often. The doctor was in his late sixties and wanted little more than a quiet, restful period to read whatever fit his fancy before his busy day of healing the world. Mrs. York had long learned his routine and she too, would read the paper, usually *The Reporter*, in silence as she sipped at her morning coffee.

This morning she uncharacteristically broke the silence of the early morning. "Oh my! Oh my, indeed, Doctor you must read this!"

The doctor grumbled as his concentration had been broken. He looked over the top of his round rimmed reading glasses, and the two stared at each other intensely for several seconds before he spoke. "My dear, how am I supposed to take notice of this obviously important piece of information unless you tell me what it is and, more importantly, where it is within the daily?"

Mrs. York continued, "Mind you not to get bullish with me darling! I will give you the exact coordinates, with the right page numbers, and the correct sub-page numbers in just a moment!" She looked again at the paper and then took a deep breath and continued, "I just can't believe this. You will not be able to believe this!" This time she fanned her face with her hand.

The doctor was getting irritated but collected himself and said in a calm voice, "I, too, am ready to join you in this state of disbelief if you would kindly tell me what has flustered you so."

His wife shook the paper at him, "Well it's right here. Those sweet Lonchers, you know that poor man and his little girl? The ones you sold the wagon and horses to? Well they have up and gone missing! Foul play is speculated!"

His eyes widened in shock, and the doctor immediately grabbed for the newspaper in his wife's hands. As his hand was only inches from grabbing the paper, Dr. York remembered that the *Thayer Headlight* still sat unopened on the table. The story would no doubt be there and possibly in greater detail. Without a word he opened the *Headlight* and on the front page was the story, "Father and Daughter Among the Growing Numbers of Disappearances!" the title of the main story read. The doctor tightened his grip on the paper as he read the account.

As Laploom always did, a flowery back story was provided to set the stage for the mysterious disappearance. George Loncher, his wife and child had moved to Independence and staked a claim. They, like so many had migrated to Kansas to take their chances and had carved out a better life on the prairie. Unfortunately, sickness had claimed Loncher's wife and placed the family in turmoil. George Loncher, fearing he would not be able to continue the back breaking long hours needed to farm his new claim, and take care of his daughter alone had decided to take his child to Iowa, where his family lived, while he dealt with getting the farm on its feet.

Dr. York removed his spectacles and wiped at his eyes with his handkerchief. Mrs. York kept her silence, as to do otherwise would have made her husband uncomfortable. There was no doubt the news had hit the doctor hard. The doctor had taken a special interest in the Loncher family starting with the sickness of the mother, Darlene. She was twenty-nine years old and a person of intense happiness. Even in her sickness she was a joy to be around. Scarlett fever still killed many, but Dr. York had a local following for his success at being able to beat the sickness if detected early. At first the prognosis had been favorable, but Darlene was unable to recover after the first rounds of treatment.

When the sickness came back in full force she did not last long. Uncharacteristic for the doctor at his age, he made numerous trips to the Loncher farm to treat the mother and even spent the night at the home during her final day. Dr. York had seen death so many times his wrinkled face seldom flinched when the reaper took the sick. This had not been the case with the mother of the Loncher family. It was as if a bright candle had been extinguished on a dark stormy night. Dr. York's grief,

while a fraction of that of the family, was great. The York's were the only two
non-family attendees for the burial at the Fawn Creek Cemetery.

George Loncher had placed all their savings into the farm and despite feeling the need to relocate his daughter, had not the means of doing so. Against his normal judgement, Dr. York gave the father a wagon and a team of horses on the promise of payment at the next harvest. In truth, the doctor never expected, or would have accepted, actual payment. It was simply the only way George Loncher would take the needed wagon and horses. He was an honorable man. Now he and his daughter were missing. Despite knowing better than to allow it, a wave a grief and remorse covered the doctor. It was as if he had somehow failed this fine family twice.

He knew the feeling to be unfounded, but it was there and it was strong. He continued reading the story. It turned out George Loncher and his daughter had traveled to Coffeyville where a kind lady had given the girl traveling clothes. Next, the two had said they would head to Ft. Scott before leaving the state. Laploom reported a team of horses and a wagon possibly matching the description of the Loncher's had just been found in a forest near Ft.

Scott, and authorities were trying to verify if they belonged to the family.

"Tell the head nurse to cancel my appointments for the day, no, the next two days. I'm going to Ft. Scott!" the doctor said as he slammed the newspaper on the table.

Mrs. York was not happy with the doctor cancelling his appointments but was less so when she discovered he would not be taking a driver and the wagon on such a long journey. This was his normal routine when simply travelling the few blocks to his place of practice. They had both become accustomed to the doctor's normal, consistent, and timely routines. After all, he wasn't a young man anymore and if there were dangerous people out there attacking travelers she wanted him to have nothing to do with it. The woman would have locked the doors and kept him from leaving had she seen the doctor place a revolver and extra bullets into the inside pocket of his heavy coat.

"I'm not for this," she said in an uncharacteristic voice filled with both sternness and fear.

"You wouldn't be a good wife if you were," the doctor said as he hugged her close. "Those are my horses and wagon and nobody can identify it better than me." He stroked her cheek gently and continued, "If I can help them find that man and his daughter, I think I need to do it." The doctor looked into the distance and said in a soft, far away voice, "I have to do it."

His wife kissed him gently on the cheek. "When you get something in your head I have long ago learned, neither God in heaven nor I can stop you, so go!" She smiled as she waged her finger at him, "I'm giving you two days, and if you're not back here reading the newspaper and drinking coffee with me by then, I'm calling your brothers!" Dr. York rolled his eyes at his wife and walked out the door.

The trip to Ft. Scott was taxing for the doctor. He rode a fine prancing mare. It was a high dollar horse, as the doctor was a man of means. His family had had money and he had invested his inheritance well. Unfortunately, neither family wealth nor fine investments can counter the ravages of time, and the doctor was finding out he was no longer built for the physical punishment of long rides on a horse. No, it wouldn't be the end of him, but by the time he made it to Ft. Scott and reached the authorities, who lead him to the horses and wagon, the doctor had sore legs and an equally sore backside. Worse yet, his back, which had given him trouble over the years and had tightened up, was causing him great discomfort.

The muscles of his entire body seemed to seize all at once as he inspected the horse and wagon. The horses had not been fed in days and despite broken bales of hay, which were before them, looked gaunt and sickly. There was no doubt the beasts had belonged to him, as well as the wagon. Worse yet, there was a folded dress in the back of the wagon with unique red and white print, that Dr. York had seen the daughter, Mary Ann, wear on his visits to the Loncher farm.

"My God in heaven." He said under his breath before nodding to the constable that the horses and wagon did, in fact, belong to the missing father and daughter. Pulling out a worn, black leather note pad the doctor had used to take notes in the field years ago during the war, he started asking as many questions as possible. He wanted to know every detail the authorities had. He was dismayed to discover they knew very little. The constable and two sheriff's deputies who were present assumed the father and daughter had been travelling northeast, but the doctor could tell they were basing that not on any discernable evidence they had collected. There had been no witnesses, no bodies, and, in short, they had no idea where to look next.

Dr. York wrote every single word of information the authorities would give him until the point they grew tired of his questions. It didn't take long for the men to see the doctor was ready to lead their investigation and they were not going to let that happen. For the doctor, the visit was frustrating. The men had good intentions but they did not appear to tie the incident involving the father and daughter to the rash of disappearances taking place in this area. They obviously did not read Marty Laploom's column in the *Thayer Headlight*.

What was gleaned was that the search effort that was taking place was happening right around Ft. Scott, and to the north and east. This was the point of contention between the doctor and the deputies, which brought about his dismissal from the crime scene. It seemed logical to the doctor the idea had to be entertained that the Loncher family could have been abducted and the criminals who did this might drop the wagon and horses at this location as an act of both desperation and misdirection. The deputies, both men acting at the direction of the county sheriff, currently worked from two opposing theories, of which they were unflinching from diverting from. The first theory was that if the family had fallen prey to foul play, it had most likely happened at this location. The criminals, wishing to get as far from Bourbon County, in which Ft. Scott was located, as possible, would travel north and east into the state of Missouri. It was a plausible theory the doctor agreed, but not the only one to entertain. The second theory, one which vexed Dr. York greatly, and of which the deputies seemed to put even more credence to, was that George Loncher, saddened over the death of his wife, might have brought harm to his daughter and to himself. The doctor's intimate knowledge of the family did not seem to divert the deputies from this line of thinking. It was over this point Dr. York was ordered to go home by the authorities. The doctor left the crime scene but he did not comply with the directive.

After two miles the doctor stopped by a field and rested his horse behind a long hedge row. Mrs. York had sent her husband away with a canteen of water and a small sack of cheese and apples. The doctor smiled as he took a large bite of the cheddar and swallowed it down with a mouthful of water. That woman of his was usually right about things. By the time he started working on the first of two apples his mind was clear and alert. Contrary to the deputies, the doctor had brought a map and had a working theory. His eyes moved slowly over the paper, and he looked for commonalities.

"What do criminals and patients have in common?" he thought to himself. The answer, beyond the fact that some do not pay their bills, was they must all take roads to travel from one location to another. By the time the last piece of apple had been consumed, the doctor had finalized his thoughts and had a plan of action. Since the Bourbon

County authorities were placing all their efforts immediately around the county and towards the state line, the doctor would work his way back west using the major travel routes in the area, which in this case was the Osage Trail. If the horses and wagon had been abandoned in Ft. Scott to misdirect the law, and if the law was not interested in investigating this option, the doctor would do it himself. He owed the Loncher family that much.

The Osage Trail was easy to find and for hours the doctor rode west stopping at each farm house. He knew better than to affiliate himself with any law agency and he didn't need to. His own credentials carried equal authority and people were quick to talk to a family doctor who was looking to locate former patients, when they might not be so quick to visit with deputies seeking out criminal activity. Unfortunately, no one had seen the Loncher's horses and wagon on the trail nor had spoken to the family. The doctor continued, undaunted.

As night approached the doctor was only eleven miles or so from Independence. His muscles ached and he was once again hungry. The horse was also tired, and he decided to take a short stop to let the animal drink water. He could also use a hot cup of coffee and a local inn came into view just as the thought entered his mind. The woman who opened the door for him spoke with a thick German

Last Meal

accent. Even so, she seemed to know exactly what he wanted as she warmed the coffee on the stove, along with a pot of stew, which had a rich smell of chicken and potatoes. A few moments later a big man in a brown flannel shirt came in and sat at the table.

He smiled at the doctor and spoke in broken English, "Soup smells good, no?"

"Yes, it most certainly does," the doctor responded as a large cup of steaming coffee was placed before him. The two Germans seemed vaguely familiar he thought, as he returned what was a sour attempt at a smile by the woman, as she served him a hot plate of soup.

The three ate in silence for several moments until John Jr. and Kate arrived carrying two small baskets of apples. The delicious fruit was out of season but the Benders had learned how to hang the fruit in the barn from the last pickings of the season, and they there were still several good apples to eat. The doctor immediately recognized John Jr. from their visit to his office.

"Oh, my boy!" he said with a smile. "I did not know you lived here. How is that head of yours?"

John Jr. seemed to have no recollection of the doctor, but Kate did and her jaw dropped. Ma and Pa suddenly stiffened but said nothing.

261

"I'm afraid my brother has limited memory of his visit to your office, sir." Kate said quietly.

"Well that is to be expected, he took quite a wallop on the old noggin." He turned, and without thinking, the doctor began to inspect the boys head. John Jr. stood motionless as the man moved his head back and forth slowly and looked into his eyes. The doctor began to ask him if he suffered from headaches and other ailments associated with such traumas. When the boy responded he did not the doctor smiled and returned back to his seat and began to finish his meal. Ma refilled his coffee, and all but Kate seemed to relax.

"An apple for you, sir?" Pa motioned to the baskets that had been brought in.

"I certainly will if you promise not to tell my wife. This will be apple number three for the day." They all laughed at the statement, and Ma began serving two more bowls of soup.

Pa began to cut the apples into sections as Kate sat down near the doctor and inquired, "I did not know you visited patients so far from Independence. It must be something of considerable importance for you to be so far from home at this hour."

Dr. York smiled, stroked at his chin and answered. "Well in my younger days it was quite regular for me to call on patients further out than this but I don't do that anymore. Mrs. York likes me home promptly at five-thirty to have supper while it's hot. Every evening we play a single, but spirited, game of dominoes before retiring. A rather small Chinaman got us hook on the game twenty-years ago, and it still hasn't lost its allure." The doctor ate two of his remaining four slices of apple and then looked at his pocket watch. "I must say, I have missed supper tonight and am at risk of missing the first dominoes game in some time." He smiled gratefully at Ma and handed her two dollars which made her smile back with much more believability than her first attempt.

The man was ready to leave and the visit had been pleasant and profitable. It was over the tip of his coffee mug on his final swallow the doctor noticed the knife in Pa's hand. The knife he was using to cut more apples slices was unique. It was of blue and green design with horses running across the handle. The doctor had never seen two of the like but he had seen the one. It had belonged to George Loncher and one night, one of the many he had spent at the Loncher ranch while sweet Darlene had laid in her bed slowly dying, Darlene and he had talked about the knife. It had belonged to her father and had been given to her husband as a wedding gift. George Loncher would never give up this item.

Now it was the doctor whose body stiffened, and Kate saw it. The doctor pulled his chair back as if to get up but did not. "Yes, I'm afraid I'm just too old to go on house calls anymore. I am investigating a crime. Maybe you fine folks could help me." All feelings of joy left the room. "Some good friends of mine George and Mary Ann Loncher may have been traveling this way. Their wagon was colored red, and they had two fine horses, which, I used to own. These people are like wounded birds away from the nest, and I must find them." The doctor reached into his coat's inner pocket and placed his hand around the revolver. He knew from the facial expressions of the group that he was among the criminals he sought. He was afraid, but his fear was surpassed by another emotion, anger.

"We don't know anything about them." John Jr. spoke and before he could say another word the doctor sprung to his feet and brandished the weapon.

"Now you might want to hold your tongue, son. We'll write that false statement off to the head injury." The doctor pointed the gun at Pa who was still at the table with the knife in one hand and an apple in the other. The doctor pulled the trigger back and pointed the revolver and the big man's chest. "Let's talk about that knife, and if you say it's yours or you bought it at some shop or something else as stupid as that, I'm going to shoot you."

Pa sat the knife down and remained motionless.

"Where's the owner of that knife? Where are George and Mary Ann Loncher? Bring them to me!" The revolver shook in the doctor's hand. His adrenaline was at its peak but it would soon wane. His finger was on the trigger, and Kate could see the pistol would fire soon whether it was of his will or not. She had to defuse the situation.

Placing her hands in front of her she spoke in a calm and soothing voice. "Dr. York, look around you. This is our home, and we are simple people. My family and I feed cows and plant corn. Ma cooks soup and we give coffee to a handful of people along the road every week." Her eyes locked with the doctor's and she continued, "John Jr. and I attend the Harmony Grove Church and we learn the Holy Word. There is no evil in us." A tear rolled down her cheek, causing the doctor to lower the revolver.

At that moment, Pa lifted up the kitchen table and toppled it onto the man, who was not expecting such an action. The gun flew from his fingertips. Kate grabbed her straight razor and started toward the men but was knocked aside by John Jr. who brought the mallet down on the doctor's skull. A loud, crunching sound exploded through the room as an arc of blood shot from his skull. Before anyone could speak John Jr. brought the mallet down two more times. From the corner of her eye Kate saw Mr. Pipps standing in the room. It was the first time he had entered the inside of the home and he stood in all his dark magnificence watching what had just transpired. Kate knew this was the end. They could not hide this deed from the public as Dr. York was a well-known and needed member of the community. They had violated one of their most important rules and killed a local man of importance. Kate looked to Mr. Pipps expecting to see anger and disappointment in his eyes, but that was not the case. Her benefactor's eyes were not on her but on John Jr. Worse yet, Mr. Pipps appeared happy at what had taken place and his joy was oriented toward the young man. John Jr. laughed manically as blood ran down his face and hands.

19 MARCH 1873: MARTY LAPLOOM'S BIGGEST STORY

Mrs. York was true to her word. She waited patiently for her husband to come home that day and even though she was surprised he did not return by evening she waited until the end of the following day to contact the doctor's brothers. Dr. York's brothers were some of the more powerful in the state. Alexander M. York was a Kansas senator and the second oldest behind her husband. The youngest brother was Colonel Edwin York who was in charge of a platoon of soldiers in Ft. Scott.

Over the next two months both York brothers searched frantically for their brother. Colonel Edwin York was given a large number of soldiers whose sole purpose was to find the missing doctor. Senator Alexander York managed to create several financial bonuses for local constables and deputies who might find his brother and bring him safely home. Soon the York family would be privy to heart breaking news, and the doctor's brothers would change from concerned brothers to blood thirsty men in pursuit of revenge.

Marty Laploom sat on his horse, his least favorite mode of transportation, in the damp, darkness of South Coffeyville. It was a cool, rainy night, which always seemed to cause fits with the reporter's seasonal allergies. He wiped savagely at his nose several times. This was not a place to suddenly sneeze unless you enjoyed getting shot. Laploom had twenty reporters under his employ at the *Headlight* and twice those numbers in private agents. Laploom liked the second of these better. These were dirty men; men that frequented dance halls, bars, dog fights, and places where criminal action was the norm. These men, for the right price, could open more doors for good stories than any law man could dream of.

The reporter had been researching missing travelers through Kansas for some time. When Dr. York, a man he had met along the course of his job on more than one occasion went missing, Laploom took his efforts to a new level. It wasn't that the reporter felt anything one could call love or kinship for the popular doctor, it was his uncanny ability to see a big story on the rise. The reporter had already been sharing letters with family members abroad collecting property information on travelers who had disappeared. He tripled these communications and soon had photos of horses, saddles, guns, boots, and more, which he began to look for in shops and thrift stores.

When these inquiries turned out to be fruitless, he turned his attentions to places for stolen goods. Laploom knew them all and he had the agents that could look around without raising attention. As it turned out, even with a large number of people reported missing, an even larger amount than he had presumed had parted with their belongings in the local area. Guns, jewelry, saddles, and more had been located in seedy black market vendors in Parson, Independence, and now possibly in South Coffeyville.

The stormy night had taken all the stars from the sky and replaced them with intermittent lightning, which created flashes of bright light, which played tricks on the eyes. Laploom now found himself a quarter mile from the expansive property of Church Mongroly, a particularly dangerous fence. His estate ran for miles and was a hodgepodge of junk of all kinds. In some areas, heaps of twisted metal were higher than a person's head, and it was definitely a place one would not want to get lost in. There were several main buildings on the property and activity there never stopped. Guards with rifles and liquor walked the grounds, and angry dogs patrolled the fields of junk. Even in Laploom's driven state to get the details for his story, he was not stupid enough to try to sneak around the grounds. Instead he paid one of his "dirty" men to do it.

Jimmy "Pinky-toe" Tulip was the designated man for this excursion. Laploom had no idea if the man's reported first or last name was real and, frankly, he didn't care. His nickname, "Pinky-toe" came from the fact that one of his smallest toes had been shot off. Tulip was a local petty thief. He drank heavily, which kept him thieving on a regular basis. Despite only having seven remaining teeth in his head and a prominent limp, when it came to entering and being seen in places of criminal business, Tulip had sterling credentials. The reporter had shown the thief several pictures of pieces of property and the man had reported he had purchased some of them that evening. As he did with all his agents, Laploom had spent considerable time teaching his fences how to acquire the goods he wanted without attracting attention. Back stories for the reasons for the purchase, and how to ask for items without seeming to have a purpose beyond what went for normal in such places were painstaking practiced. Criminal kingpins like Mongroly did not stay in business and out of jail by being stupid. Even when people of Tulip's pedigree offered cash for one of their stolen items, questions were asked. Again, Laploom didn't care if men like Tulip were gut-stabbed and left to bleed out in a ditch. What he did care about were the pieces of evidence they would bring him; evidence he would document in his newspaper, which was now selling more than ever. Worse yet, he worried a blundering agent might bring men of Mongroly's employ to his doorstep to see who was really purchasing these products. He had no intention of bleeding out in a ditch alongside Tulip.

Laploom looked at his pocket watch and waited for the lightening to strike to see the face. It was midnight and the man was an hour late. This was not a good sign. Worse yet, the storm was picking up, and visibility was worsening. Finally, a man on horseback came down the road. Even in the storm Laploom knew Tulips slumped left shoulder. The reporter had no intention of having this meeting in the road, and, instead, the two rode in silence for several miles stopping at an abandoned farm house a good distance from the Mongroly estate.

The farmhouse was meager, but the windows were still intact, and the roof only leaked in a few places. Laploom had met Tulip here several times, and a table and chair were there for the using.

Tulip broke the silence as he dismounted his horse, "It weren't easy getting these here items." The man's voice was shaky from lack of drink. Laploom demanded that men such as Tulip be sober during these transactions, and the man was dry beyond his tolerance level.

Pulling two bottles from his own saddlebag the reporter shouted above the growing storm. "Get it all inside and we'll have a drink." Laploom knew that if the man had been successful, he would attempt to raise the fee for his service. He also knew that by the second bottle of whiskey, he would forget his plan entirely. Tulip brought two large items wrapped in burlap into the farmhouse. Each item was unwrapped and the reporter used the burlap bags to cover the windows. He was taking no chances on prying eyes. A single lantern illuminated the small room and the items on the table. Tulip began to speak, but was silenced by the reporter who shoved a bottle of whiskey in his face.

"Well, I don't mind if I do," Tulip responded before drinking straight from the bottle. Laploom was oblivious to the man's actions as he was already retrieving his photos to compare to the items. Slowly, and with care, he compared the saddle and a set of men's boots with photos of the same. Several times he brought the lantern to the items to scrutinize stitching and other unique branding marks of production. There was no doubt these were the items he sought. The saddle belonged to W.F McCrotty. It had the insignia of the 123rd Infantry, in which McCrotty had honorably served, along with his initials. The next item was a pair of boots belonging to John Greary, a card player

272

from Missouri. The boots bore his initials, along with pieces of silver and turquoise obviously of Indian construction. They were unique, they were traceable, and Laploom now had them. In total, he now had over fifteen items belong to missing travelers over more than a two year period.

Now for the final piece of information for this night's work and it would have to come from Tulip, who was now half way through the first bottle.

"Hold on now, you drunken fish!" Laploom shouted as he grabbed the bottle from the man.

"Aren't you happy? Why are you taking my reward from me, Paper man?" Tulip showed his disapproval in a voice that was already slurred.

Laploom placed a shot glass he had brought on the trip upon the table and filled it. This got the thief seated without delay. The reporter filled the glass slowly as he spoke, "Remember all of our practice before you started visiting this place for me?" The man nodded in agreement, still looking at the shot glass. Laploom continued, "What were you to do?"

The man reached for the shot glass, but the reporter restrained him from lifting it to his mouth until he answered the question. Irritated, he responded, "All right! I look for the items in the photos. If I see them, I don't get excited. I tell my story about having some dumb folks I can make a big profit selling them to, out of towners of course." The man rolled his eyes and went on, "I haggle a bit on the price, buy it, and get the stuff to you." The man smiled exposing four of his seven teeth but was immediately upset when the reporter refused to let him drink. After a moment of contemplation, he understood what was keeping him from his drink and he continued, "Oh yeah! Carefully, not pushy like, I ask about the items and who brought them in."

Laploom nodded his head and released the man who immediately consumed the drink. After a moment of silence, in which nothing else was offered to the shot glass, Tulip gave up his last bit of information. "It weren't easy, that part. Mongroly is a careful man, but over several visits and passing out some of your cash, not too much but enough, he gave me what you wanted. It was a big man, a German with broad shoulders, followed by a young man said to be his boy. They done the bargaining most the time taking the usual rates like everybody else, but when there was hard bargaining to be done, these people brought in this young darlin', a siren, the devil's imp, as Mongroly put it, and she walked out more often than not with the higher dollar than what was preferred."

Laploom's eye's narrowed. It was the same story over and over. Despite it seeming completely out of rational thinking to be so, it was. The people who were making traveler's disappear where the quiet little inn-keepers—the Bender family on the hill. Even stranger, this criminal enterprise was ruled by the young and beautiful girl, Kate Bender. His story would be front page news on the *New York Times*. Better yet, he would write and publish a book to detail how his groundbreaking journalistic investigation had broken the longest chain of killing in the country's history. *I will be a national sensation*, he thought to himself. Laploom noticed his breathing had become ragged and he calmed himself. He was close but he wasn't there yet. He had lots of circumstantial evidence and some low-life testimonial evidence, which could be used in articles but not in a court of law. He still lacked the most crucial piece of evidence. Where were the bodies of the victims? Without the bodies he was still dealing with conjecture. However, Laploom had a plan.

Since the disappearance of Dr. York, the reporter had had several meetings with the York brothers. He was welcomed by both brothers as his paper's readership had the potential to bring forth witnesses, who were hoped to lead to the rescue of the doctor. As time dragged on, Colonel York began to get reckless, and his soldiers became more like a brute squad than government paid investigators. Senator Alexander York was more restrained, and Laploom worked through him to get the governor to strategize with three local sheriffs to create a multicounty search warrant decree. It was uncharacteristic, but due to the fact that Dr. York was so beloved in the area, and the fear that others would be plucked from existence, there was likely to be support for this invasive maneuver to catch the illusive killers. The governor had signed off on the blanket search warrant, which would be unveiled at a multicounty meeting at the Harmony Grove Church two days from now. The warrant would, effectively, give law enforcement the authority to search the properties of every homestead, farm, and livestock facility in Labette, Montgomery, Wilson, and Neosho Counties. The sheriffs and deputies of all four counties would conduct the searches, but the owners of the property being searched, and the neighbors of the adjacent properties would be allowed to be present. In short, everyone and their dog would be there.

Laploom had to know the bodies were on the Bender property before the searches began. He already knew through his own sources that the searches would begin in Neosho County, and if the Benders where the blood thirsty killers he believed them to be, they would have plenty of time to flee before their farm came up. Laploom had to be able get authorities to start their search at the Bender farm, he had to have proof. He had to know the bodies of the dead where on the property and exactly where they were. This was a huge story and he would unfold it to the world. With that said, he had to see the graves, and the bodies of the dead himself. It was not a job he could pay a man like Tulip to perform. His lackey was already sleeping soundly in his chair. Laploom smiled and placed a few bills on the table. He had avoided having to listen to the little, dirty man try to negotiate for a higher fee. He would have to be especially careful in his dealings with the Benders if he was to get his proof from the inn and come out of it all with his life.

The following day the reporter put his plan to quietly invade the Bender property into action. The rain of the previous night continued with a seasonal mix of fog. It gave the Kansas landscape an eerie feel but for Laploom, yet again, it could serve as an opportunity. For several weeks the reporter had observed the Bender Inn property from different angles from below the hill. He did so today from several miles out using a single-scope binocular, which had served him well on many investigations. Despite the coverage of the fog, there was no denying the geographic advantage the location of inn had when it came to keeping activity private. From all directions of travel, and at almost every distance, the human activity from the inn was obscured from view.

"Yes, that has to be the place if there is any." The reporter said to himself as he slowly took in everything his eyes could see of the Bender Inn from the magnified vantage point of the binocular. The apple orchard was the perfect location to hide the bodies. It was next to impossible to know how many people the Benders had killed since establishing the inn. The reporter was also not sure if the apple orchard would be the only location where the killers would hide the corpses of the dead, but it was the practical place. He reviewed his notes from his previous trip to the inn. His visit had left him questioning things. Despite Kate Bender's ability to always seem innocent, in retrospect she had seemed nervous about his interest in the barn and orchard. Could the barn hold hidden bodies as well? Laploom scratched his chin as he pondered the possibility. That question would have to wait. The reporter planned to sneak onto the property that evening and reconnoiter the orchard but he had no intention of looking at the barn. It was too close to the inn and he did not want to take that chance. In fact, he hoped to be taking precious few chances at all.

Laploom dismounted his horse in Cherryvale at a local tavern. This establishment, "The Lazy Dame," was a particularly lower class dive but it was exactly the place the reporter could get what he needed for the evening's covert excursion. Sitting at the bar, staring at empty shot glasses where the Green brothers, John and Joshua. They were both tall Irish brutes in their early thirties. They were built like bulls, with thick necks, broad shoulders, huge arms, and almost identical in every other way. When someone mentioned the Green boys, it was almost always tied to a brawl of some fashion. When they weren't in jail, they were fighting in the bars, on a job, or with each other. The Green boys liked their drink as much as fighting but they never stayed employed long enough to have the money required to quench their insatiable thirst. They were the perfect thugs to hire for short-term, clandestine work. For the price of a shot of whiskey, Laploom got the men to sit in a quiet corner and listen to a business proposition.

"So, boyo, let me see if I'm hearing you right," John Green said with a smile. "You want me and the wee one to ride out with you tonight, in the rain, and trespass on some honest man's property. What you're after there, you're not saying, but if we run into trouble, you want me and the wee one to make sure no one wrinkles your fancy clothes."

"Stop calling me "wee one" you daft bastard!" Joshua, the younger brother shouted.

"Ah, shut your hole! Can't you see I'm talking business with this wriggly little paper man?" The older brother flashed a tenacious look at his sibling and then smiled back at Laploom who feared the brothers might start fighting right on the spot.

"Would that be the long and short of it?" he asked, with his smile widening.

The reporter swallowed hard and ordered the men a second drink. "Generally, yes. I offer you both five dollars apiece now to commit to the job and then ten dollars after for your silence. I do not plan for us to encounter anyone during this project, but our success will be hinged on absolute secrecy. If we are to run into anyone, your task will be that of security"

"So the saps in this little caper are likely to call the constable if they find us poking around their place or maybe put a knot on our heads?" the younger brother asked.

Laploom's face was deadly serious when he responded, "No, they will more likely kill us."

The Green boys sat in silence for a few seconds before bursting out in laughter.

"Yeah, right, Paper man! John responded, slapping his knee.

"The only person who can put down a Green boy is another Green boy! Don't worry, boyo, we'll keep ya safe!"

When the reporter said he needed sober men to complete this project, John responded, "We'll be sober enough. Now give us some money and be where ya say you're going to be tonight. I'll get the wee one there on time."

The younger brother was too busy ordering drinks to respond. The reporter made his payment and left.

Laploom spent the rest of the day preparing for what he hoped would be the story of a lifetime. Despite having a mind for detail, he found himself fighting not to daydream about all the fantastic things that would come to him after the story broke. He would, of course, be the first to break the news. It would then be covered by all the major papers in the country. He would no doubt be interviewed by all the major news organizations, but within a series of exclusive articles, written by himself and only available first in the *Thayer Headlight*, he would break down his brilliant investigation into sections. He might get an accommodation by the governor or Colonel York. It would be the perfect catalyst for a major book to follow.

Laploom shook his head to clear his thoughts. There was plenty of time for that thinking later. The reporter packed all of his evidence against the Benders and locked them in his personal safe. Also within the safe was a detailed letter of his investigation, and his planned trip to the Bender farm. If things went awry, his safe would be eventually opened and the note and evidence discovered. It was his backup plan. He did not dare share his plan with any of his newspaper staff. His philosophy of "never trust a man with a deadline" kept him in fear that if any of his writers knew about the story, they might attempt to publish it as their own. It was a risk that no one knew about the late night trip to Bender mound but it was one he was going to take. He hoped the Green boys would be all the necessary insurance he required.

John Jr. and Pa had done morning chores, and Kate had collected the eggs, but little else. The rain had kept the Benders indoors most of the day. There was little chance of any travelers stopping regardless of the weather. Since Dr. York's disappearance the locals had become suspicious of everyone. Despite the fact that people from the area had been disappearing for some time, the sudden vanishing of the local doctor had brought the realization home. The Temperance Societies in Cherryvale, Thayer, Independence, Coffeyville and Parson had placed a strict

9:00 p.m. curfew on their towns, and anybody out after that time was met with harsh scrutiny. Even the late night opera houses and bars were shutting their doors early. In short, people were scared.

The Benders turned in early. Ma, who had always had difficulty sleeping at night, took an herbal mixture that helped her rest. Pa, who had plied himself with considerable alcohol, was the first to sleep. Kate could fall asleep with ease and did so this evening. Only John Jr. had difficulties with turning in. He had spent the last few days seeking out his new fixation, Mr. Pipps. As was with his nature, the supernatural being often did not appear during inclement weather. There was no way to know if the being was affected by rain, snow, sleet, or any of the other weather conditions Kansas had to offer, but for reasons that were his own, he had been nowhere to be seen by the two people who could view him. This had saddened John Jr. greatly, and he had pouted openly. Kate was also in turmoil over her benefactor's absence but she kept her feelings to herself. She had to appear strong, now if ever. By 10:30 p.m. John Jr. closed his eyes and went to sleep.

Two and a half hours earlier, Marty Laploom met the Green boys at the Johnson Eatery. The place served evening meals, and Laploom bought large servings for himself and the big men. He wanted their bellies full, as it could be a long night and he did not want hunger getting the group off task. He also hoped the food would absorb some of the alcohol that was sure to be in the men's systems.

The Green boys were in good spirits, even better spirits when the reporter showed them the cash payment that awaited them. There were a few questions that came when the reporter handed the big men shovels and lanterns, but the promise of an additional five dollars apiece ended all inquiries. The group rode to about three miles north of the Bender property. The rain continued to fall at a slow, steady pace, and the fog which had maintained itself all day, thickened. Laploom dismounted at the edge of a thick hedge row, which led to the south into an empty field. The men followed and tied their horses behind the trees. Then, after climbing over a rock fence, the three began moving north toward the apple orchard, which was located near the top of the mound. It was two miles of hard walking through the muddy pasture. Laploom had dressed for the weather and the Green boys were young and tough, but it was rough going as the ground began to incline and they neared the area of the mound's apex. The reporter stopped the group once as a small herd of cows had congregated in the short distance and he made sure that they made a wide arc around them.

This was the country, and the reporter knew sound traveled farther here, unlike in the towns. Also, he presumed the Bender Inn to have little insulation, and if they spooked the cows, it could draw the attention of the family, even at this distance. They moved by the cattle quietly.

As was agreed before they set out, their lanterns were left dark until they reached the orchard and would only be lit if there was a need.

"Okay boyo, what are we doing now?" John Green asked with a less than intelligent look on his face, as they reached the orchard.

Laploom placed a finger to his lips and responded in a whisper, "What we're doing is being really quiet!" Now, one of you go twenty feet to the west and the other goes twenty-feet in the other direction. Watch for anyone approaching from the main house or the barn. Stay behind the trees for cover. If you see someone, don't shout, just come to me and let me know." Laploom started to walk deeper into the orchard to the north and stopped, turned, and went back to the two men and continued, "Also, watch me, just in case you see anyone approach me. You see that, come running and earn your money." Laploom looked at the men with his most serious face.

Both of the Green boys smiled as they could see there was more than a bit of fear on the reporter's face. The eldest brother spoke, "Don't you worry, boyo, their all asleep up in that main house, and no one but us midnight adventurers and the cows are out here in the mud." The younger brother nodded in agreement.

Laploom wanted to say he was not as confident of that being so but made no reply. In fact, the reporter had felt their approach and presence here in the orchard was being monitored. The Irish boy's logic was sound. Who would be out in the middle of this miserable rain in the dark of night? Whoever it was, if not simply his imagination, made Laploom want to move fast. He fought the urge to rush. Failing to pay attention to details was what made most reporters mediocre. Marty Benedict Laploom was better than that.

The first thing he did was focus his eyes and mind. When he concentrated, he noticed the moon, still present through the fog, illuminated the landscape. His eyes went to the orchard. It was extensive and had been planted in stages. He deduced possibly as many as seven different species of apple trees were present. Someone had paid special attention to creating this place. His assumption was that fast growing seeds had been used along with direct transplants. The cost of this would have been extensive.

The reporter did the math in his dead and concluded that the creation of the long, thick orchard with its interesting variety could have cost as much as a third of building the main house. This was especially unusual as the Benders had never attempted to monetize the orchard. He would have known if a thriving apple business had been running up here on the mound.

Next, the reporter looked at the pasture itself. The orchard had a short rock fence, which kept the cattle from trampling the apples during the season. Even on a stormy night like this, he could tell that fresh grass sod had been planted in the orchard. The grass had not fully taken hold yet, but he could tell it had been planted at the beginning of the year. Again, this was a big investment, but why? There was no monetary value for high quality grass to be planted here, and yet here it was. Was this freshly planted grass for the purpose of hiding graves? Laploom then got down on his hands and knees and waited for the moon to cut through enough of the fog to show him the orchard from this lower level. He cleared everything but the earth and grass from his mind and scanned the area slowly. From this vantage point the world was different. He could see the peaks and valleys of the ground. He could see the irregularities within the dirt and as he looked on, he saw many. There, in long, rectangular sections, the grass was thinner than the rest. It began to make sense, and there was a uniform pattern to it all. Rows and rows of rectangular blocks were present where the newly planted grass was thinner. The reflected moonlight on the wet earth marked the locations if one was looking directly at it. Laploom counted the patches. He counted forty-three. His mind raced. Were there forty-three graves in this orchard? Forty-three bodies under the earth? Forty-three murders yet to be discovered? There was only one way to know. The reporter grabbed his shovel and began digging. Upon the branches of the highest tree sat Mr. Pipps, observing the trespass of the Bender property.

Cool wind splashed across Kate's face like water. She felt weightless and at the same time with the power of flight. Well, that was not exactly right, she could fly but not of her own volition. She wore a white dress that fluttered in the warm breeze and she was wrapped in love. She was safe from all danger. For a moment she thought of her current lover, Dr. Kegan. He was by far the most interesting man she had met in Kansas. He was intelligent but also dangerous. He had the means to give her a great life. He was clever enough to outsmart the law and, most importantly, he accepted her for who she was. Dr. Kegan was an amazing man. She had contemplated spending her life with the doctor and it had been an internal conversation longer than any she had ever had about a man. With that said, she knew here, in what must be a dream, she was not in the arms of the doctor. She was in the arms of Mr. Pipps. It was the dark one, her benefactor in both life and death, who had the ability to keep her safe at all costs and from all forces.

Tears rolled down her face as she looked into his red, burning eyes. She felt the heat of his presence, and his power through his touch made the hairs on her arms rise. Together they sored over land and water. His boots clipped the tree tops, and towns shot by them at amazing speed. Finally, as all the breath in her lungs had been consumed, her benefactor stopped his rapid flight and came to a rest on the edge of a tall mountain. Below them was the inn. She knew it was a dream but the clarity, even at night, was amazing. Mr. Pipps pointed to the pasture and she viewed the cows lazily grazing in small groups. He continued to point, and she saw the reason for the trip. Three men with shovels were now digging at separate graves in the orchard. Kate's mouth opened in shock, and at the same time Mr. Pipps and the mountain upon which he stood disappeared. She was now alone. Falling, with nothing to grasp hold of.

"Catch me, my love!" With a shout, she sat up in bed.

Her cry woke the family, which came to her side.

"The reporter, Laploom, is in the orchard with two men, big ones." Kate had immediately collected herself. They had a very short time to act. Without hesitation, she gave her orders. "Pa and John Jr. get rope for three. Ma, collect the chloroform and three rags. We're going to the orchard now!"

Everyone moved with purpose except John Jr. He had heard Kate's waking statement and he knew who it pertained to. His jealously was front and center. "How are we going to get to these men without being detected? Are you going to lead us there in the dark of the storm?" Kate opened the door to the inn and the wind brought a wave of wetness inside. Mr. Pipps's dark silhouette was present only feet away.

Kate responded with authority, "We'll be fine."

Anyone in the orchard had a clear view of the inn. That is, if they were looking. While Laploom had placed a great priority on having the Green boys watch for anyone who might approach them, once he had discovered what he thoughts were graves, he quickly assigned both of the big men to digging. If he was right, with all three of them working at separate locations, they could locate and identify three separate corpses, more than enough evidence for authorities, and be gone quickly. Laploom's face was transfixed on the wet mud he was moving with his shovel. He quickly grunted an agreement to pay the men an additional five dollars apiece for their participation in grave digging, a detail he had left out of the original proposal. As his shovel bite deeper into the earth, Laploom's eyes scanned the area of the inn less and less.

Meanwhile, unbeknownst to half of the gang, Mr. Pipps lead the group by way of the shadows to the orchard. Through his guidance, every step they made was sure and on solid ground and they never were in a straight line of sight. At times the group moved quickly, at times they moved slowly and even stopped. Soon they had made their way behind the orchard and approached the men from the rear. Ma poured her special blend of chloroform thick upon the rags lest the rain dampen the effect. The men were on their knees which diminished their size advantage. John Jr. and Pa got behind each of the big Irishmen and Kate move slowly upon Laploom, who was now totally covered in mud. Even above the stormy night she could hear his labored breath. It had a sexual nature about and when his shovel hit something solid, his ragged breathe stuck in his throat. Without hesitation the reporter thrust his hand into the black water and pulled forth a partly decayed arm. The rotted appendage flapped in the wind, and Laploom squealed like a pig in exaltation.

Holding the arm like a trophy from the fair, the reporter turned to show his find to the Green boys. To his shock the big Irishmen laid face first on the ground, and at their feet were the Bender men. Before he could form a word, his face was thrust into the grave he had dug. The reporter could feel his nose and forehead being push into the wet, slimy chest cavity of the corpse below. Air bubbles escaped his throat as he screamed. After several seconds of this, the reporter was pulled from the watery grave by his nose and a rag was place over his face. Everything went dark.

The first thing Marty Laploom noticed was sound. It was the sound of dripping water combined with a squeaking door. Somewhere, a door was being open and closed and it emitted an irritating *sqeeeeeak* sound over and over. His eyes fluttered open and closed. He struggled to see as the room he was in was brightly lit. Rubbing alcohol. He smelled rubbing alcohol in great quantities and a metallic scent, which seemed to increase by the second. It was the smell of blood. His mind registered this fact at the same time his eyes adjusted to the light.

Something is wrong with my body, was the unspoken thought that crawled through his slow working mind. A man in a clean, white lab coat had his back to the reporter and was diligently doing something.

"Where… where am I?" the words came out of Laploom's mouth in slow motion.

The man turned to face him. While the back side of his lab coat had been a pristine white, from the front, it was soaked in crimson. The reporter could only moan. The man smiled and shouted over the squeaking sound, which was getting louder all the time. The man smiled again and raised a blood soaked finger as if to ask for a moment of patience.

It was then the reporter came to grasp what the man was doing, and the danger of his own predicament. Before him was a high backed, metal chair. Inside the chair was the big Irishman John Green. His arms and legs were strapped in with thick leather bindings. His head was strapped to a metal support, which was made into the back of the chair. From this metal support rods and pins jutted forth and had been screwed into the man's skull at different angles. The top of the man's skull had been removed with a surgical instrument, exposing his brain. The brain was a pink fleshy thing, and currently a series of clamps and metal wires had been inserted into it at different places.

"My God," Laploom managed to get his mouth to make the words. The squeaking door sound, which now grew louder, was not a door at all, but the screams of John

Green. The man in the blood soaked lab coat placed a clamp in an upper quadrant of John Green's lobe and squeezed it tight, and the screaming suddenly stopped.

Smiling, the man turned John Green to face the reporter. The Irishman's eyes darted in all directions, and his breathing was rapid, but he said nothing.

"I'm sorry for that. I don't tend to hear it but I know it can be annoying to others." The man laughed as he spoke. Moving closer to the reporter he introduced himself. "My name is Dr. Author Kegan. You are in my private laboratory, just outside of Independence, Kansas.

"Whyyyyy?" Laploom gasped.

"Oh my, dry throat. One moment please." The doctor said as he left and quickly returned with a small cup of water. He gave the reporter a few sips of water and then continued. "It's the air down here, it dries the vocal passages. I drink my weight in water some days here, I tell you." The doctor's smile seemed to be almost painted on. After several seconds of silence he spoke again. "Oh yes, you are surely feeling the effects of several sedation drugs which may slow your speech functions." Laploom attempted to form another word but could not. "I do apologize but the air here degrades brain tissue so quickly, I must attend to things. However, I do have a friend for you to interact with before I'll need you to help me with a few experiments."

With that, the doctor was back to work and in his place Kate Bender appeared. She was smiling as well, but her smile was different. While the doctor's grin had been detached, the girl's smile was one of revenge.

"I am told that your eyes are the only mobile part of your body. If that is the case, then I know you are currently lacking all the details your curious nature requires. I believe I should be able to get you some much needed data." With that, the girl used two hand mirrors. Placing them at different angles she showed Laploom that he was strapped to a metal chair like the Irishman. Deep within his head were rods and pins, and a cut had been made along the top of his skull. His skull cap had not yet been removed and his brain had not been exposed, but this seemed to be a foregone conclusion. Laploom could not feel his arms, legs or any part of his body. He was completely defenseless as the girl began to wheel his chair around the large laboratory.

"Mr. Laploom, I'm told we have about ten minutes" Kate said in a soothing voice.

"More like seven, my darling" the doctor returned.

"Well, time does fly. I guess seven minutes it is. I think that is just about enough for me to tell you everything. Oh look, your other compatriot." She pointed towards a surgical table to the dismembered body of the youngest of the Green boys. Joshua Green's arms and legs had been removed as well as his tongue. His skull cap had also been removed and a number of metal rods were deep within the brain.

"Let me show you what I learned today!" The girl skipped to the dissected body and pushed on a rod connected to the man's brain. Suddenly the corpse's eyes opened. When she pushed another, the dead man winked at the reporter, which made Laploom go into a fit of moaning.

"Oh quiet down, I'm about to give you the details to the story of a lifetime. That's what you want, right?"

For the next few minutes Kate told Laploom everything that had transpired at the Bender Inn. The killings, the burials, the gold, nothing was withheld. As a bonus, she told the reporter about Kegan's full criminal operation, including his illegal medical experiments. As the doctor began to swab copious amounts of alcohol along the surgical cuts around his head, Kate whispered the details of the existence of Mr. Pipps to the reporter. She had told it all.

The doctor grasped the man's skull cap and pulled it free. Laploom's pink brain was now free for inspection.

Kate leaned down and placed her face in front of the reporter. Their eye's met and she could see the man was still in there. She extended her finger and reached forth to touch the fleshy meat of his brain while looking Laploom in the eye. Dr. Kegan grunted his disagreement with the action but her smile melted him, and he quickly gave his reluctant approval. She brought her gaze back to the reporter and pushed her finger deep into his brainy flesh. Laploom's mouth opened and a low, long, sound escaped his mouth.

"Awwwwwwg," was the sound he made, and as soon as she removed her finger from the brain, his mouth clamped shut.

Kate's smile widened, "Well you finally have it all, sir. No detail has been excluded. Does it make you feel as good as you hoped? I'm sure whatever feeling you are lacking the good doctor can help you achieve."

The girl walked from the room as another moan escaped Laploom's lips.

20 MARCH 1873: DEATH OF A LOVER, FATE OF A BROTHER

With the delivery of the reporter and his henchmen, the contractual obligations to Dr. Kegan had been met. Cash in the form U.S. currency of various denominations were counted, recounted, and loaded into two large travel cases. The gold was removed by Kegan's staff the following day from the Bender Inn. This was the only current development that sat well with the entire gang.

The elimination of Laploom, while necessary, was just another in a line of high profile disappearances that would soon be discovered. Kate had no idea who might know what Laploom was investigating, and how fast it would lead to the Bender Inn. Discussions began on evacuating the inn and moving on. Ma was ready to go at a moment's notice. She had never liked the rural setting and was anxious for the cosmopolitan allures of the big cities. Pa was less anxious to leave suddenly as every neighbor and road was being watched by the citizenry, who were in a state of fear. John Jr. refused to partake in the discussions as he was both jealous and angry at Kate for her interaction with Mr. Pipps during the storm. This morning he roamed the pasturelands near the orchards looking for the dark one in hopes he could bring the supernatural creature back to a stronger bond with him, or keep him away from Kate.

By late morning Pa had collected John Jr. They would attend a multicounty wide meeting at the Harmony Grove Church. It would be mostly men in attendance as they were the heads of the households, and despite Kate wanting to attend, the last thing they needed was to stand out at a time like this. As the wagon pulled away the women packed their immediate belongs. They had collected so much money, no one had room for many cloths. In the event they had to run, each person had three outfits they would bring. Two sets would be city clothes they had brought with them. Some of New York's finest vest suits and silk dresses they had in their possession.

With these outfits they could immediately shed their Kansas personas at a moment's notice. They also brought an extra pair of clothes made at the inn. This was just in case they were required to go somewhere where appearing affluent was not in their best interest.

Since the acquisition of money had played such an intricate part of the operation, they devised plans never to be without it. The men would place money in their boots, hats, pockets, and specially made money belts. The women would carry money in their purses and hats, as well as bills sown into their brassieres. Then, of course, each carried two large travel bags filled with the riches of Solomon. Kate had ordered them to pay initially with coin money to lighten their load. They would have to be quick of mind and body while on the run. She would like to have practiced how they would talk and act while traveling. This had been a part of their success at the inn. At the inn, they knew their parts and acted them out so well they had become a true family. However, they were not prepared to greet fellow travelers, and especially authorities and keep a convincing cover. When they ran, they would be in constant danger.

Pa and John Jr. got to the meeting early. Having attended the Harmony Grove Church many times, they knew the capacity of the building was limited to about two hundred people. Following Kate's instructions, they secured themselves back, aisle seats where they would be able to hear everything but draw little attention to themselves. They would not leave until the meeting was adjourned no matter what revelations took place. Kate felt confident law enforcement agents would have a keen eye for anyone present who acted out of the norm. What Kate had not taken into consideration was the melee that would take place.

Over three-thousand people arrived to hear word about what was being done to save Dr. York and other missing loved ones. This created all kinds of problems for those who had come to speak. Several men came to the podium and they found they would have about three minutes of speaking time before the roaring crowd got so loud no one could be heard. It would take at least ten minutes to quiet people down, and for time purposes the next speaker would try his turn.

The longest quiet period was afforded John Wilkons, legal aid to Kansas Governor, Osbourne. Wilkons explained the multicounty search warrant, which would allow any and all farms and farm land to be searched. The sheriffs from Wilson, Labette, and Montgomery Counties almost seemed shocked when the crowd applauded the warrant. Next, came the fighting and the arrests. Sheriff

Roy Grundy who was a popular sheriff in Labette County actually incited the violence. The sheriff was facing his first strong election challenge in twenty-five years and wanted to show scared citizens crime would be punished in his county. Bringing a hangman's noose to the pulpit, the elderly law man held the rope in the air as he promised attendees the "wrath of God" on whoever was committing these crimes. The short speech was well received but it got an already scared and angry group past the boiling point. The Irish in attendance blamed the German immigrants for the crimes, and several cross racial accusations began to fly. Soon angry words turned into angry fists and a fight that started in the church spilled into the overcrowded parking area. The Harmony Church Choir tried to sing the violence down but were simply reduced to background noise in an environment where people didn't trust each other, were angry, and wanted payback. Pa and John Jr. quietly left amongst the chaos.

As the men arrived at the inn, they found John Lockheart, one of Kate's many local suiters, had stopped by to visit the girl. Lockheart's father owned the Cherryvale lumber yard. Like many of the men in the local area, Lockheart was smitten with Kate. The girl had made sure the young man kept pursuing her while affording him only a belief in possible future pleasure. In truth, she had kept the eager young boy around to eventually square off with Rudolph Brokman, a local vendor who had been pressuring her for marriage for some months. Lockheart hated Brokman and it would be an easy confrontation to create. Lockheart came from money and was quite spoiled. In his mind, no matter how things were going in the present, he knew he would eventually have Kate Bender. He wanted her and he always got what he wanted. His arrogance at this perceived inevitability clouded his judgement when it came to the girl, who constantly manipulated him. She would manipulate him again today.

While Lockheart sipped lemonade in the kitchen, Pa and John Jr. briefed Kate about the town meeting. She had to make a quick decision and she did, they would flee tonight by cover of darkness and they would be on a train headed away from this place by early morning. All they needed was a small local distraction to make sure prying eyes were not looking in their direction. John Lockheart would serve this purpose.

With the men checking over the wagon and feeding and watering the horses, Kate excused Ma from the house which placed her and Lockheart alone. This was a first in his perceived courtship of the girl. Kate had always kept Ma's harsh, judgmental eyes on the poor boy and used it as one of many excuses why she could not be romantic. As soon as Ma left the house Kate embraced the boy and kissed him hard on the mouth.

"Finally that old woman gives us some peace," she said between passionate kisses.

Lockheart began sweating profusely but after several seconds of indecision, pulled the girl close and began to run his hands over her body. Kate giggled seductively, which further aroused his passions. Thinking quickly, she formulated a plan and sent the young man on his mission.

Placing his hand on her heaving breast she spoke. "I can't stand these games any more my love. I want you forever."

His response came in gasps, "Y—yes, me as well!"

As if coming to a terrible realization, she pulled his hand from her warm flesh. "There is only one obstacle." She paused for effect, as if the mentioning of such a thing caused her great pain. "It's the butcher in town, that Johan Smith. He will never let me go." Lockheart looked at her curiously as he did not know the man. Kate almost broke character at her own creativity. She had never meant the two men's paths to cross or she would have spoken to each about the other to create tension, as she did in many cases with men. As she thought about it, Brockman's business was not in town, but the butcher's was. She needed a fight that would occupy the law in Cherryvale. A real knuckle buster; one that disturbed the peace and ended in arrests. This would do it.

She placed the boy's arms around her waist and pulled him in close. "The butcher plays the peaceful man's game but he has claimed me as his own against my will. If he is not bested, he will see me as his for all eternity. I must be free of him, and only a man of true action can attain this." She kissed his neck in several places until she could feel his pulsating heart beat upon her tongue.

"It will be done today! I swear it!" he said with a strong conviction.

As planned, Ma made noises outside the house to announce her approach. The two jumped apart, but not before Kate brought her mouth to his ear one last time saying, "Do this today, brave one, and I will lay with you tomorrow by evening."

The lumber yard owner's son ran from the house with fire in his eyes, and it would be a wonder if he did not kill the butcher.

As quickly as she had been pretending to be in the throes of passion, Kate was orchestrating the Bender's escape. Their bags were organized on the floor, and everyone checked their personal belongings. There would be no doubling back for missed items. Thayer was their quickest departure route by train. People would see them get on the train for sure, but it had to be done. They would change trains several times and soon they would blend with travelers. That is if nothing out of the ordinary happened.

Kate desperately wanted to visit Dr. Kegan one more time. The night the reporter had discovered the graves in the orchard she had made her decision. She could never be with the doctor *and* her benefactor. Their forces were two powerful and in opposition to one another. The events of that night brought her back to what she knew to be the truth. Mr. Pipps had always been there for her. His power, while mysterious, was absolute and even though he had punished her for straying, she knew they would soon be back together. His love for her was a fire of unquestionable heat. She did not want to hurt Dr. Kegan but she had to let him go. Maybe quietly slipping away in the night was fitting. No words, no last glances, just the memory of the special moments they had shared.

As darkness approached they began loading the wagon. John Jr. gave extra food to the animals, including the pigs that had so drastically changed his life. The mallets that were used to slay so many people were left behind. Whatever lay ahead of them, these items would not be needed. There was talk of collapsing the tunnel from the house to the barn, but even that idea was abandoned. If scrutinizing eyes inspected the Bender Inn, and in time they would, incriminating evidence would abound everywhere. The existence of their secret tunnel would make little difference in the scheme of things. They were preparing to leave when a man on a horseback came riding in at a full gallop. Pa reached for his rifle that was in the wagon but Kate stopped him. It was Dr. Kegan. The man dismounted quickly, and Kate met him at the well.

"I waited until nightfall to come. I see I was almost too late." The man's face was forlorn.

"I needed…I wanted to talk to you but we don't the time." Honest tears ran down Kate's face.

"I was at the meeting today and I know that danger is coming your way." He paused for a moment and then took her in his arms, "You could leave with me. You know that, right?"

She nodded her head. They had discussed it many times with her never making a final decision. She knew now her indecision then was because in her heart she already knew she could not go with him.

She kissed his cheek and said in a low tone, "I cannot, I'm sad to say. Go now, dear doctor, and do your experiments, achieve your feats, and find joy and happiness. I wish all this and more for you."

She stepped back and they looked at one another. The doctor was sad but he held a smile. In his uncanny wisdom he may have known she could never stay. He nodded his acceptance and turned to mount his horse. As he turned, a thick, long knife drove deep into his chest. John Jr. held the knife, and a twisted smile was on his face.

"No!" screamed Kate.

Kegan, who did not expect the attack, grabbed the boy by the shoulder. John Jr. quickly removed the blade and stabbed him a second time in the throat. This time the blade came out the back of his neck. With a blood-soaked hand, John Jr. pushed the doctor into the well where his body splashed to the bottom after several seconds of descent.

"Why did you do that?" Kate screamed at the top of her lungs.

John Jr. pointed the bloody knife at Kate. Blood covered his face making his eyes and teeth seem to glow as he spoke. "You take love from others and use it how you wish. It's time you feel the pain of losing someone special. It's time you feel alone and helpless."

A man on a horse road by at that exact moment and John Jr. turned his body away from view. Pa placed his arm around Ma, an extremely odd move, and the two elder

Benders waved together at the traveler. The man on horseback waved back and continued on.

When the man was out of view, Pa growled at everyone, "We go now! Everyone get in the wagon!" He grabbed Kate and pulled her to the front bench which separated her from John Jr., who after being handed a wet rag to clean himself, got in the back with Ma. They rode for hours in silence. The evening air was warm and they had not eaten. By late night they abandoned the horses and wagon in a secluded area and walked the last half-mile into Thayer. They purchased four tickets on the Leavenworth, Lawrence & Galveston Railroad bound for Humboldt. Pa and John Jr. went to watch the stowage of the large travel bags on the train. Ma kept a subtle watch for law enforcement from just outside their passenger car. Kate stayed with their carry-on bags and personal belongings in the sleep cab where they would rest when the train departed. Despite the haste of their departure, Ma had brought a large, thick crockery container full of chicken soup. The soup had cooled but smelled delicious. Kate filled four large bowls full of the soup and handed Pa and Ma a bowl as soon as they entered. They eagerly began eating. Kate also handed John Jr. a bowl which he accepted reluctantly.

As she handed him a spoon she looked at him and said, "John Jr. no matter how you and I feel toward each other right now, we have to work together or we will all hang. Can we have a truce for the sake of everyone?" She looked at him with as gentle a gaze as she could muster.

"For the sake of everyone, yes." John Jr. said and nodded at the same time.

"Well good, then eat up everyone! This smells like the best soup ever!" Kate said as she grabbed up her own bowl. As the Bender gang ate hungrily of their food, Kate nonchalantly patted the little green metal container that was within an inner pocket of her dress. The container that held Ma's secret, slow-acting poison was with her. She had quietly lifted it from the kitchen over a week ago. It was the same poison that had just been applied to John Jr.'s food.

21 PRESENT DAY: THE FINAL CONFRONTATION

Detective Johnson allowed himself to be blindfolded and moved several miles from the Island of Death. In return, Jesse James gave him three days rations, his weapons and ammunition, and most importantly, the location of the Benders.

The gang had decided to flee the country and had secured travel to Columbia. With a supply of money that surprised the outlaw James, they had purchased safe travel into Mexico to the small port village of Torta Madreena. From there, a sidewheel steamer would take the gang on to South America where they could disappear forever. The captain and crew of the steamer where known to carry less than legal items back and forth between America and Brazil, Portugal, Columbia, Venezuela, and anywhere there was a stop they could make a profit at. Jesse James and precious few others at the Island of Death knew the Benders true intentions. Despite the detective having missed the boat's launch at Torta Madreena three days previous, there was still a chance for him to intercept them at St. Aleandro Vargus, a common launching port for thieves smuggling items around Mexico's southern border. The detective had two days to get there.

Determined not to let the boat leave the port without him, Johnson threw caution to the wind and road non-stop to the location.

"My apologies, friend," the detective said to the horse as he left the tired beast at a holding stable to be cared for while he approached the small shipping yard on foot. The horse eyed him angrily until a young Mexican boy brought a bale of hay and water to its stall, then all seemed to be forgiven. Johnson knew if he were to stop at a teletype office there would be a stack of messages waiting for him. Most of the communications would be angry message from his employer, Clint Parker. It was out of character for him not to pass information back to him. Not doing so was against his training, which went all the way back to the war. Information was the most vital part of winning battles. Unfortunately, he did not have the time. He was so close and he could not let this opportunity pass him by.

It was 11:00 p.m. and dark when the detective made his way close enough to see the boats. He breathed a sigh of relief when he saw the ship he sought in the harbor. He had been given a detailed description of the boat, and the vessel had no standard name written upon its hull to mark it. A true smuggler's ship it was. The steamer was a large beast of metal and wood. It was American made but had long been running South American waters by its worn out appearance and lack of maintenance. The vessel had once been a marvel of construction but was at least twenty-five years past its prime. The cargo hold most likely contained stolen goods, anything from spices, to guns, to things even the detective did not want to think about.

About twenty shipmen worked the docks. They were loading what the detective thought were barrels of liquor, but upon closer inspection saw they were actually gunpowder.

"Great! Murderers and explosives," he whispered to himself as he approached the ship. Looking along the deck, there was no sign of the Benders. Not a surprise, this was a short stop along a much longer journey, and the gang most likely did not wish to take any chances with being viewed until they were further away from American authorities.

The detective would have loved to have found the criminals wandering the beach away from the crew, vulnerable to arrest, but life seldom offered such great opportunities. He scratched the stubble on his chin and debated his next move. He knew he had to enter the boat and he could tell there were only minutes until the vessel launched. He could see the mooring ropes being removed and without hesitation, he ran through the night to the pier.

He used his swiftness to cross the long wooden platform with speed but not at a full run. Even with his rifle in hand and looking nothing like the Mexican shipmen, he walked with purpose and passed by several men loading goods into the ship without drawing attention to himself. Once on board, he went immediately below to the storage deck and found a small room full of rifles, ammunition, and strangely enough, fancy ceramic masks for Mexico's celebration holiday known as *Día de los Muertos* or in English: the Day of the Dead. There were thousands of the masks in different sizes. Some of the masks depicted humorous faces while others were twisted and ghoulish. The masks gave a surreal feel to an already strange situation. He waited until the ship had set sail and most of the crew was likely to be topside. When that had taken place, he took advantage of his location and went through everything in the cargo hold. Johnson needed to perform a task before he faced the Benders.

Most smugglers who took passengers on covert voyages got paid twice. The first payment came at departure and the second was upon successfully getting the travelers, and whatever they were hauling to their destination. In the criminal world this was an amicable system as it kept both parties as honest as possible. With that said, the captains of most smuggling ships tried to get as much leverage as possible on their travelers, and Johnson presumed this captain would require the Benders to stow everything but a personal bag in the cargo hold to help ensure final payment. After a short search, he found eight large travel bags that had matching copper colored pad locks. These had to be the personal bags of the Benders. Removing his bowie knife, he worked on the padlock of one of the bags. The bag was heavy and the lock was of high quality, but he had been trained in circumventing locks and after a few minutes the locked had been breached.

Unzipping the large flap, he opened the first travel bag and saw that it was stuffed to the hilt with cash. Thousands upon thousands of dollars spilled onto the floor, and it took him a while to get all the bills back in the bag. People with this much money could disappear forever, no matter how many people they'd killed. That is, if the bandits who were giving them a ride never found out the undeclared fortune these killers had on their boat in the Gulf of Mexico.

The last piece of luggage was a wooden box of about six feet long. Johnson attributed it to the Bender's property because of its lock, which matched the others. It was probably full of cash as well but something about the box made him pause. Though he needed to move, he couldn't help himself. He removed his bowie knife again and went to work on the long box. After several minutes, the locked open and he placed his hand on the lid. He froze as he heard movement near the door to the hold. After a bit, the sounds moved away, and he focused his attention back on the wooden box. He raised the lid and gasped in shock. Inside, lying on a bed of cash was the body of John Bender Jr. His body was well preserved and did not overly smell, but his face showed the anguish he had felt as he left this world. Jesse James had been accurate about the young man's sickness and Johnson knew the physical signs of poison. For one reason or another, one of the Benders was now facing judgement, just not on Earth. The detective hoped with one of the Bender men dead, he could arrest the rest of the group with less danger to himself. Grabbing two of the large traveling bags he began to carry them to the exit of the cargo hold.

The legal landing ports in Mexico, and all the countries of South America were clearly known. To dock and to load and unload goods without the permission of each country's government was illegal. In South America, smuggling had become so rampant the governments seeking to curb their losses by the black market had ships constantly patrolling the waters near all usable ports. Ships on the seas could be boarded and inspected several times by representative of several countries during the course of a single day. That is why many smugglers traveled at night and most often without any visible lights, which was also against the law. There were many near misses in the night by smuggler's ships, and occasionally catastrophe struck. To make things even worse for the smuggler, during the summer months government ships with cannons and filled with soldiers were doubled. To combat detection, smugglers often took their ships dangerously close to Scorpion Reef, located within the Caribbean Sea east of Honduras. If boats traveled near the north shore of the reefs by nightfall, they could circumvent authorities and by morning would be in safer waters. In was dangerous going on any trip, but the strong rough winds that blew this night would make it even more treacherous. Most of the men were either shoveling coal into the ship's burners, securing loose cargo, or up in the eagle's nest looking for the first signs of the reef. In other words, they weren't looking for a stowaway searching for cold blooded killers.

By the time the detective made his way to the sleeping quarters, the ship was beginning to rock hard back and forth on the choppy waters. To make it worse, Johnson had to move in almost total darkness. There was very little moonlight, and he almost fell down a set of stairs as he made it to the first set of sleeping quarters. This was the crew's quarters and he walked by quietly to a set of eight wooden doors. He could see light shining from under all eight doors. They all appeared occupied.

"Great." He thought to himself as he leaned his rifle against the wall and withdrew his revolver. He needed the freedom of movement the pistol gave him and at some point he would have to get a lantern. He couldn't keep stumbling around the boat in the dark.

Hmmmm, eight doors. Which one feels lucky? he thought. Would the family be sleeping together? It was possible, and he hoped for it. If he could get the drop on them all at once he could end this chase. The problem was, if he opened the wrong door he would alert everyone and the element of surprise would be lost. He would listen and collect data before he acted. Moving near the first door he stuck his ear to the wood and heard snoring. There was little sound behind the second but the third door seemed promising. He heard female singing, and it came from not one, but two females. He heard a male voice but could not discern the language of the speaker. It could be the family relaxing together having thwarted the law. The other doors either had sounds of sleep or no sounds at all. He made a choice, it was an educated guess, but action had to be taken and Johnson was a man of action. Opening the door quickly he stepped in with pistol drawn. Standing in the corner of the room were two naked Mexican women in their forties. Both women stood around a naked Mexican male who sat in a wooden chair. The man wore a large, blue sombrero with silver etching. For a moment all three looked at Johnson in a state of bewilderment and then suddenly all three were shouting at him in indistinguishable Spanish. Johnson stepped back out of the room and was suddenly struck in the jaw by Pa Bender. His revolver flew from his hand as he crashed to the floor. The big German packed a wallop but he intended to do much more. Sitting on top of the detective's chest, the big man rained down punches on his face. Ma and Kate ran by the two and went topside. After a couple seconds of attempting to retrieve his pistol, the detective decided he had to just simply stay alive. Rocking his body back and forth, his managed to get the big man off balance; this finally allowed him to be able to get free and onto his feet. The German ran up the stairs grabbing Johnsons rifle on his way.

"Damn it!" the detective cursed, having allowed Pa Bender a weapon. He retrieved his pistol and followed.

As soon as Johnson exited the hold and was topside gun fire rang out. Pa was handy with a rifle but nothing akin to the detective's skills. The first shots were high as the German fought to keep his balance on the swaying ship. Johnson fired back which made Pa take cover. Ma and Kate were nowhere to be seen. The deck was almost completely clear, which afforded the detective nowhere to hide. Pa, who was positioned behind some barrels opened up with rapid fire. Johnson knelt and fired back knowing his bullets, while fewer, would be more accurate. They were. Before Pa's rifle went empty, he took a bullet in the shoulder. He screamed in rage more than pain and charged the detective who squared his pistol and pulled the trigger.

Click, was the sound the empty weapon made before the two men where again entangled in mortal combat.

"The reefs ahead!" shouted the men from the ship's eagle's nest as they prepared to make the treacherous crossing. The drama unfolding on the deck of the ship would not be interrupted by the crew. The winds that had been rocking the vessel were a precursor to the storm that now erupted. Rain began to fall in sideways motions as the wind took it.

The two men punched each other with blows that were staggering. The German man delivered thunderous hits even with an injured shoulder. Johnson targeted the injury and after getting the man in an arm lock, broke three of the fingers on his left hand. This took a good portion of the fight out of him. Unfortunately, his free hand brought forth the sturdy blade belonging to George Loncher which cut deeply into Johnson's left forearm.

The pain was intense but it was not the first time the detective had tasted a blade. As the big German rushed him on the slick deck, the detective didn't flee. If he had, he would have died with a knife in his back. Instead, he moved toward the big man and ducked the blade intended for his chest. In one movement he removed his bowie knife and cut the man deeply from chest to belly button with one fluid motion. Pa Bender fell face first onto the deck of the ship as his entrails escaped his body.

No sooner was the big German down then Johnson heard gunfire behind him. Ma Bender had retrieved a pistol of her own and had crept up to the two men during their fight. She fired four times striking the detective twice in the hip. She would have killed him right then and there had not the rocking of the ship taken her balance. She fell and slid for a bit in the fast moving water that flowed back and forth on the deck. When she had her feet again, the detective had crawled twenty feet up the deck and now was on his knees by some of the ship's barrels.

"We should have put you in the orchard!" she said in anger and then laughed as she raised the revolver. Her laughter stopped when the detective cut free one the items secured to a main beam. It was one of the Bender's large travel bags.

"How much to you think is in here, twenty thousand, more? Well, easy come easy go." The detective pushed the bag, which slid upon the ship's deck. The large bag glided underneath the safety railing and off the side of the ship into the storm. A cracking sound echoed around them, and shouts of warning from the crew went unheeded. The ship was catching the reef and its frame was shaking badly. Ma fired wildly at the detective but missed. Quickly his knife cut free two more bags.

"Is this yours, Ma? Hope not!" This time he sent two large bags sliding toward the edge of the ship at the same time.

"Not the money! No!" Ma could stand it no more. She dropped the pistol and jumped for the bags. She grabbed them both, but their weight and momentum took her over the side of the ship. Her final scream was quickly lost in the storm. The detective rose slowly, the bullets in his hip causing him pain with every movement. He picked up Ma's revolver seeing a single live round was left in the chamber. There was still one more to go and she had disappeared during the battle. Somewhere was the pretty twenty-something Kate Bender. As accounts seemed to mount, she would be the most dangerous of them all.

The shipped lurched and then seemed to stay in one place for a moment, bobbing up and down. They were stuck on the reef. This was a death sentence in such a storm. Johnson took little notice of it as Kate Bender appeared. She stood in the center of the vessel in a white night dress. Her clothes were soaked, and her magnificent body was in full view. She smiled at Johnson in the strangest way. It wasn't a smile of revenge but something friendly; a smile that might be shared between a man and a woman during a tea social. Her voice was sweet like honey on the ears.

"Quite a storm we're having. I thought you would never come. Take me in your arms! I am yours forever, my darling!" She raised her arms as if anticipating an embrace.

For a split second, the detective felt the presence of something approaching behind him. He turned to see a dark figure only feet away. A big man covered in dark leather and wearing a large brimmed hat. His eyes burned red, and even within the storm he emitted heat. Johnson raised the revolver and fired his last bullet. The round struck the thing in the center of the forehead, but the bullet passed through like mist.

How can this be? Johnson thought, as Kate's straight blade went across his throat. A crimson arc shot from his body, and the detective staggered before falling onto the deck. The main sail mast fell as the waves began to tear the ship apart.

"My dearest Mr. Pipps, you have shown me what is possible and your absence has taught me I could never love another. My heart, my body, my soul are yours!"

Gasping for air, Johnson could only watch what unfolded next. The dark figure walked over and grabbed one of the large traveling bags full of money and moved to face the girl. Kate looked at the creature with both love and desire. It could have been loss of blood, but Johnson swore the hooded man's face moved as if bugs crawled across his flesh. He was shrouded in darkness, but there was no confusion about the smile that crossed his face. Kate smiled back and embraced him. She kissed him deep and with an open mouth, and his blackness slowly enveloped her entire body, like bugs crawling across a carcass. Within moments, her entire body was as black as the storm, except for her eyes. Her once blue eyes where now red like the fires of hell. Without a word, the travel bag filled with thousands of dollars was dropped back to the deck of the ship. Where Kate Bender was going she would no longer require money. Floor boards broke from the ship's deck and the entire vessel split into two pieces. Johnson's vision was going dark and rain from the storm was filling his eyes, but before he saw no more, he viewed Kate Bender and the creature, now both dark things, fly from the disintegrating ship together into the night's storm.

A WORD FROM THE AUTHOR

I hope readers have enjoyed my fictionalized version of the Bloody Bender story. As most writers do at about this time in the story telling process I would humbly ask readers to leave a review on Amazon for the book. I want to hear what you think about the story and reviews on Amazon have a powerful effect when it comes to a writer reaching more readers. I thank you in advance for your honest review.

Having lived my entire life in Kansas I learned about many historical giants of the 1800s such as Wild Bill Cody and his traveling Wild West Show. I learned the stories of Wild Bill Hickok and his brushes with danger. Even of General George Custer, who is best known for the Battle at Little Bighorn, has a rich Kansas history. These men are all part of amazing pieces of American history, and most people everywhere learn at least a little about them.

When it came to criminals and Kansas history of the old west, I learned about the Dalton gang. Television shows and movies have documented these outlaws, who met their fate in Coffeyville, Kansas in 1892, while attempting to rob two banks at the same time. Amazingly less than twenty-miles away from the location of the Dalton raid was the biggest serial killing in the country's history in the 1870s. Yes, it was the Bloody Benders. It was real, and it was on the front page of news in the *New York Times*, and yet today, even locals in Kansas don't know their story.

Between 1978 and 1979, I visited the Bender Museum near Cherryvale, Kansas as part of an elementary school field trip. I wrote a report along with a school chum about the visit. I was amazed at the story then and still am now. Such savage killers. Such cold calculation. The gang was never caught. In that regard, the Benders fared much better than the Daltons.

I would like to say a special thank you to Fern Wood, a feisty and creative writer for her documentarian on the Bender saga. It has kept my interest piqued on this, all but untold, story years later in my life. For many years, Ms. Wood operated the Cherryvale Museum where three of the mallets used as murder weapons by the Benders still reside today. Much of Ms. Wood's data was used in the writing of this book.

Lastly, I would tell readers I am a fiction writer and much of my story of the Benders is shrouded in the world of make believe. Still, beyond being entertaining, a little scary, and I hope a page turner, I wish for the real life story of the Bloody Benders to more fully reach the public consciousness. It's an amazing tale. Remember, the Bloody Benders where real people, they lived, they killed, and they were never caught.

Check out these other books by Dr. Paul A. Ibbetson and No Compromise Media

Last Meal

Last Meal

'50s Ville

The town you will absolutely love, or else...

EVERY THING

is going to be

OK

Vol. 5

A mini-serial novel by Dr. Paul A. Ibbetson

Last Meal

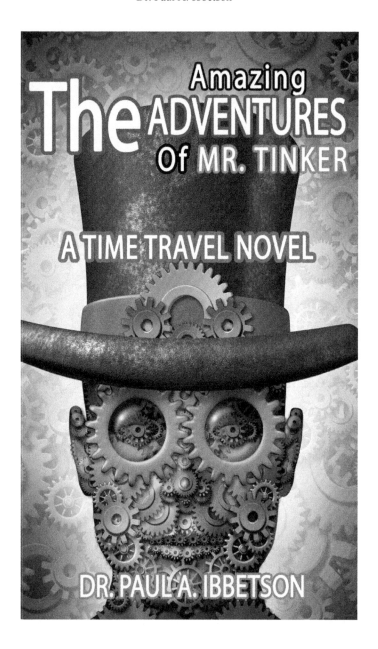

The Ghost Mystery Collection

You decide the ending!

Dr. Paul A. Ibbetson

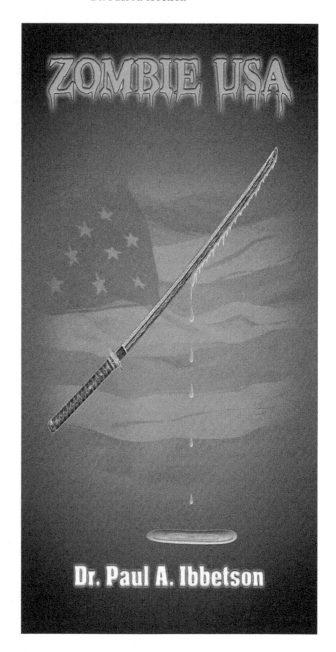

Last Meal

Made in the USA
Middletown, DE
21 May 2023